Lonely child...
to an abandoned teenager
to an abused woman.

Produced by:

FriesenPress
Suite 300 – 852 Fort Street
Victoria, BC, Canada V8W 1H8

www.friesenpress.com

Distributed to the trade by The Ingram Book Company

Introduction:

MY STORY AND memoir is about what I have lived through, how I overcame adversity, pain, and suffering, and how I should have left my husband sooner but never did. This Series will show what I put my children through by staying and how we, together as a team, not only left and never looked back, but also how we have grown and now smile at the good memories. Now we are a unit, a stable foundation with strength, and courage. We are a family of three united as we move forward and cope with whatever life throws our way.

This story shows the pain of being abused emotionally, physically, mentally, and sexually. My road was a road from self-loathing to self-discovery. It was a series of paths, choices and events that lead me to not only being victimized but also to a life I wouldn't wish on anyone, a life that people might think was glamorous, fun, and exiting when in fact it was horrifying, wrong, empty and unfulfilling.

I married a man who is everyone's friend but my worst nightmare, a man who is the father of my children. This man is a monster who hid behind a vest, a man who used his power and his control behind closed doors. This man was a full patch Hell's Angel. I was his girl, the mother of his child and then I became his wife.

I had lived quite an extraordinary life by the time I was twenty. I left home when I was young because I felt I had never belonged, from Christmas dinners, to school events or just plain everyday life.

My sisters and family constantly made me feel out of place and alone. I was a shadow and felt as though I had never belonged. That was my life then and this book is about the series of events that lead me to the place where I met my nightmare.

I clawed my way back from the very depths of my own self-imposed prison walls, to a life of sunshine and happiness.

I shall touch on a few obstacles that were in my way while I was young and how it lead me to self-destructive behavior and later, how I found my own self-discovery, how I was then and who I am now. What it is truly like being abused, how one feels, and what a woman really goes through when she is in an abusive situation.

This book shows how it occurs, how hard it is to get out, and the dynamics behind how my upbringing shaped me for what I felt I deserved. Every thought, action, moment and every word you speak in your life can change your course. Every action has a reaction and my own delusional dreams as a child gained me an unrealistic view of reality.

My thoughts were of a knight in shining armor who would love me for me, sweep me off my feet, and take me away to have the family I always dreamed about. There would be love and stability with ups and downs and yet it would all be going okay. This dream of love turned into a hope to survive, and that hope to survive helped me find myself with the two little men who are my sons, my world, my everything. Together we all found each other.

My commitment and promise to them, was to never allow them to have the pain and loneliness I had growing up. I fought with all I had to never make the same mistakes twice, by using my strong heart and the gentle love of a mother to break the cycles that had been created.

I want the world to know you can change and break the cycle, because hope and faith are all you need. No matter how lonely you think you are, you are not alone because we are one with ourselves, we are as

lonely as we want to be. We are here for a reason, people just have to learn to believe in themselves. No matter what it will all be okay, for everything bad that may come from your mistakes, there are blessings to be had.

Somehow, somewhere, my inner power came from inside me and my fight to survive, my truth, and my beliefs found me in the most horrible depths of hell, the hell from which I felt I couldn't get out, but, I did. I started not knowing me and I started believing everybody else, and wondering what they would say and what they thought. Then somewhere, deep within my very soul, I found the strength and I fought all the obstacles. I started questioning those people who had always put me down, and mistreated me. I didn't want to surround myself with ignorant, self-centered, mean malicious people who hurt others to get ahead. I didn't want violence and I didn't want that around my children any longer. So I removed myself from those I did not want to be near and started surrounding my children and me with good people and positive, healthy energy.

I shall speak out and share my story with all of you. Perhaps I might help others who are on the same road that I was or simply help a parent who has a child going through something similar. Perhaps he or she did not <u>purposely or intentionally</u> label his or her own child. If I'm lucky, I might be able touch another woman or child going through what I did, and reach out to them, telling them they are not alone, others have been there, and perhaps shed light to them in their deepest dark hours .

I want to spread awareness to youth who are influenced by the bling, the cars, the money or life of the untouchable bad boys. It isn't always as pretty or sweet as you think it might be. It can be only as good as you can give. Inevitably you will be hurt in some form, or even raped of all your own self-worth in order to accommodate the lifestyle of gang banging thug life. All those secrets you hold inside are like a black cloud that slowly seeps into every part of you, tainting your out-look on life. It could be that man that you're holding does have a wife and kids at home. It is not fair or even right. I was that wife and that mother who was hurt, stolen from, and beaten while supposedly held above all others.

Here is the beginning of the hell I had to go through to get to where I am today.

Kerri On

KERRI KRYSKO

Book 1

Part I

History

I NEVER KNEW the consequences of meeting certain people, or hanging out with a certain crowd. I was young, to live you have to learn, to learn you indeed have to live, unless you have proper parents that teach the difference between right and wrong, and do their best to protect you as well as teach you the consequences of certain actions. If you don't have that, then you are left on your own.

My heart from an early age, was always kind and caring, forgiving as well as understanding. I was the type of girl who brought stray animal's home to nurture, a girl who would do my best to help other children if they were hurt or sad. I loved people and I enjoyed the simplicity of life, nature, and dolls. I dreamed as any young girl dreamed. I wanted love, children, and a prince for a lifetime, just love.

My mother married twice, which is common nowadays. I have two sisters. My older sister, Sabrina, is only a year older than I. My younger sister, Sam, is six years younger than I, a stepsister from my mom's second marriage. My parents divorced when I was only two or three years old. I don't remember much of my childhood, only certain moments that are forever embedded in my mind.

I always had a hard time letting go of things, people or even routines. I believe it was a huge impact on my life when my parents divorced. My mother and father fought constantly.

My father told me this one story when I was asking if he could remember anything from my childhood, because I had trouble doing so. He related this story to me.

One day my mother came to pick me up from the babysitter's where I stayed while both my parents worked to make ends meet. She told the babysitter that Frank (my father) would be picking Sabrina up after work and she was only taking me. During that day, my mother had packed up all our things, furniture, dishes and clothes from the home where we as a family were living, and moved us out. She took me with her, so when my father went to the babysitter's to pick up both of us after work, he was shocked, when the sitter told him that his wife had already picked me up, but not Sabrina. He went home and was floored as he walked into our home to find the house bare except for the necessities for him and Sabrina. In his mind, he felt as though my mother had cleaned him out and took off with his other daughter. During that time, my father only had Sabrina, and not a word about where my mother and I were. My sister and I, being only eleven months apart, were very close growing up together as young children. We were not only sisters, but best friends and to be separated like that, not knowing where Sabrina or my dad were had a huge impact on me. One of my biggest problems as I was growing up was letting go of people. A month after my mother had done that, my father found out where my mom and I were. I guess we were living in an apartment in the city somewhere. My sister

and I were re-united and my parents ended up getting a divorce.

I don't know much about that time because I was so young, or perhaps blocked it out. I never felt close to my real father and I always felt uncomfortable around him. I was turning into a young girl. My mother always put my dad down, saying horrible things such as he made her deaf in one ear. He often didn't show up for his visits, but when he did, he was always bearing gifts, matching presents for my sister and me, one in pink and one in blue; from jackets to jewelry boxes, they were always in the two colors. I received the color blue, but never wanted blue, I wanted pretty pink or even purple. I was a little girl too and that would always bother me, but I didn't complain because I would get in trouble for being disrespectful. I started to feel as though I wasn't as special as my sister, Sabrina.

I tried to talk about it numerous times with my mother, father and even sister, but they only frowned upon me. They laugh about it to this day, all of them. No one understood my feelings that were so sensitive. I just tried to mention how I felt; the lines of communication had been severed early.

My mother met my stepfather, Tom, a year or two after her divorce. My mom would always be out with her girlfriends or they'd be over sitting around the table in our townhouse drinking coffee, smoking cigarettes and gossiping. I was always in awe, watching them put on their crazy blue eyeliner and two or three different mascaras and back combing their hair. I enjoyed watching them and always thought they were all so pretty, wanting to be just like them when I grew up. They were typical 1980s ladies: outrageous, fun and exciting, music blowing through the house, of yesterdays and love, mixes of good ole rock 'n' roll. I loved music from an early age, often putting myself in every song as it played, singing at the top of my lungs only to be told how horrible I sounded or annoying by my sister, Sabrina. I would get under her skin, a lot. The pet peeves of a sister. Music quite simply touched my soul.

I remember exactly when my mom met my stepdad and brought him home to meet us. It was as if one day she went out and the next day he was there. Usually everyone cooed and awed over my sister, Sabrina, but not him. He treated me as an equal to her and he involved me. He often would sit and play with me, making me feel wanted. My mother was the happiest I'd ever seen her. When they got Married, I could really call him dad, even though I often already called him that, purposely letting it slip when Sabrina wasn't around as she didn't accept him as I did. I knew he was making our home a home. I loved him. He never once gave me an uncomfortable sensation in my stomach that I would often get around older guys, even my real father. I was very happy at that time. They had my baby sister before they were married and to me she was perfect, a porcelain doll with the most beautiful large green eyes.

I thought Sabrina was happy about our sister. I knew she loved her to pieces just as I did, but I often heard her say, "Oh mom and her own private family." With jealousy and snide remarks daily, it was as though in my older sister's eyes we were separated somehow. I didn't grasp the whole meanness of her words, until much later. I was thrilled about our little sister and was ecstatic when she was born.

Sabrina didn't like it that there were more rules for her now that we had a step- dad or that she wasn't as much the little boss she thought she was. She would sit in our room and say she wanted our real dad. We were about six or seven at the time. She didn't like it when she didn't get all the attention. She was like that from the time I was born, full of *do this* and *do that*. When she got in any sort of trouble, she would blame me or not play with me, using that as a way to coax me to do her bidding. She knew how to get her way and was stubborn enough to wait until she did. She didn't like my stepdad being around and was never afraid to express it when we were alone, or even to him. I was worried my stepdad was going to get hurt feelings like those I had when she acted in that manner. I continuously worried that he wouldn't love me anymore or think I agreed with her in not loving him.

It bothered me how mean my sister could be towards people, no one ever saw it but me, I thought. She was the cooed at first- born child to the grandparents and everyone or she was just very vocal. It often surprised me how crass she could be and have no feelings of remorse.

My real dad and my mom would fight over Sabrina all the time. Some of my first feelings of sadness were when I was sitting in my room hearing my mother on the phone yelling at him, saying all he wanted was Sabrina. Always I would hear my mother saying, "What about Kerri Lynn, Frank, what about Kerri?"

It was then, I found the closet where I knew I could cry all alone and wouldn't be sneered at by my sister or anyone for being hurt. Everyone said I needed to toughen up, and laughed at me when I'd get upset, for being a baby. I had huge feelings for a little girl. Often feeling so alone, almost as if no one noticed me, constant feelings of being overshadowed by my sister overwhelmed me with loneliness. I don't remember having many friends. Everyone on the block played with my older sister, never with me unless I was permitted to play by her. Even cousins of ours always clung to her, more times than not. They would only play with me if she wasn't around, then I could be me, then I wouldn't feel as though I were the odd girl out.

It's tough being a child; children are mean. The behaviors are learned and for me to have felt so alone, for it to have stuck with me throughout most of my life, is truly sad. Somehow I was missing the normal attention a little girl craves or needs.

One day I woke up and my stepdad was gone for no apparent reason other than that he had to go away for a while. He would be back, I was continuously told. I stopped asking after a while, hearing my mother tell me over and over, "Imagine how I feel or your little sister." I felt more alone than ever. We lost our house and all of our belongings; it was as though everything I knew was gone. We started, being able to see our real dad again, he would take us for the weekends. I felt homesick and queasy all the time and couldn't understand why I never felt comfortable around him; he never did anything to me. I wonder now if it was due to hearing my mother always ranting about him, as him with her or just the otherwise sensitive feelings I have always had.

Our real dad would take us over to his best friend's house where Sabrina and I always hangout with their two boys who were so much fun, but the guy's wife would always pick on me often giving me portions of food to eat. It was a place where I hated going, especially when she was there. I felt out of place, but did my best not to show my feelings. I just wanted to go home. The woman hated me, she always did. I even tried to bring it up to my father and he said, "Oh, that's just her, Kerri Lynn, she's miserable." He and Sabrina would laugh as if to lighten up the serious note in my voice. I heard, my sister saying, "She's not like that, Kerri, GOD." Once again, my sister being the favorite, I would be sneered at and receive looks that were horrible for any girl growing up.

We came home one day from dad's weekend and my mother had another boyfriend who drove a cool brown Camaro. I loved the car but definitely didn't like the guy. His children were too forward and they scared me. It seemed we were continuously meeting new guys and their children. I wanted my stepdad back. My sister seemed to just flow with things. She was my anchor during these times as we were growing, moving and always switching schools. I would wish at night for my step-dad to come home and everything would be happy again with the regularity of a normal family home. I craved routine and structure and would always be the first one up as soon as the birds chirped. I loved the sounds of the early morning hours, the peaceful bliss of it, quietness. I loved nature.

A few years later, or a lifetime to a young girl, my stepdad did come home. It felt as though I had a family again, my voice and opinions, my little plays in skits that I put on would be noticed. I used to jump on his back and backcomb his hair as he watched TV, it was a regular occurrence, something my little sister, Sam would do with me. Things seemed to be so much better for a little while. I say this because what I remember as a little girl isn't very much. I loved my whole family as they were all I knew. I remember always craving my mother's attention. I would watch her as she got ready in the morning, cooked and even cleaned. I wanted to be a mother just like her; to me she was the moon, the stars, everything.

We moved to an acreage and I loved it. I felt free, building fake teepees in the wooded forest behind our house, playing, singing and roaming throughout all parts of that quiet acreage subdivision on the outskirts of a small town. It was peaceful and beautiful. My sister was getting more into makeup and friends and I was free, running in those backwoods behind our house. We were growing apart, but everyone seemed to be happy. I even was able to have my own room and loved it; finally, having a beautiful floral pink bed set, I had always wanted.

It was wonderful and exhilarating living on the acreage. I even had my own special best friend, who had a wonderful horse ranch. She introduced me to another woman who owned a farm, and would pay us to clean out her stalls. I loved working with animals; I loved being free and wanted. I truly had found a place to call home. Those were the truly happy moments I remember from when I was young.

My sister, Sabrina, was instantly popular. She was a true beauty growing up. I admired her because she was someone who acted in the role of my mother much of the time. We shared a room most of our lives and were close as sisters should be. I would drive her nuts because I was her shadow a lot of the time and then her words would sear into my heart when she made fun of me, or taunted me to go away as she was my role model. It hurt like hell when she would act as if I were a boy, or ugly, laughing at me as she spoke critical words. She would love me when it suited her and then push me away with her words. I didn't understand. When we were alone she'd be nice, most of the times, but it was changing, she was changing. She and I were as close as we had to be at home, but in front of others like her friends, she would openly ridicule me and laugh at me, especially at school. I didn't have very many friends at school growing up because of her behavior and the way she treated me, being openly treated like that by my own sister at school left quite an impact.

Those kids she hung with would never even give me the time of day. They felt they could not only laugh at me, but also gossip about me. It made me out to be exactly like her jokes, an ugly little duckling who could fit a bulldozer between her teeth. As I said my sister, whom I adored and looked up to, was popular. I would just suck it up and try my best to ignore her and her friends. I loved her and did not know any better as I was only a child.

Those initial moments of starting to understand the dynamics of others laughing at me hurt. It was a crushing emotional agony that only amplified my feelings of worthlessness and forever stayed within my mind.

My little sister, Sam, was a little younger and babied. She is the baby of the family after all, and to me she was never a threat, just my cute little sister. We were able to play after school and on weekends. As I look back, I never have any memories of even that, almost as though she was perhaps kept separated from me.

After supper on one of those school days, Sabrina and I were doing the dishes, when my mother came in. I was drying, Sabrina was washing, as we always did every night after supper, giggling and making our own selves laugh at our jokes of fun. My mother came in and started yelling at me that I hadn't dried one of the glasses properly. It wasn't so much just yelling as it was the insults she was swinging my way, with a force of hatred, not love, pure, evil venomous words that have forever stayed in me.

She said that I did nothing right, that I was nothing; she wished I could be like my sisters. I couldn't talk, my stomach plummeting as it often did during my moments of self-worthlessness. I tried to do it the right way again but she was yelling and saying I don't do anything right, that I don't belong. I was shaking by this time as a little girl can only handle so many hurtful words. I felt absolutely little, beneath the ground we all walk on. My mother was not only scaring me, but telling me I was worthless when I already felt like that most of the time.

I couldn't breathe, my sister was watching shocked. I didn't understand what was going on, or what I had done. Sabrina and

I were just laughing and doing the dishes, as we always did every night. The pit of my stomach was in knots. My mother was saying she didn't even like me. I had always felt as though I wasn't special, or loved, always trying to reach out to love that wasn't there. Sabrina tried asking my mother to stop and took the blame for me, because she could see how depleted I was. My mother never listened and continued on as before, becoming more enraged.

My sister, Sam, was red in the face from crying because of the way Mom was freaking out. Sabrina took Sam into the other room at mothers request and demand. I was terrified, that terrifying moment when I was hearing the words out loud of something I have always feared. My heart broke in so many different pieces. I just wanted to run away and hide. I was humiliated, alone and scared, it the worst moment of my life at ten years old.

My mother doesn't love me was echoing in my head, in my heart and my bones, that was punishment enough. I remember falling to my knees as silent tears rolled down my face. I was so scared I couldn't talk. She was asking me something, yelling at me, but the rush in my head was blocking her out. My self-pity, my sorrow was so evident I couldn't hear anything as the blood was rushing through my body, and air through my ears as she grabbed me by any limb she could get ahold of and started dragging me down the hallway, yelling and screaming at me.

Somewhere, I found my voice and started begging her to stop, "Please, please, Mom. I will do better at the dishes." By then we were going past Sam's room and Sabrina was in there holding my baby sister who was crying just as loudly, my mother dragged me by them, and by now now I was trying to get away. I saw the look of horror on my older sister's face and her own silent tears cascading down her cheeks as little Sammy cried, pinned to the ground by

Sabrina(so she wouldn't run away)and upset mom anymore then she already was. In an attempt to make it better, but when she saw me, being dragged by our mother, she rushed at Mom to protect me.

My mind was starting to hold onto to any love I could find, echoing within my sad, sad heart, "Sabrina loves me, and someone loves me." My mother lost it as Sabrina tried to help. She started ripping the baseboard from the wall, freaking out in a manner that was horrible and delusional and all the while yelling at me that I'm an awful child, she never wanted me. *My mother hated me!*

She locked Sabrina and Sam in my little sister's room and came at me, fast and furious. I was huddled on the floor crying, "Mom, Mom, please, NO, NO. . ." I was a child of just ten years on the ground begging my mother, "Please, Mom, don't hurt me"! She raised the wooden piece of floorboard that she had ripped from the wall and started hitting me, over and over and over again. I was in a ball on the ground begging her to stop as she continued hitting me, pounding down on my back, legs, bottom and even my arms, everywhere. I vaguely remember the screaming from my sisters as she stopped. I was that child beaten into submission, a perfect picture of a broken innocent girl, curled into a ball.

The sorrow was so deep in my chest, more so than any of the painful feelings that were all over my body, or the bruises I was sure were on my arm where she had grabbed me and the floorboard she had hit me with. I had tried to cover myself from each hit to prevent injury to my body, but eventually I just gave up. I don't remember when Mom left my room, I dont remember when she stopped.. All I remember is Sabrina creeping in, horrified as her face took in what my mother had done. My sister held me on the ground and cried with me, saying over and over, "I will never forgive Mom for this,

Kerri-Lynn! Don't worry, I love you carebear, I love you. I will get us to Dad". She was shaking in anger and sadness.

I remember thinking that she was the only one who loved me as the loneliness crept in. I tried to sit up after the tears were spent and remember looking down at my legs, as these huge, long lashes of purple welts were rising high up on my body and down my back where I had turned away from my mother.

I just wanted to be alone in that closet I had found years before, as my sister left my room, she vowed to me she would never look at Mom the same way! She wanted to leave and runaway, as she tried to hug me, without hurting me before she walked to her room horrified. That moment is forever etched in my mind with weeping and inconsolable sadness echoing within my feeble, fragile broken heart. I was alone. The verification of a mothers love gone after all these years so far in my short life, was permanently stamped in my mind.

I took the blankets from my bed, but made it look as if I was asleep in it and made a bed for myself in my closet(where I felt I belonged) I curled in a ball, trying not to make a sound (so Mom wouldn't come). I cried my silent tears as the whispers in my head took over about how no one loved me, all I wanted was just to be rescued and loved.

I hated myself, God hated me and I was gross, ugly and disgusting. I didn't know when I woke up that next day that I hadn't even been missed. Mom was doing her normal things around the house as if nothing had happened. Avoiding her, I went up the driveway to my sister and our waiting school bus. She just hugged me and kept silent. My bruises took weeks to heal; I don't believe my heart ever did.

My sister has tried to bring that moment up to me a few times over the years but I always had to pretend to her as if I didn't remember as I wasn't ready yet to deal with those painful memories of my early years, much less acknowledge them in a room full of people. It was such an empty sadness; I couldn't bear discussing it, as if I was over it or it didn't matter or was normal. It was my defense mechanism, not wanting to remember the moment I knew my mother hated me as much as I already disgusted myself. Perhaps, if my mother caught wind of it, she wouldn't hate me any more than she already did or hurt me again.

I didn't know at that time that abuse comes in so many forms. Or that it is wrong, and to myself I would continuously think," Who would ever help anyone so gross anyhow". I thought that as long as I did my best, to be what everyone wanted, it wouldn't be so bad or I wouldn't be so bad.

I kept that in me for a long time and I know that was the day I started walking with my head down. I would laugh at my own self along with everyone, when I was made the butt end of jokes or I would just look at the teacher when there were groups to be formed, because by that time I knew I wouldn't be picked. I never looked to any of the regular kids to be my friends anymore. I didn't need to, I was nobody anyone wanted anyhow, so why bother. Inside, I would often dream, of people picking me, even wanting to date me, in a kiddish sort of way. I started practicing in the mirror someone telling me they loved me, just to see what my face would look like. I started reading novels around that time, as it would fill the voids in my otherwise empty existence, give me inklings of love that I dreamed and thought about, what I craved as a child.

It was a moment I will never forget and a turning point on the way I looked at things and people differently. Instead of looking at things in a grey light or a dark sense, I would always do my best to look past the bad side of people and try my hardest to find their good side. No matter how bad that person is, there has to be good in them, because I knew somewhere inside there was good in me. Despite my mother saying I was bad and no good, I knew there was greatness in me, that I did indeed love, and that greatness I kept guarded.

I felt more than others who were labeled bad, I knew everyone had to be good somewhere, because I was. That was my perception and my way of coming to terms with the fact that my mother never really loved me, or just maybe it was because I needed to make myself understand, why I had been treated that way. *It was a young girl's way of dealing with the hurt and pain; **it was my way**.*

I never asked anyone for help nor did I tell anyone. I never wanted to go through that again. I didn't know it was wrong, I just knew it didn't feel nice. It only made me feel as though I was even more of an outcast.

> *As I look back now, knowing that I'm older and wiser and have been through much more than some people, that perhaps Sabrina had been affected in some way, perhaps she had seen more than me and that's why she became so hardened or guarded with me. She never wanted to see me hurt like that again, or feel the raw emotion of helplessness. Everyone handles things differently in that we are all unique.*

Teenager

It gained me an unrealistic reality that set my course on the friends I would gain, and the guys I would date. My own delusional dreams as a child gained me an unexpected path, a path that would lead me to places I should have never been.

WE NEVER STAYED in one place long, so a few years later, it was no surprise, we moved. My parents, Tom and Mom, decided they were going to start a business in another province. I was just on the verge of hormones and my older sister was in full swing. She had just gotten her period at age thirteen and boys, music and television were her priorities. I loved her a lot back then. She had a way of entrapping you with her style and prettiness. My sister, to me was stunning.

She always had her long blonde hair curled down her back. Her best friends were just as pretty and all the boys always wanted her. Seriously, my sister was a knockout; she had DD boobs by the time she was thirteen. That was why she seemed way more mature than I did, even though we were less than a year apart.

Anyhow, my sister and I were devastated that we had to leave the province we had always known. Sabrina swore up and down she hated our stepdad for this. I believe, that was when she started seriously wanting to move in with our real dad. I was upset because I would lose a great friend I had recently made, who had horses, which we would ride every day and the part-time job I had with a stable down the road cleaning out all the stalls.

It hurt knowing I was leaving a place where the neighbors all liked me, even favoring me a little, often asking my mother and father if I could go riding with them. The only part that really upset me about moving was leaving all the animals I had come to love and my friend. I wasn't nearly as devastated as my sister. I was somewhat of a free bird, a gypsy.

As long as I was with my family, not left behind, I would be fine. To me it was more of a grand adventure, with new beginnings. That Christmas we moved supposedly to a place where it never snowed and the flowers blossomed all year long. I had to laugh when just shortly after we moved, there was the largest snowstorm in recorded history, with record-breaking results and five feet of snow outside. I loved it and felt like we hadn't even left our small town/acreage in snowy Alberta.

Sabrina got the basement room and I was upstairs in another room with Mom and the family on that floor. My sister instantly became the popular girl at school, as usual. We were separated then, in different schools. The curriculum was different and the school system had other rules. She was officially in middle school and I was left to my own devices in elementary. I didn't make friends easily, so it was a time of loneliness for me. I was shy.

Sabrina was starting to act a little out of control. Guys would be driving to pick her up lots. It was late one evening, after a night out, she tiptoed into my room and asked me to come downstairs. She said she was, *tripping hard*. I had no idea what she was talking about, so I went downstairs and making sure I did not wake up Mom and

Dad. As we approached her room, she turned on a light and she floored me. Her eyes, which were normally blue, were pitch black, and she was laughing so hard she fell down on the ground. I was instantly afraid and worried about her. I wanted to go wake up Mom to ask for help. When I asked her if I should, she stopped laughing immediately and threatened me if I did by saying, "You don't want to lose me, do you, Kerri? Mom will send me away. "My sister was my lifeline. I loved her as much as my Mom. She always had a way of manipulating the situation and I never broke my promises, so I never went to get our mother.

She started doing her makeup and getting ready as if she was going out again, all the while zoning out for minutes at a time. She was starting to freak me right out. She said she was getting picked up again to go to a house party and needed me to sleep in her room, just in case she got busted for sneaking out and I had to let her back in. I would always have her back; my sister was almost perfect to me. She went out that night and it took me a long time to fall asleep as I was so concerned about her. I wanted to say something to Mom and Dad, but she would kill me.

I woke up to her falling in the window. She was beaming and it was almost daylight, as if the birds were chirping, "there's my sister." I was happy she was home, but wowed by the whole situation. My sister amazed me. She said she had met the man of her dreams. She was so in love on and on . . . I listened to everything she was saying and understood why she had left. I loved love. I was so in awe. My sister was a goddess and I wanted to be a princess just like her. Then she told me she had lost her virginity as if it was a normal thing. I had no idea what that was. I was a complete juvenile and not as mature as she. I remember asking her what that was and she told me she had had sex, "When a man goes inside you dumbass."

I was horrified, shocked, never wanting to have that happen to me, it was dirty. I thought for years, after I kissed my non-cousin, that I was pregnant. I was completely convinced one day I would have a baby and have to tell Mom that I kissed a boy and get in so much trouble. The idea would haunt me, keeping me up at night.

Then it registered as she went into detail about it that she was drinking, smoking pot and doing acid. She loved it here. My sister, lifeline and best friend was scaring me. I felt as though I was losing my sister and I had to tell someone, but I was sworn to secrecy and I couldn't hurt or betray her. I never told anyone as she started going out more and more, late at night.

The fights escalated with our mother something fierce. It was as if Sabrina hated our mom and loathed our stepdad. She was always saying she was going to run away and move to Dad's. That's when she and our dad started talking on the phone more and more frequently. I don't remember ever talking to my real dad on the phone at that age, but then I was young. My sister was only thirteen years old, having sex and trying drugs. She was blowing my mind. I was still playing in the backyard with some toys and so happy if I could go to the mall on my own.

I met new kids at my school at the bottom of the hill from our new house on the island. I will never forget the day when I was invited over to one kid's house after school. I never needed parent's permission; it was exhilarating and fun. Her parents were divorced too and she lived back and forth between her mom and dad's houses. That's when I found out that the guy my sister lost her virginity to, was her older brother, my own first real friend's older brother. I was amazed at the new city I lived in.

He came bounding down the stairs as we walked into her house one day. He was totally hot like she had said. He and his sister were exact opposites like me and mine. I really liked knowing that it wasn't just me; I was starting to grow up and find my own way. I was happy. My friend was a little dark, Goth like but still liked Pizza Pops and chilling, as she put it. We only lived a few blocks from each other so we started walking to and from school together every day. I was becoming my own, young lady; I even had my first crush, not that I told anyone.

It turned out that the guy I had a crush on was a Jehovah's Witness and didn't celebrate Christmas and other traditions. That made me like him even more with that blonde streak in his bangs and knowing he was different. I will never forget that blonde streak in his dark hair. I loved that he started walking to and from school with my friend and me, too. I also made another friend, a straight-A student, who wrote as if it was an art. I was friends with either the really nice girls and boys, or the darker type, never the popular ones, ever.

My sister was fast becoming wild and Mom was thinking seriously of sending her to our Dad's. I was afraid one day she would be gone. It was starting to feel as though Mom was separating our family and my sister's words were starting to play havoc with my brain. I noticed that Sabrina and I were left out of certain events with the family and that my little sister wasn't allowed to play with us (me) a lot. I also noticed that she was in every activity a child could dream of and had lots and lots of love. I started believing what I was seeing and what Sabrina was saying, that Mom had her own family now and we weren't part of it. It was obvious how much more my little sister had and how they doted on her.

My mom truly loved her, never yelled at her, as she did me, never spanked her or hit her, or ever laughed at her. Even down to the chores, my little sister never ever had any, as opposed to Sabrina and I who were doing dishes since we were five years old. Definitely, there was a lot of favoritism; Sabrina was right. I saw it with my own eyes. When I would get scared at night or have a bad dream, I had to endure it alone but baby Sam could be with Mom and Dad. It didn't hurt as much as Sabrina made out, but to me, it was more of a clarification. Perhaps, I had just started growing up. I wanted to be a big girl anyway, so it was what it was.

The fighting and threatening had to stop between my mother and sister. Somehow, my mother started saying if she goes, I would be going too. Now that frightened me and I wondered why they were doing this. It was hard, feeling that I was placed in a category, being left as an outcast, never being enrolled in anything or going on special outings as other children did or simply being heard or cared about enough. Why, couldn't my mom just hold me once in a while? My thoughts were starting to take a course I didn't like, even when she did hold me, my sister would taunt me and laugh in that, "You have to get off the tit," kind of cackle laugh. In those odd moments when my mom would do my hair or hug me, I soaked it up. I needed the love. It had nothing to do with nursing; they were special moments and the only moments when I ever felt accepted.

Abandonment

VERY SOON AFTER that, arguments escalated between my mother and sister. My life took a drastic turn. I had just come home from elementary school one day and my mom was frantically packing up all our things from around the house. Sabrina, was in her room, doing the same, all smug, like she got something she wanted. No one, not anyone told me what was going on. My stomach was doing flip flops based on intuition. I knew something was bad, very bad and I wanted to run away. I didn't want to be in my house. I had to leave. As I never really had a voice back then, I was somehow always in the shadow or in the way. No one would talk to me, but when my mom finally came to the bottom of the stairs, she didn't hold me, or ask me what I might've wanted, or how I even felt. She never even took a moment, as any normal mother would've done. She said, in a rushed tone, "You are catching the Greyhound bus and going to live with your father and sister in Alberta!"

Tears were rolling down my face. My knapsack was still on from school. I panicked, I was completely and utterly destroyed. I yelled, "NO, Mom. Please, NOOOOOO." She proceeded to tell me at an arm's length away, "You are going to do this. Be strong with your sister and go. It's what YOU guys have always wanted and YOU ARE GOING!" She walked away, ranting that she couldn't go through this anymore and that we would be best there, on and on she went, as I stood there falling to the ground crying my eyes out.

Once again, Sabrina came out of her room and held me, said it was better this way and she would take care of me." Mom was a bitch", Sabrina yelled at my mother, "Why are you doing this to Kerri, Mom, why? So you can have your family?" As she went on that Mom has her own family now with our little sister and new dad, the words echoed in my mind. I knew I would never be the same again. My mother had made good on her taunts from years before, she never wanted me. I tried begging, screaming, even hiding my shoes.

We were rushed into the car with only our suitcases and dropped off at a Greyhound station in the middle of winter, aged twelve and thirteen years old. That moment, being given away by my mother as I begged her not to, was such a turning point in my life. I had truly and utterly been given away and was no longer loved even the slightest. It was horrible and sickening. As we arrived at the Greyhound, my sister and I never even had our shoes, and were put on that bus, with the knowledge that snow covered the ground all over Alberta. We were headed to a province where it was -30 deg. C, with only our suitcases and bare feet to travel across a whole province to our new home and to a dad with whom I was never close, a man I felt I barely knew.

When we arrived in snowy Alberta, there was a blizzard outside blowing cold and more snow. I barely remember about my father picking us up from the station. All I remember is crying and begging for my mommy to please come and get me. "Please, I just want my mom." I curled in a ball when we arrived at my father's trailer. I was in a room that never smelt like home, a bed that was hard and I cried over a period of weeks.

I tried calling my mother, begging her to get me so many times that she no longer accepted my phone calls. I had never felt more alone in my life. If I hadn't had a sister who crawled into my bed to hold me in my darkest, saddest hours I would have died. Those moments were suicidal and sad. I was gone, forgotten and alone. My worst moments as a child or teenager were that of abandonment and abuse.

My father put us in school; as usual my sister was the star of the show and I hung in the shadows. I never fit in with the regular kids, never wanted to be there. I was sick to my stomach, and was often left out and walking alone down the hallways or not getting picked to be part of a group in class. I just never had self- esteem. I no longer cared so much about my grades and my marks drastically declined. It was not because I needed help. The cause was that I didn't care, I was sad.

My sister had it spread all around the school that she hated our mom, so being in a small town gossip spread. People looked at me as if I was completely dysfunctional and living with a single guy (my real father) in a trailer didn't help. No one looked at my sister, even though she was sleeping around with all the socially acceptable boys, the ones who came from prominent families, with good names. I couldn't handle that. It wasn't that I was jealous, I just didn't like seeing my sister, who was only eleven months older, prancing around the town, and running our dad's house as if she was an adult and the only woman of the home, my sister who was still just a young girl. She naturally was taken for being older than she was, and perhaps that's why she and Mom always fought, she was ready to grow up. I will never know as I am not like them and I promised myself then to never ever let my children feel like that.

Sabrina would be cooking, cleaning, being picked up in vehicles by her friends, partying and enjoying life as if she wasn't just a girl, who had just turned fourteen. I was lost.

I didn't know who I was, as I never adjusted there at all. Her friends were starting to notice the smart-ass remarks about me from my sister, and laughing was allowed again, about my bulldozer teeth and short hair. I was the ugly duckling and it caused me to have a huge complex. I didn't want to smile or people would see my teeth. I didn't want to dress up as I was flat chested like a boy, compared to my sister who was fully developed. To top it all off, I still hadn't had my period like everyone else had, as I was still just a girl. Needless to say, I never fit in and was ridiculed constantly.

The few friends I had made were the outcasts of their families, too. Because of that and the small town attitude, I was instantly labelled the bad seed, the ugly bad apple, when in fact I was only sad, under developed, wanting my mother, and needing love in a lonely place so far from home. It sucked and I would silently cry at night from the insults. I cared more than most, my heart and life were being mapped out in front of me, and I had no voice where anyone would validate me. I was the black sheep and no one wanted me or to even be around me. If my sister and dad could see it bothering me, they'd say, "Kerri, stop it, learn to take a joke." I tried but silently wished it wasn't always about me.

I was emotionally beaten down, ugly and not wanted, and even with the best make up and clothes, I was still just plain old ugly. Simple, the ugly on the inside, definitely had its toll on the outside. That's how I felt during my early teens; I would beam when I received praise from anything, or anyone. Those moments touched me above all else. My romance novels became my only salvation. Even those became taunts from my family.

As time went by, I realized a few things. I was adapting to my surroundings, as well as starting to make a group of friends outside my sister's preferences, which meant I didn't have to be laughed at anymore because my friends were a lot like me. The feeling of acceptance I relished. I would never let them down, to me it was a vow I took in my own mind. A few of those friends became some of my closest confidants with whom I shared the feelings of how my family made me feel. They understood, but, *I NEVER* said anything about the beating I had received. It's as if I knew I would be judged and then they would hate me. I did not want them to know I was weak, begging my mother to stop, or that my mother didn't want me. I never wanted anyone to know that, or maybe they would do the same to me. I just didn't want to lose that feeling of acceptance; it was what I treasured beyond all else.

My sister would continue to laugh at me about my group of friends, saying they're grease bags, and it would hurt me because I cared about them and they cared about me; To me they weren't!

I finally got my period, and didn't understand the huge life-changing experience that my sister had made it out to be. I tried to ask her what to do, or be excited about it, as she did to me when she had gotten hers, but she just looked at me with a sneer, as if I was gross. I didn't know what to do or use. I did not turn into the beautiful swan from that ugly duckling, never got any boobs, and boys never liked me. I didn't understand why this was so huge. But one thing was for sure, I don't know if this was my innocence coming out, but that thought that I was pregnant all those years ago because of that kiss, this definitely confirmed that I wasn't. I always felt so ashamed and worried because of it. With no one to talk to about the idea, it was a notion that had left quite a tremendous impact on me. I realized later I needed pads. Somewhere I learnt about tampons, but never knew how to use them, they felt wrong to me, to this day, I don't need them, and perhaps my angel or angels are watching over me after all.

After many tears, bouts of loneliness and my feelings of acceptance with my new group of friends, my mother and I started conversing on the phone more regularly. I didn't feel like an abandoned child any longer. I was growing up and accepting what life threw at me. *You can only hurt so much before you build a callus or wall around your heart.*

I was well into my teenage years, liking it, and enjoying that my friends wouldn't hurt me. I even had a crush on a boy with an identical twin, who of course was considered the wilder one. Mom started playing on the feelings, "Are you sure you are all right, Kerri, you don't need to pretend." It was weird, as if she was insinuating that I should feel differently; it was all so confusing, but, No, I was happy. I didn't fit in with her and her new family. Sabrina was right. Her opinion was definitely wearing on me, now that I realized no matter how many tears I'd spent crying for my mother and begging her to let me come home and she would not. Now, I didn't want to be somewhere I wasn't welcome. It was very nice though, that she was asking how I was and it made me feel whole. It made me want to try to be who she wanted, it made me feel love, it made me want to go home again, to be with my mother ,not that I ever wanted to leave her or them in the first place. I just couldn't please everyone.

I started dating the twin and with an adolescent mind, I believed I was starting to fall in love. He acted as if he liked me, but I believe any type of emotional feeling would have had my heart. I craved the feeling of acceptance and love, needed it as if I was addicted and it ended up scaring off the one person I thought I loved. I will never forget him telling me, "That I was going to be so beautiful, one day and he had to let me go, because we were never a forever, I was meant for different things." It tore my already fragile heart in half. I almost didn't survive; I wanted to die. In my mind once again soared the thoughts of…" No one ever wanted me, I was an ugly, ugly, person, not pretty and never lovable".

I called my mom and just cried and cried. I wanted my mommy and finally she wanted me home. She started blaming Dad that he was doing a horrible job as a parent. I tried to say it wasn't him, but Mom had it out for Dad, always had it out for him, as did he for her. It was her excuse to finally want to be my parent again. I was shipped back across two provinces to my mom's where she was waiting with open arms. When I saw her, I started balling my eyes out, I had missed her so much. She hugged me, not the hug of a mother who hadn't seen her child for a year, just a hug that was at a distance. She seemed unsure about me and informed me that a lot had changed since I was with her. She had moved and bought a house with Tom, my stepdad. It was now where their new company was based. It was hard on me hearing all that, when all I wanted to do was relish the fact that I was home, back with my family. She was standoffish.

She had the perfect school picked out for me, as my little sister was in elementary and I was now in junior high, except I was going to be in a school for grades 8-12 now. It was supposedly known as a very posh, high-end school. She and I needed to get me a whole new wardrobe.

As much as it felt good to be home, back with my mom, it felt different. I had grown and that feeling of being not wanted by her as well as by my first crush was still such a blow to my feeble heart. I remember **Wind Of Change**, the song by **Scorpions,** was so powerful. The weeping within me cried out, such feelings overwhelmed me, I was devastated. I didn't have anyone to talk to as she was out with Sam and her activities. I locked myself in the bathroom, put the stereo on repeat and grabbed a knife. I was a hormonal teenager, with a broken heart and no one to talk to. I had heard my mother talking to her brothers and sisters and her parents telling them that I was no good, that somehow my father had a been a bad influence on me. It broke my heart hearing her gossip and degrade me. As the distance between myself and family members had already severed any normal life that I thought I could have, I was a mess, in need of love. I never wanted to kill myself; I just wanted to die. I was losing a battle and there was nothing but emptiness, no one cared, no one understood that I was so alone, or just lonely.

The feelings I had were so extreme it was dangerous and when I cut myself it didn't hurt, so I did it again. I could never hurt other people, my own inflicted pain was enough, but it wasn't right, it was wrong. Thoughts whirled in my mind: I never wanted to be caught or I'd get in trouble; I never wanted to cause my family hurt; I never wanted to cause pain to anyone else; I never have wanted anyone I ever met to be hurt by me.

That was when I snapped out of it, the depressing feelings were overwhelming me. I quickly left the bathroom, washed the knife and put it away. I was crying out inside. I wanted to be noticed, not for bad attention, just to be validated or told loving words, anything. I needed to be enveloped with loving arms and told I was worth something. I wanted to be loved. Instead, I wrapped a bandage around my wrist hoping it would be noticed, or that I would be kicked out again, shipped off, and unwanted. In my dreams I would wish, maybe my mom after all these years would see my hurt and pain, wash away all the raw emotions of helplessness and defeat and just tell me she loved me. She never did, and those two little scars

I carry with me to this day as a reminder of how strong I was and how silly.

I never did that again. That day is another moment that will forever stay within me. For how weak I was in the heart, but also for finding the strength in myself, to survive. It was a revelation of sorts, me against the world. I enjoyed not living in the shadow of my sister. I had clothes from all the coolest stores, my own room and a little sister I could now become close to. My stepdad, was awesome and always made me feel included in everything. Mom seemed to be happier, not struggling so much financially and enjoying decorating their new home. There was officially a sitting room, as opposed to all our other small homes. It was considered the white room that no one sat in. I loved it and that is where I would read my books. I loved reading fantasy as it was an escape from the world, always a happy ending of love and bliss. It was beautiful as I would escape to reading in this room when my life was in turmoil, to feel the emotions I was otherwise lacking in my own life.

My mom still had a way of not trusting me and I often felt her watching me to see if I was going to screw up somehow. I don't know why she would do that or perhaps it was just that inner voice of mine thinking she didn't really want me there. I would call her out on it now as a teenager, in that it would only add confirmation in her eyes that I was out of line.

School was a success, because in my teenage eyes, I was instantly popular. I never was before and it was awkward being liked by so many. It was new but I loved it, people saw me for me and I could now be me. I met so many amazing new friends.

I was catching a lot of slack at home and couldn't understand why, but hey, I was a teenager. We're not always pleasant to be around. My broken heart had healed and was now on a new road in life. I had much more freedom now and was able to catch a transit bus if I needed to, and it was doing just that, that lead me to meet my second boyfriend and fall hopelessly in love.

He pulled up in his car, shared with me I was beautiful, wanting to take me out sometime, handed me his phone number and kept on driving. I didn't phone him that day but many weeks later. I was going through the regular drama at high school with all the girls who I thought liked me and who turned on me just as fast. I've never had any friends that were ever like that. I never fit in with the popular crowd. I couldn't be vindictively mean or cunning or talk gossip. I hated that, it killed me, because my family had been doing that to me for years. I felt like my ship was sinking. Some girl accused me of stealing her boyfriend, but I never did as I wasn't into anyone at school. One of the guys said it was because they were jealous, that I was pretty and someone liked me. I couldn't understand that. These kids grew up together and I was on my own.

My popularity faded just as fast as it had happened. I would cry at home and not want to go to school, trying to voice my thoughts to my mother only lead to being even more labelled as a screw-up. They were all bullying me and wanting to fight me after school. I didn't know how to fight. I liked to pretend I was strong, but really wasn't. I was scared when the girls all showed up one Friday night at my house where my family was and started yelling for me to come out. I was terrified. I didn't know what to do My stepdad chased them off and my mother acted like my mother, threatening to kick me out, yelling at me the effect this is having on Sam. I was back to feeling afraid, lonely and scared. Butterflies flipped in my stomach, my mind did its crazy thing in my head: "Why did everyone want to beat on me, or hurt me? Didn't they realize how sad I was? I wouldn't steal anyone's boyfriend. I wouldn't hurt them, I liked them, I really liked all of them."

I had a moment of clarity that no matter where I go no one liked me. The only people who did like me were the crowd who didn't fit in, or the truly kind-hearted kids who were labelled nerds or had reputations. It was astonishing to finally have this three-dimensional, four-dimensional thinking I had acquired now. These people who thought they knew everyone, prestigious and popular, were stuck within themselves or just stuck up. They caused rumors and lies, and belittled people without a care as to how someone might feel. I became stronger and would be friends with anyone who was an outcast or labelled because to me they had heart.

Growing Up

To know Life now, I wish you to Live it, Tastefully and Gracefully… Always think before you Do…..

THEN I REMEMBERED that phone number I had of that guy who had offered me a ride I didn't take and instead gave me his number. So I called one day shortly after that horrible episode at my mom's. Whom never even came to make me feel better. I saw compassion in my step-fathers eyes, the humiliation of that night, me being a coward, and scared had bugged me, I needed to feel wanted, heard or even special. So when I phoned and he remembered me, I quickly said yes to going out. We met and he took me out for supper. It was the sweetest thing in the world. I had never been on a date before. I was so excited; instead of being cooped up at home, I could go out. He was older than I by five or six years, but he liked me and to me, that's all that counted.

He told me how he was adopted and we talked every day for weeks. Being validated and accepted was something I craved and needed as a young teenager. He asked me to go out with him again a month after knowing him, we were officially dating. He made me feel safe, would pick me up from school in his car. No longer was I picked on by all the girls, because he would scare them off. Right from the first day, he picked me up. He was my hero, "Action ", the bad boy I never knew existed until then, who understood what it felt like not to be wanted.

It was a whirlwind of feeling. I was liked for me and he wanted to be loved as I did. Little did I know, I was headed down a self-destructive path that would take me years to get out of. He hated it when I wasn't with him and I hated not being with him. He spoiled me. I would always get the most special presents and loving messages. Action, made me feel alive and worthwhile. It was a ride I never wanted to get off.

My mother would kick me out over every little thing. He gave me an aura of self-defiance with my mother, putting things in my ear, "How could you kick a young girl out of your house and how could a mother do that?" perhaps validating my own perceptions.

I had put up a protective wall after my heart was ripped out years ago. I wanted so much to be accepted by my mother, but no matter how hard I tried, I would never be equal to her idea of perfection. Simple things like asking to be enrolled in a sport or dance was answered, "No, you will never finish it," or I just wanted a hug that didn't happen. Don't get me wrong, she had love to give, just not to me.

The remarks were becoming too much, the looks were overbearing.

I realized she had never wanted me to come home, she had given up on me a long time ago, never really wanted me to begin with. I was never invited to family gatherings. She was ashamed of me, it hurt like nothing I could describe. The comfort a mother usually gives a child just wasn't there for us and I was now realizing that I was old enough and strong enough to be on my own. I had Action to watch out for me now, a guy who was strong, wasn't scared, a man who stuck up for me when no one else did, a man who would be enraged if someone hurt me.

My mind echoed his remarks, my own inner child was validating all he said, "Why stay somewhere I wasn't wanted?" I gave up trying to be the daughter I was never going to be to her. It hurt like hell, for me knowing my family didn't want me.

It scared me. During one of our many arguments, and me leaving, Action showed up as I was running as fast as I could to God knows where, held me and heard me. He made all that hurt and pain go away. He, in that moment became my lifeline.

He was able to take care of me, he promised and had money, sometimes a lot and sometimes a little. He almost always kept me fed and a roof over my head. He took care of me when no one else did. I was a little teenager in need of guidance. During these times, I vowed to myself I would never treat my own children like that. There would never be favoritism and I would never ever let them feel alone. I made all these promises to myself. I believe all the hopes helped me survive throughout my teenage years. My dreams and visions gave me strength to know I was growing up and soon would be an adult. To me, I would make it work. My idealistic dreams were just that dreams and it wasn't long before the walls I had built around Action came tumbling down.

I never thought anything Action did was bad. There were times when we had no food. I mean we had to eat, so I would have to sneak into my mothers garage when I knew they weren't home and raid their freezer so I could cook at Action's house. His friends loved me and all appreciated the fact that I kept a clean apartment and knew how to cook. It was all such a new experience to me, being on my own, no guidance at just barely fifteen years old, still oh so young.

I had many bouts of homesickness, and whenever I did, the guys would all tell stories about how they've been on their own since they were fourteen years old. They were in and out of jail. In the winter they wanted to get caught, as it was warmer and at least they would be fed.

I never wanted that in my life. I wasn't a thief but I was in awe and their stories fascinated me and were amazing. It was a protective feeling knowing no bad guys could hurt me, because these guys were tough and crazy, not afraid of anything. They treated me as if I was their baby sister, in turn I made them my family.

Action made sure that if I needed money, I had money, eventually. Soon that life started gnawing at me, I didn't like it. I was always holed up inside, many times all alone. If Action's roommate was home and Action wasn't, I heard about it when he came home. Action started getting very possessive. He would freak out and smash things, but then tell me he loved me, and that I worried him. It was a freaky feeling and something I wasn't sure I could handle. I never realized how crazy it could be. I felt safe from bad guys, but was starting to feel unsafe with the guy who said he loved me. It was weird. I had nowhere to go and I didn't want to feel lonely, better to be with someone who loved me, than places where I didn't fit in.

I was stuck in a situation I had no idea how to handle. Somehow, whenever I tried calling home, everything was my fault and I had to say sorry, sorry for feeling a certain way, looking a certain way. I hated it, I was damned if I did and damned if I didn't. I hated feeling as though if I brought anything up, somehow, some way everything was never anyone else' fault, only mine. I was a burden. In order to go home, I had to beg and plead, and go through all the emotions of hurt all over again. I didn't think my heart could handle much more, but I did know I couldn't live this lifestyle with the thieves and criminals I had met so far, it was downright crazy!

One day, I said how I felt to Action. He looked panicked and guilt ridden, he then promised that he would move us away. We could catch a bus and live at his family's house in the mountains. We'd live a good life! I wanted to meet his adopting parents and have a normal home. I wasn't cut out for this street life. Soon after, Action and I caught a bus out to his families in the middle of the Kootenay Mountains.

I don't know what I had expected but it wasn't anything like I envisioned. His parents were in retirement, a lot older than I expected. Their home was beautiful, but was also secluded in those mountains, on a cliff overlooking a waterfall with white rapids. They had a private cabin just off from the main house down a short trail. It was breath taking, something I would have appreciated more if I had felt more secure, the way I did back on the acreage. The seclusion freaked me out, that's where I'd go into hiding in my closet or somewhere far away and dark, when I was hurting, feeling alone and sad, when I was younger. I was more homesick than ever, but where was home to me? I never knew where home was, it left such a dark void within myself that I fell into a depression.

His parents did not seem impressed when we showed up. It reminded me a lot of the way my mother would look, when I tried coming home, not impressed and wanting me to go. I felt sick to my stomach, what had I just agreed to? It never seemed right, my intuition was always hitting a chord that would set off an alarm within me, my way of knowing what was right or wrong. I never trusted anything more than that.

Certain smells still remind me of that era in my life even now like the handouts of pear shampoo and conditioner. That's what his mom would buy for me or allow me to use. I felt as if we were asking for handouts and were delinquent.

I had pride. I didn't want to be there unwelcome. I knew that feeling all too well. I know Action was trying hard and doing his best to take care of me. He knew I wasn't into that lifestyle where we had been before this and he had all the right intentions, but he could feel me slipping away. His jealousy and true character were coming to the surface. The feelings I received when I feeling abandoned or alone, were his feelings as well, he just reacted in a different way. I looked to the light and would do my best to see all the good around me, the love in a person. Others going through whatever they did, would often only find the darkness and negativity.

We stayed in the cabin, closer to the cliff than I wanted. He was becoming really possessive of me. I had no one to look out for me, like a parent or friend, just me. I believe my instincts were kicking in, but I was still growing and wasn't as perceptive as I could be. I'm sure the reason he started acting so crazy, yelling and calling me names, was that he felt I wanted to leave and perhaps he knew I was going to.

This man I thought I loved wasn't who I wanted to spend my life with. It didn't fit with my childhood vision of a wonderful man, with a beautiful stable home and kids. It seemed a little too hard to live his lifestyle. I didn't like it when he would come home with money or presents knowing he had taken them from someone. That wasn't me, it never was. Sure, the presents were nice but to me they were never mine and I knew in my heart, I didn't want to live like that. I had to leave, get out of there. The name-calling soon turned into hair pulling and shoving me anytime I even mentioned wanting to leave.

I was petrified and the isolation started kicking in. I was treading very carefully and felt I had never really taken the time to get to know this guy or his life until I was already with him. I didn't have the proper voice when I should have to speak out to him about how I felt. I was only just fifteen years old and I didn't know very much about this commitment stuff or relationships at that age. It was my first real relationship and I was living with a total bad-ass in the middle of the mountains, far away from anyone I knew. This man who said he loved me was yelling at me, "You look like a boy."

It was my fault he kept losing his temper and breaking things around our cabin. He was starting to belittle me with words that were leaving marks upon my soul. He had slapped me at that time and I never knew any better as I had been slapped before. He would cry afterward saying how much he loved me, begging me not to leave him as he had been so alone his whole life. I would hold him, understanding his pain, try with love to heal this otherwise broken soul, this young man who just needed to be accepted. I was one person who completely understood.

One day, soon after a few good blowouts, he told me he wanted to show me that I shouldn't be so scared of the mountains, so he took me on a long walk. Then disappeared and left me there by this rushing river. I was so panicked I could barely scream, that gut-wrenching fear, where my legs were jelly and I wanted to scream but it wouldn't escape my mouth. I was lost and couldn't find my way back. My mind was calling out to anyone close by, my heart tumbling within my fragile body. I was scared. So, I walked carefully and slowly, finding my way towards the road before nightfall. I knew that once I hit the road, I could find my way back to his parent's house. As I was about to cross a path to the road, all of a sudden there he was, leaning against a rock, laughing at me. He was trying to fish. I was instantly upset. He thought it was a joke, and that it was funny.

I lost all feeling of safety with him. I wanted to go home, wherever that was. He walked me back towards the cabin. When we got there, I told him I was leaving. I was truly upset at his delinquent behavior as there were cougars in these mountains and I was petrified. It didn't dawn on me to tread carefully. He freaked like a thunderstorm that comes on too strong. He snapped pinning me to the ground. I was crying and screaming for help but no one could hear me. He started slapping me across the face to make me stop. He was choking me and as the stars were approaching to the point of passing out, I stopped fighting him in order to get him to stop. I just trembled with my silent tears as he ripped open my shirt, said I was a boy and that no one would want me. He spat on me and walked out the door. I felt dirty and gross. I felt humiliated and deflated, but most of all I felt as I had when I was a young girl, alone and afraid.

I don't know how long he was gone, but when he came back he had a whole bunch of money. He didn't just say sorry, he cried and begged me to forgive him. He was like a child begging me not to leave and said he would never do that to me again. I was his life and he loved me. I just held him as he balled his own eyes out and fell asleep. In the back of my mind, I had a plan to escape in the morning and try to get a ride to town. From there, I didn't know where to go but I had to leave, I had to. I knew from experience you can't change a person, but you can love them from afar.

If I could survive these last few months on my own, I could survive. I tried that morning to sneak out, quietly grabbing the bag I had packed the night before when he was gone. He came to so fast it made me jump. I looked guilty and he knew, like anyone who lived a sad life, he knew I was trying to leave. He snapped, jumped out of bed, grabbed hold of me and as he pinned me to the ground, he wrapped his hands around my neck and started choking me, slapping me, and spitting on me. Then he collapsed, realizing what he was doing. The profanities he said were horrible and truly disgusting. He snapped out of it for the briefest of moments, and as I got to that door, I ran as fast as I could, not looking back. I screamed for help. I believe his parents came out of the house, but I vaguely remember that, as I was running to the road

My instinct told me not to go into their house for help, not to stop. I didn't want them to get the brunt of his temper as I was running. I hit the main road and I could see an old truck coming around the corner. Whoever was driving could see me trying frantically to get them to stop, as my arms were flailing in the air,

"Help, help!"

Just as the truck stopped and I was jumping in, Action was coming up the drive. He was booting it fast. He had an axe in his hand that he must've gotten from the logs piled up outside the cabin. I told the guy, "Go, go, go!"

I'm so grateful for that man because if it wasn't for him, I wouldn't have gotten out of there. All I know is, I cried and told him everything that had happened. I didn't want to go to the police. My parents wouldn't come and get me and I wasn't risking being killed because I went to the police. My boyfriend was one crazy guy and I was scared.

I asked that man who picked me up, with bruises around my neck and swollen eyes, from tears and a red swollen face from his slaps, and said, "Please sir, just drive me as far up the road as you can in the opposite direction and I will hitchhike to my dad's in Alberta, please." I knew after the way my mother didn't want me around her precious family, I wouldn't be welcome there. I still had my daddy and he wouldn't turn me away. I made the decision where I was going in that instant.

I don't think that poor man knew what to do, but he had seen Action running for me, so he knew I was going to get hurt. I could see the calculation in his wise eyes, as I remember. He had such a friendly face and most importantly, I felt safe with him, safer then I had felt in a long time.

I know this, because that man drove for six hours, so close to exhaustion. I only explained as much as I could between crying, about everything, from my childhood to whom I had dated. I bared my soul to a stranger. It did me wonders because after that I slept better than I had done in years. He drove me as close as he could get me to the Alberta border and woke me up with such a nice gentle, fatherly voice, when we were at a truck stop. He had found a trucker who was going directly to my real dad's home town.

That man saved my life. I know it. If I could, I would wish to know who he was and where he was, because I would like to thank him. I know he must have wondered about that young girl that he saved, when she was being chased by a crazy man, who he drove all that way.

I would never know, as I didn't realize, being as young as I was, that regular children, teens aren't living at their boyfriends or going back and forth between parents, as well as getting kicked out. I'm not saying I was innocent by any means, *I was a child in need of love and guidance.* The people who I should've been able to get that from had all labelled me long before it was ever necessary. I was looking for love in all the wrong places. I should never have been able to do half the things I was allowed to do. I should've had security and protection. My little sister sure as heck wouldn't have been able to do those things. I wouldn't allow my own children to ever be unsafe or anywhere close to harm's way. There is no excuse for a parent to just let go and give up on a child, no reason. I felt like a little girl in a big, big bad world. My dreams were of a prince, who would take care of me, when I had no one else.

It turned out Action was not only the black sheep of his family as he had been adopted and had feelings of trying to find his place in the world, but he was also a career criminal as I found later. I was still feeling unsure, I wasn't happy where I was at and wanted my mother, I wanted a home. I couldn't understand why or how I could be told to leave home; don't they ever wonder if I'm okay? Why did I feel so utterly alone, I should know which way to go, where to go, I should have someone. Instead I often lied to strangers so they wouldn't know the shame I held, the pain I felt in not having anyone to turn to. My parents would say they were there, but when I would try to explain how I'd been hurt, they'd blow me off, put me down or walk away, trying to find some other place for me to go.

I was always a clean fanatic even at an early age. I relish routine and have always enjoyed getting up when the birds started chirping. It had been great being loved by him and my bad boy made me feel safe and not alone, but he put me in harm's way with his own personal demons. I couldn't handle any more of people's words, it caused a deep, deep hole within my heart. His words and slander would hurt more than any grabbing or choking.

I wasn't the perfect teenager, but I had heart. I never would've steered the wrong way if I had love and understanding, or had been allowed my own individual character. I wasn't bad or mean. When I would get upset it was because no one would listen to the truth or acknowledge me.

A huge piece was still missing from my life, I wasn't happy or satisfied and when I started voicing my thoughts to Action and never once did he ever say my parents were horrible. He treated me as he would a treasure that he wanted keep safe and secure. I didn't know that was a form of manipulation or control. I didn't know any better, until it turned violent. Even then, I had no one to turn to, so I stayed as long as I could, until it became too scary, and intimidating, until he made me feel what I had always felt, unwanted, scared and alone.

I learned then how to survive on my own. As the other trucker and I approached my father and sister's home town, it was late, dark and most people would be sleeping. I asked to use his phone and called a friend of mine with a super cool dad. I quickly explained I need a place to stay. It was in another town five miles past my dad's. They were excited to see me. That was such a good feeling, a moment I relished and held within me, to be wanted and not turned away with a sneer.

I will never forget the look on this trucker's face as he said, "You don't ever get stuck in this situation again. You are a good girl, too young to be out by yourself!"

That was a kind reprimand from a person who liked me. The feeling of acceptance was something I craved, I valued what he said and I still hold those memories close. I look back now and see how most other people genuinely accepted me, liked me, even cared, until they met my family, and heard the slander. He drove right through that small town and dropped me off at their front door. I remember my friend's dad coming out to see what was going on and him talking to the trucker as my girlfriend and I embraced. It was a reunion of complete happiness. I needed to talk to someone and come to terms with all that happened.

As her dad came in, he looked grim so I think whatever that gentleman who rescued me had said to the second trucker was now told to my friend's dad. I was so scared he would kick me out. I started crying and crying. As my friend was holding me, he leaned down and said, "GIRL, you are not to be doing that again. You have a home with us for however long you need it. Why your parents aren't around is not mine to question, but you and my girl can bunk up together and share a room." I was going to be okay. I had a home and I wasn't alone, resonated through me. The joy must have been written all over, because he leaned down and gave me a huge hug and said, "Guess I have two daughters, now don't I." My girlfriend and I, jumped up and down.

Living on my Own

I look back now and wonder why I held onto my family, how I was beaten and hurt, why I couldn't go home, isn't that what family is? I see now, I raised myself, it was a slow process to becoming comfortable in myself. Or a smaller sentence, coming full circle to finding who I really was, where I did belong.

IT WAS A new beginning with a new home and family, what I had always wanted, to be accepted for myself and have stability. I didn't think to call my father as I had thought to do before, or I was going to have to grovel to be able to go back there. It never crossed my mind for a few days. I was too busy enjoying my new sense of family and home, too busy to hear the speculation or grimness in their words. I just needed to relax, enjoy and relish the moments of acceptance.

I didn't want to call my parents, because it would mean explaining, the criticism and putting myself into these situations, as opposed to them accepting responsibility for never wanting me in the first place. I did eventually call my dad, but never told him what happened. It was too hard to relive, and he seemed okay with me living with my friends. He said I couldn't stop by unless he was there. It truly broke my heart that my sister or dad never even wanted to see me, or didn't rush over to hold me, hug me or even love me, when all I needed was their love . I was to them all they'd ever thought, NO Good.

I never, ever received any type of welcoming, like I did by my friends. I lived there for a whole year and got a job as a waitress at the local restaurant so I could pay my way. I think I was happy, but often flutters of yearning would engulf me when I thought of my family.

I was keeping in contact with my friends in BC, and it was nice, almost as if I didn't want to stay forever. My thinking was developing along the lines of My Family Are My Friends.

My sister would turn her nose up at me or shake her head at me in public when we would run into each other. The love we had once shared where I had thought of her as my idol and a second mother was long gone. Suffice it to say, I was hardening myself towards the careless way I'd been treated.

Sabrina was a total small town girl who found her place in the world, dating one of the In guys and soon to have a baby. It only showed me people do grow up fast. My dad, I felt more apart from him than ever, because he never took the time to see who I really was, or even how I was. He was my dad, the one who was supposed to save his little girl from heart ache.

It was hard, but my girlfriend and her dad, made me feel good and loved. He really did treat me like a second daughter. I opened up to them about what my ex did. He said," if he could get his hands on that Mothe%&&$, he'd shoot him!" It really touched me not to be judged by him, but encouraged, even stuck up for. It gave me a peace I'd been missing in my life, as if I was worth something. Her dad told me I was too nice to people and needed to toughen up and never allow anyone to hurt me again. He said it in a lesson sort of way, as opposed to a sneering remark. I stayed single after Action for a long time.

My family didn't really contact me and my mother never even tried calling once. Who knew what she had told my grandparents, aunts and uncles. I never even belonged or was ever invited to any family dinners or events, almost as if I was never part of any of them. That's a heavy burden to feel in one's small heart. I felt like the outcast because I was. It opened a whole new beginning in my life, it gave me worth knowing it was me against the world.

It was getting hard to be in the small town where everyone whispered and taunted me. No one really acknowledged me, except to purposely barb me, only people who were working from out of town would invite me out or ask me to do things. It seemed everyone I knew was a pothead or rather that's where I fit in. I wanted something more out of life instead of being stuck in this small town.

I mean my sister fit in, but me I knew I couldn't have any children here because all they would grow up seeing would be people who put their mommy down and I wouldn't allow that to happen. I knew the ramifications of that. So living here long-term was never going to work for me. I didn't like the snow much or the windy cold weather. I wanted to go home to BC, where it was rainy in the winter, green, beautiful and lush all year round. I loved the natural world of BC where there was always beauty and a sense of peacefulness. I would often when I was there, take long walks enjoying the surroundings as long as there weren't any roaming dogs. My fear of dogs is legendary, even poodles.

I was getting excited about going back. I was working and saving money for a Greyhound bus ticket and then from their flight back to BC. I was welcome to stay at another girlfriend's house in BC, until I contacted my mother. If that didn't work, I would get a job and my own place as I was almost seventeen. I wanted a place where no one knew my name, a place where it seemed that people really did like me. I wanted a place no matter how big, small, or any race and color, brown, white or black, where I could fit in. I wanted a home.

Vancouver is a city of dreams, and so much more. I was never a small town girl. It was a good escape for me to get my bearings after being with my freaky ex. It was never an idea to stay in that town, it's a place where everyone knew your name, what you did, cliques were formed and people shaped, all because of one person's opinion. Unless you fit in there you were never at home.

So, off I went to that city I loved, with many thanks and hugs for the people who had taken me in. I was ready to start out on my own, or maybe be accepted by my mother finally. I was so excited to get back to BC that I had butterflies the whole way.

When I landed, true to her word, my girlfriend who was perhaps two years older than me, was waiting for me. She was a bigger girl, a well-grounded person, with a huge heart who lived with her dad. She was another pothead. I was coming to realize almost everyone I knew was a pothead. I was growing up, not needing so much to be accepted by my family, my friends were my family. Every day I still wished for them to just love me for me, or see the Kerri I knew I was, while others saw but they were too blind to notice.

We walked out of the airport and jumped in her little white Omni car, and rolled down the road, laughing. Ahh, it was good to be back to this beautiful land, in BC. She was going on about how everyone missed me and were happy I wasn't with Action anymore.

As she was telling me about the bar, I wondered how she got in, she wasn't of age. She then said she had fake ID and she also had some for me. She said our friend's older brother and his best friend would be meeting us there later. I was so in, a new experience, with my wide eyes and gypsy attitude. I was excited, not to mention that I had a huge crush on my friend's older brother. He was one of those oh-so-cool but yet oh-so discreet guys with class, good looks and a fast car. There was no way I was going to miss out on seeing him.

Seeing her and being back in Beautiful BC was amazing. I loved the green grass and the sounds of the waves crashing against the rocks. BC was my home, a place where I was happy and everyone loved me there. I was known more as girlfriend material, and because of my mother and stepdad, I was known to be a wealthier girl. Not very many people knew my stepfather wasn't my real dad; to me he was my dad. Everyone knew me. The *me* I could be. That loyal, loving friend, who helped where needed and never gave up on others, who loved life and people. The side I wanted so many times to be seen by my judgmental loved ones, whom I still loved, no matter what.

I was going to move in with my girlfriend and her dad, for a short while until I could find a job and a place to rent. All my friends now had cars and it was pretty cool not being so young that I had to constantly lie to other parents that my parents knew where I was or make up a story for them allowing me to have sleepovers on school nights, even though I really had no place to go. Being seventeen was different; even though I felt much older than that. My friend's dad in BC was awesome, he knew the truth and welcomed me with open arms. Yep, I had found my place, I belonged. I was single, young, carefree and happy.

The girls had given me the fake ID, and it was going to be my first night ever in a bar. Their older brothers who were above legal age by a few years, were all showing up. I felt safe. Safety was a huge issue and always a priority. Growing up without guidance, I had to have some principles and that was mine.

It felt good walking into that bar, "Cheers." The bouncer loved me and instantly named me "Jody Foster". I felt amazing. We were all having a blast. When "Kane", my friend's brother walked in with his best friend, I melted. I sure hoped he liked me. He was beauty incarnated and I was head over heels crushing on that bad gentle boy/man, hard!

The music was blasting and I felt it flowing like the alcohol in my veins. My friends were giggling that Kane and his buddy only showed up because I was back in town, I couldn't understand why everyone lately had been stating I was pretty, I never felt it and it was a compliment I would often shrug off.

As they strolled up to us, Kane grabbed me, swung me around and almost carried me away in his arms to the dance floor where he kissed me, random and secretive. I was going to melt into a puddle on the floor. I loved every moment of that night, being back, and now the one guy I liked when I had first laid eyes on him, was kissing me as if I was the only person in the crowded place, unexpected and totally consumed. I did not notice that we kissed like that for well over forty-five minutes as the bar's lights came on and it was time to go.

My friends were still laughing and in their own world with Kane's friend, who was a complete joker, a fun guy with huge muscles, but not Kane, he was an open book as opposed to the invisible guy , that was Kane. As fast as the lights came on, Kane was gone, with his buddy and the girls and I jumped in her car and drove home.

I remember thinking," What a night". We all talked until we fell asleep, I was just thinking, "WOW."

Kane wasn't the sort of young man you would date or marry and live happily ever after with (not that you wouldn't want to). He was discreet, intelligent, and beautiful to the point of essence and substance. He had an air of darkness with a touch of all loveliness. He was Kane, to be kissed by him softly as if you were the only person in the room was nothing less than magnificent.

His best friend, Zak, was just as cool in a sort of light instead of dark side. He was funny, wild, made everyone laugh and was built along the same lines as Kane. Those two were best friends and complimented each other beautifully.

New Beginnings

They never took the time, to truly see the impact they've had on my life, how it hurt and what created the dynamics surrounding my existence....

ZAK SHOWED UP at my friend's house later the next day in his hot rod Trans Am, roaring the engine, as he was pulling up on the front lawn. Having all of us girls hanging off the balcony laughing as he yelled up, "Kerri, come to the store with me, quick." I quickly put on my sandals and ran out the door. I jumped into his car (with the sun roofs off in the back seat) and we ripped down the street. I felt alive, more alive than ever. I was laughing, carefree and really did feel pretty. He had the music cranked up as he did a donut: honking the horn, we sped off.

We listened to music for a bit, then he turned it down, and said, "You do know Kane has been with the same girl and she basically lives with him, for LIKE, two years now, right?"

I had no idea, but I wasn't hurt, far from it. Kane was like an invisible god, whom anyone barely saw. Now I knew why, I just smiled and said, "Now I do, Zak." He laughed as he cranked the music back up.

It was a special moment making a friendship that would last for years. We cruised for a bit and then stopped at a store. I remember him coming back with a rose and giving it to me. That was totally cool, almost adoring. We talked for a while then we made plans to go out sometime in the next few days. As he dropped me off at my friend's, he gave me his number and sped away, revving the engine as he took off.

My friends were all chill, probably baked, as I walked in. I told them what was said and they told me I should date him," Zak". It was amazing to have friends like that, no bars or walls, just us being girls, wanting what all girls want, love, infatuations and being carefree. We all as teenaged young ladies agreed that Kane was the type not to date, many have tried, and none succeeded.

I knew I had to call my mother and let her know I was back in BC, but I regretted having to do so. I was a young girl who had already been on my own for over a year and I didn't want to hear the disappointment in her voice. It still hurt that she didn't care enough about me to give a shit, that's how I felt during those years. Perhaps I needed her to say I was worth something and that she wanted me, wanted to be a normal, loving parent. It's like setting yourself up to be hurt and that wasn't what I wanted. I was too busy enjoying being around all the people I had missed, who missed me. I knew I couldn't live at my girlfriend's even though the offer was there. I wanted to go back to school and graduate, like a normal girl. I had Dreams and it did not matter what I'd already had been through. My dreams were alive, well and ready to transpire. But I could not go to school without a normal residence.

I put it off for a week, just enjoying being with my friends who were my family. They were my sisters and in some ways, were even my parents. I was starting to realize for all I had been through by the time I was sixteen and a half, I was much older than them in some ways. I could only laugh and screw around, do my nails and such for so long, before I was bored.

I had had a job by the time I was fourteen and was used to supporting myself. I loved my family of friends always, even still to this day. I just wanted more intellectual conversations that would leave me more fulfilled. Also, I had plans for my future, it was me against the world. No matter how many times I've tried to be that girl everyone wanted, I wasn't. My own self-talk was often negative, my own worst critic, saying that I was no good or no one would want me. I set myself up for failure as I was starting to believe what was drilled into my head when I was young.

Zak stopped by every day and was worming his funny little way into my heart, but I was holding off. He was three or four years older than I, which made it easy to hang out with him and converse. He had his own place and understood me more than anyone but I was still scared and scarred from my life with Action. I really didn't want that whole relationship stuff and was also self-conscious, overly worrying about what people would think of me if I actually did date Kane's best friend. Zak was the complete opposite of Kane. He knew how to touch deep places within my heart. He was growing on me and my vision of a life-long love wasn't far from the surface with him.

It was he who understood me the most. I could open up to him, as to no one else, and with his insanely funny nature, he could make me laugh or smile no matter what. His mother was a Christian, an exceptional woman who accepts everyone as they are. She is known as a pillar in the community and takes in children who have a hard upbringing and have been taken away from parents by social services. She raises them as her own. She never judged me out loud, but I could tell by her facial expressions that she didn't believe Zak and I should be together. She was a wise woman and later on in my life, I could completely relate to her, and absolutely respect her.

Zak started pushing me to talk to my mother and try to live with her and Tom again. He brought me to my mother's front door, instead of phoning her to say that I was back in town. He knew that I wanted to go back to school. Zak heard all of my thoughts as he was one of my closest confidants.

I can remember that day clearly. I did not receive the welcome I thought I would get when I knocked on the door on that beautiful spring day. The sun was high in the sky as my mother opened the door. The look of shock was priceless. She never smiled, never embraced me, like a mother who had missed her child would, as I said she was in shock. I had left my luggage a block down the road with Zak. I didn't want my mother to think I was showing up with friends on a party kick, since that was what I always heard them say now, their own speculative assumptions. I wanted her to believe in me. I needed her to believe in me. As she invited me in, I felt awkward and more than a little out of place. As this was my mother's house, I shouldn't have had to knock, I should've been welcome to come in. I should've been loved.

I gave her the normal rundown of what I was doing in BC because the last she knew I was in Provost, Alberta. I told her I wanted to come home, be with my mom, and small towns weren't for me, I just wanted to come home. I know I was begging her with my eyes, as I carry my heart on my face and sleeve. I was the type of teenager who has seen a lot in her sixteen and a half years. I would cry tears of happiness when I met someone I hadn't seen in a while, often gushy over little mishaps.

She was looking at me and asking why I was there with speculation in her eyes. I remember quickly saying I can go and find a job or apartment to rent. Not that I had the slightest clue as to how to rent a place, let alone find one, or the fact that you had to be above a certain age. I said it nonetheless. As soon as I said that, insinuating I didn't have to stay with her or that I didn't want to impose, she started laying down the ground rules. Still there was no hug or even any happiness in her eyes, even though my mother hadn't seen me in over a year. I couldn't understand why my ten-year-old sister whom I could clearly hear in the front room playing, didn't even run up and give her big sister a hug, or say hello. It hurt me to the core. I was unsteady, tears were filling my eyes fast, that was when my mother leaned in and gave me a hug, saying, "I love you, Kerri, everything will be all right." She said it as if there was something wrong with my life and me, as if I was a delinquent, as if I came home because of trouble. I never did. I came home because that was where I belonged, where I should be. She just kept holding me saying everything would be all right, which made me cry even more. I had learnt silent sobs from when I was a girl and never spoke the words maybe I should have. "Do you even want me, do you or have you even ever loved me?" Instead, I let my mother think whatever she wanted as I didn't want her to kick me out again.

She then asked as the tears were fading and convulsions of sadness subsiding, where my bags were. I mentioned I left them down the road around the corner block, as I didn't want to bother her. She told me to go out and get them and come home; we would discuss everything later. I remember walking out the door with a feeling of sadness and shame, but also happy I was going to be with my mother, I loved her, I needed her.

As I went up to Zak, I put on a façade of happiness, but I also thanked him for pushing me to do this and I truly meant that. His mother lived just ten minutes away, and he said that he would be coming to get me all the time and visit. I was so happy knowing I had that one loyal friend, even though I had all my girlfriends too, but girls are harder for me to trust as they always end up turning on me, even though these hadn't, and so far after two years they have been more family than anything. In those moments, and that path it felt good, it felt right, I had finally made the right choice, at the right time, and I had to try one more time with my mother. She filled a void I always thought I was missing.

Zak true to his word, would come whisk me away lots. He took me on all sorts of adventures, most of all just made me feel special. He never took me over to Kane's though, not that: that was a big deal.

I ate at his mom's lots. My favorite dish was pork chops with mushroom soup. He and I went to his mom's church many times and when I think back to that time, I remember thinking how lucky he was to have a mother who completely loved him no matter what, totally devoted as she was. I always noticed families and their relationships with their children. It struck a chord in me more times than I can remember and I cried at the pure loveliness of it, often longing for it myself.

Zak had already been in a huge serious relationship where he had a baby girl with an older woman who already had two other children. He was the essence of a man in training. He was a guy who knew how to say all the right things, his shoulders were big and you could put a lot of baggage on them that he took in stride. I believe he got that characteristic from his mother.

One night, after many of our excursions, rolling around in his car and jamming to his rock 'n' roll music, as he sang at the top of his lungs, he kissed me. I mean really kissed me, his lips were soft and succulent, the kind of kiss that knocks you off your feet, a kiss that was ultimately gentle and soft.

To a girl who craved love, it completely took me by surprise. That was when I did indeed fall hopelessly in love with my friend. The power of a touch, a gentle touch does wonders to a broken soul. We couldn't stop kissing, from red lights, to driving, to sitting on his couch, our lips were inseparable. What made that even more special was that he was my friend and confidant beforehand. We did things together with his family that I loved. He was my love, my young high school love, we couldn't be apart.

My mother even liked him and I would see her smile at his jokes and laugh. It was special to see my mother accept me more and more. It touched my heart. My stepfather never liked him, but tolerated him, for my sake I presume. I was growing up and to me he was the moon, the stars, my light. My Zak.

The day our trust wavered, was on the day he pulled up outside of a house and went inside. Soon he came running out, like a bat out of hell with a French fry sticking out of his mouth as a woman in her thirties was chasing after him, freaking out. When I say freaking out, I mean running for his car as if she was going to kick some serious ass! I was in complete shock as he jumped in the car and tried locking the doors as he was speeding off. She started banging on the windows, kicking the doors, my side in particular, and screaming, "I'm going to kill you, Zak!" I was shocked, completely shocked, I had no idea what that was all about.

Zak looked at me and tried to kiss me. He said that was the mother of his child. He had just broken up with her and where he had lived, as honest and true as he could only be. I thought he loved me, swarmed in my mind. No wonder his mother acted as she had towards me. I was a home wrecker and I was ashamed, that I looked like that to his family. That was a betrayal of my heart in the worst degree. I asked him to drop me off as we were now in one of the worst argument of our lives.

I remember coming into to my Mom's, sad, crying and told her what had happened. My stepfather didn't look too impressed and said, all casual, "See that's why I didn't like him, I knew something was going on." My heart was shattered, and broken. I believed in trust or wanted it so bad that I believed certain things hurt me more than anything. I couldn't understand how he could do that to me. I was his friend and over the few months we had spent together, how come he never told me, that they were still together or even before he kissed me like that. Or why didn't I ask?

Questions and unknown answers flooded my teenage, young adult head. It was the beginning to another broken wing and a blow to my heart I was feeling little inside. To top it off, I missed him as if a part of me was missing. I ignored his calls and kept on with my everyday life as a now student in school.

One day, I'm sure no less than a week, he pulled up in the parking lot in a huge 4x4 truck, lifted to the hilt and he showed everyone in my high school he was my boyfriend. How romantic, right? Yep, I forgave him. I missed him and felt he loved me and they did break up right? This was my common mistake of making excuses for a wrong done to me.

He took me to his mother's where he was now staying in her basement. We started talking about moving in together, moving away and him working on the drilling rigs to make money. I would laugh, yeah, right, a BC boy in the heart of cold winter weather in Alberta? But a dream is a dream and we often would lie awake talking of forever. I was just happy he was back. I loved him and I could forgive him. I always believed in the goodness of people, always. I didn't know that one day it would save me.

In my heart of hearts, I knew one day we weren't going to be together. A doubt had been placed and it created the vicious cycle of jealousy between us. Once a trust is broken, it's broken. I wondered what else he was hiding. Sure, when we were together, we were the only ones who existed, but he never took me around to see what kept him always so busy when we weren't together. When we were together, we were too enthralled in each other to do anything else. The seed had been planted in our minds about running away, and building a future of our own.

During this time, I was adoring my older sister Sabrina, who had a baby a year or so before. I thought she was the luckiest girl in the world. I wanted the feeling of my own family, as it was unconditional love, a forever love that never fades or leaves you alone, a love that lasts forever. My dreams were what had kept me from sadness. My dreams had kept me alive throughout some dark days of my childhood; my dream was having a family of my own.

Even though we were planning, my mind was working on the feelings of trust and hurt. Often I would ask myself why I accepted certain things from the people I loved, why I would forgive so easily? I believed in the good, that good would always prevail, and did I take him back, of course, I did. I understood him. He gave me love or I believed that is what love was. I never knew any better, that even though I forgave, it would eat me up inside until the betrayal by ones who said they loved me hurt me too much and it would come to the surface. I never knew any better. I was still very much a young girl inside, even though I wanted to be a woman and I even thought I was an adult, I hadn't learnt to be strong enough to walk away or to know my own limits of what my mind, body, heart and soul could handle. My beliefs, and dreams helped me to *Kerri-On*, not let go, and never give up. My friends had never given up on me, why would I ever give up on them, in particular him. He gave me back a piece of myself that I was missing, acceptance. My Zak truly loved me.

My father's 40th birthday party was fast approaching. My mother was planning like crazy, inviting people my step-father hadn't seen in years. I was super excited. Zak and I were waiting until after the party to leave for Alberta, to embark on a whole new life together with the dream of having a home and family. The only thing that sucked was I wasn't eighteen yet and he was, so he could go to the bars. That would bother me, you know, petty jealousy.

The party was a blast. We broke the news to both our parents and left the next day. Zak and I had asked his mother to pay for a hotel room for a month until his first paycheck, when we could rent a house. He started work immediately. I will never forget walking into the town's small restaurant and one of my sister's friends was working there as a waitress. She had to take a double look at me and said, "Are you, Kerri? Sabrina's little sister?"

I said, "How are you?" all pleasant and happy.

She said, "WOW, you sure have changed. You look so different now, as opposed too, as opposed too," she lingered with her innuendo, then she laughed and gave me a hug.

I felt elevated for sure, but it also made me feel as though it was okay for my sister and her friend's to belittle me all over again. I became very self-conscious with Zak. Is he going to hear how horrible I am, and not love me, or start treating me badly? That girl's remark stayed within me, haunting and even taunting me.

I went back to our hotel, after finding a job at another restaurant in town and waited for him. I was extremely happy when he came in. I felt immediately better and he told me all sorts of jokes about working. Then we started a new day as we had been in town for a few weeks already.

My sister was out here, as it had not worked out with her and the father of her child. She was starting over as well. I tried visiting with her and her friends, but was still not accepted, no matter how much I tried. They would look at me as if there was something wrong with me, and my sister would make me the butt end of jokes and laugh, they in turn right along with her. No matter how well I did, there were past mistakes I would be sure to hear about, past mistakes that made me a joke. My unhappy feelings were starting to creep in again, so I stopped going over there.

Zak came home from work one day, jumped in the shower quickly and started putting gel on his hair. I asked what he was getting ready for and he said he had a safety meeting. I didn't believe him at all. He went out and as I was lying in bed ready to fall asleep, I heard the phone ring. It was my auntie who had recently moved to town calling to say she just caught Zak in the bar making out with a girl who was one of my sister's friends!

So she, knowing what it felt to be the black sheep of the family, and how wrong he was, punched him off the chair. I didn't know that till later, my head was elsewhere. How could my sister's friend hurt me like that, always taking a piece of me? I was devastated, those lips and his kisses were mine. I cracked and finally lost it, my heart was pulverized.

That was a breaking point with me, after all the years of being lied to and treated like a shadow, I had had enough. I was so upset; I didn't want to hide in that closet anymore. I didn't want to crawl into myself and take it. I snapped; I became a horrible jealous monster. I dumped spaghetti in his clothes, packed them all up, cut holes in all his socks, jeans and parked them outside the door. Then in a stupid immature state, I called one of the guys he works with and had him come pick me up. We had a few drinks together and then got a hotel room as I needed Zak to see I was not going back to our room. Being as foolish and young as I was, I made out with his friend, nothing more. It was completely immature and a petty thing to do.

I was devastated still by my love doing that to me, so I drove all over town the next day, in his friend's truck. I talked to a few of my own friends, that same day and found a place to rent a room, the person I rented from was a guy who used to date my older sister.

I took a stand for the first time in my life and I was going to prove to everyone that I could do it: work, live on my own and be an adult. I was only seventeen and a half, but I had enough of living under people's thumbs. I had enough of being hurt, and being treated like a nuisance. I gathered strength from my pain. I moved my stuff out of the hotel that day while Zak was at work. He never came home either . . . hmmmmmm. . . oh well, I was done! I later found out that he actually did and had to phone his mother to rent him another room for the night.

I heard a few days later that he was living with a friend he had met in the oil patch, was still in our small town, and in the bar living it up. He had realized we weren't going to live together, because of my rashness. I know that if I hadn't set my mind on succeeding and being on my own without parents or friends, my boyfriend that day, I would've taken him back. Its what I always do. Soon after all that happened, Zak caught a bus and went back to BC and I stayed in town. We were over, and another chapter in my life had ended.

I was having the time of my life being on my own and mending my broken heart with work. The thought of soon being eighteen and an adult finally was a bridge I was preparing to cross for so much more opportunity. I finally went out and got my license on my own; life was falling into place. I just couldn't allow anyone or anything to bruise my once feeble heart or self-worth.

I was the happiest I had ever been at that point in my life. I was no longer a shadow, also becoming my own person. Sure my sister and her friends, talked about me and I still received sneers from people in town, and put downs but I was starting to make my own group of friends. They were completely separate from my sister's. I was coming into my own, learning my voice and my thoughts did mean something, but my family didn't like it..

The ironic thing was that my mother respected me more for it. When I looked at her or talked to her, it made me pause sometimes as I would see a woman, a lot like me trying to please her family, from buying them gifts to just dropping everything she was doing to be there for any one of them. It was a revaluation of sorts as I approached adulthood, or was forced to grow up. I often watched people and what they did, as their actions spoke louder to me than any words. I knew I couldn't constantly worry about what my family thought, if they loved me, or even wanted me, it was around that time in my life, I built a wall around myself, and accepted me for me. I chose to forget all about my lonely inner-self, my hurt, what they made me feel, and just to live for me, and be the best I could be. No matter what, I wasn't going anywhere and if anyone of them ever needed me, I'd be there, because that was who I was, a young woman full of heart. That was me. I was done denying that part of myself, to simply toughen up as they would say.

Adulthood

Every time someone cared about me, it gave me strength and a will to survive, a hope that someday there would be love for me out there, in that big world, a love that would last forever.....

WELL, THE DAY came that I was officially an adult. I was unbreakable, alive, kind and loving. I could no longer be told what to do. It was a special day. The restaurant where I was working, asked me to start working in the lounge and bar. I was excited. I remember taking the first legal drink of a shooter and having a blast with my roommate, who was a guy, a friend and nothing more, he truly was my friend during this time. He gave me confidence and self-worth. I valued him as a person.

My sister wasn't there, of course, no one in my family ever was, but I was okay with that. No one could tell me what to do or that I was no good. How wrong I was. My choices were officially my own. I felt way older than my eighteen years, but I could do this. I missed BC a lot, but the money and work were here, at least until I was nineteen and could work there, make better money, perhaps gain a career. I had always envisioned myself as a lawyer, or just so much more.

I was still in contact with my friends in BC and often wondered about Zak, how he was doing. I missed my friend, not in a romantic way, it had been a fleeting romance where two people join for reasons they never really know, souls joined to uplift one another, when they were lacking something.

I was working in the bar about four months later when I received an unexpected phone call from Kane. I was super happy, excited and had those dang butterflies he always gave me. I told him about all the money he could make here in Alberta, how well I was doing, how awesome it was, about my own place and really built up where I was. He wanted to come out for a visit. I was super excited to hear he was coming in a few weeks.

I will never forget the day when I actually received the phone call that he was at the Greyhound station in Edmonton, shivering and completely out of his element. I had to drive three hours to get him. When I finally got there, he jumped in the car in relief and we chatted the whole three hours back to my small town. I had never had so much conversation with him in my life. He had always been so discreet, to some it would seem eerie.

He was in town for a few weeks, loving it. He found his own room to rent. He was working and making good money. One day in the bar where I worked, in walked Zak and Kane; I was floored. They purposely did that for the shock value. It's who those two were together, trouble. Zak came up and swirled me around as we laughed and hugged.

Gosh, was it nice to see familiar faces, it's crazy but in BC I wasn't frowned upon, I wasn't talked about, I was me. I was so happy they were both here, my two best friends at the time. Definitely cool to have these two here, I had missed them tremendously. They were slamming back drinks in my workplace, singing Cherokee, having a blast. I had a few shots with them as well, it was allowed. Those two best friends would always dare each other to do the most foolish things. They were misfits I swear and it was hard not to admire the friendship they had, two peas in a pod.

Spice girls came on Kane dared Zak to sing it. Normal city boys as these two were, would never have done that back home. Completely hammered, Kane said he would give him a hundred dollars, to sing it. Good for Zak's outrageously funny character, he did it. The funniest thing in the world was these two" GQ" BC boys partying with a bunch of farmers.

I had no idea that Kane was upset because Zak and I had dated. So being mister conniving as he often was, with his secretive, gentle nature, he dared Zak to do all sorts of foolish things and provoked him until Zak was very drunk. Kane dared Zak that he couldn't take any of the girls in the place home that night.

Zak did take a girl home, but did not know that the girl was not someone he normally would have. It's called the country booze goggles. I laughed so hard, as Zak tried to wink, as if he was mister boss. He strolled out of the bar. He made a huge scene asking for the keys to Kane's place, tucked that girl's arm under his and strolled right out that door , like he was something else!. I was almost on the ground laughing, my gosh was it nice to have a bit of home here in Alberta. That night I laughed, laughed and laughed some more.

Kane was paying a lot of attention to me, acting suave as usual, so when Zak walked out of the bar with the cross-eyed girl (that I actually liked, as well as went to school with, when I lived with my real dad) throwing a wink at Kane and me, we almost wet our pants laughing, Zak you're awesome! Kane stayed until after closing and came back to my place as his was otherwise occupied.

We walked in the snow down two back alleys, arms around each other, sort of a romantic way, but so much more a friendship way. He was telling me that he and his girlfriend were finally over. He was enjoying himself out here and then all of a sudden he stopped me, leaned down, lifted me up and kissed me. It was not just any kiss, but the kind that made me oblivious to anything but the moment. (Kane had no idea, how I needed that). It was a long time since I felt those inklings of a real Heart to Heart kiss.

I was still that insecure girl who needed and craved intimacy, not in the sexual form but the power of a touch meant the world to me. I wasn't the sleep-around type of girl. We continued walking and talking as Kane had never really opened up to me before or to anyone for that matter. He was an aphrodisiac of the mind for me. I loved that about him, intelligence.

We went directly to my room and lay on the bed, fully clothed as *Honey Moon* Suite was playing and snuggled all night long. We just talked and bared our souls to each other, still kissing here and there. In the early morning hours, was the only time, Kane and I made love. Do not take that lightly, it was sensual in every way, every brush of his hand, a true gentleness. In the morning, Kane went back to his place whispering sweet nothings in my ear as he left. My roommate, shook his head and said I should be careful. I did not hear from Kane after that for a couple days, which was weird to me, but just the way he was.

The regular upsets those two were involved in caused Zak to freak out and he had to move to our basement, who knows with those guys. Then one night as I was walking to work down the same dang alley I always used, Kane came running up it with only a tank top on. He was saying he loved me, and wanted to be with me. I didn't understand at the time what had transpired, but a moment of revelation, if that's what it was, came to me. I was sick of being hurt and the games. I never wanted to lose my friends, Kane and Zak. I needed to think.

I was still a little offended that he'd just come here to visit me, but was hanging out with new people, and living there. We had done something, which to me was the most special thing in the world, and then he shut off and shut down. Then Zak showed up saying that I got played and he needed to stay with my roommate, and me until his bus left back to BC. He dropped hints, without being abrasive or rude, it all just came to me. It was not worth the price I would pay with my heart if we continued. Secretly, I wanted to, but Kane had always been so secretive, so I made a choice not to listen, but still to be a friend. Even though he was begging for us, I didn't believe it. I thought, how those two boys could come here, lift up my world with their light, and within a few weeks treat me like that. I felt used.

So Kane running down the alley, yelling he loves me, seemed very abnormal. Having lived through enough mental and emotional bullshit I could see the signs; this was not forever. I had to protect my frail, kind, forgiving, loving heart, and think of me. I was getting along amazingly well before they showed up and would continue to do so. But I would always keep a place in my heart for them both.

Zak left on his Greyhound bus with words of advice. Kane left shortly after, with a complete snub to me as if I wasn't worth a thing. He was always discreet and invisible, so when he becomes non-existent, he leaves hurt in his wake. It wounded me, but I didn't blame them. I knew it wouldn't last, my BC boys in Alberta, the dead of winter, what did I expect.

My ordinary life still took precedence over following false promises, hopes and dreams. I was a little wiser, but still would dream of a forever love, one day. I would never forget that feeling, I had lying in Kane's arms. I swear to this day that I felt the slightest, warmest glow flutter within me that night. Kane's and my music will forever be *Honeymoon Suite*.

Month & Half Later

I WAS FEELING very sluggish, but lovely and didn't want to go out. I felt more grounded than ever, confidant and sure of myself. I knew something was going on in my body, so I had to know. I went to the local drugstore, with employees who were known to gossip about customers, so buying a pregnancy test kit, was definitely going to be talked about. I went home, peed on my stick, and few moments later screamed. My roommate came rushing in as I was hunched over in a ball, looking at the test.

He hugged me. I don't understand why I screamed, because I knew in that instant, my Angel and my prayers had been answered. I knew that I was the luckiest woman in the world. There was never one doubt in my mind. I was having a baby and Kane was the dad. The only part was contemplating how to tell him. My baby was my baby; I was happy. I finally had a wish come true after all these years, I would have unconditional love. I never had a doubt, as some women talk about, ever within me. It was clear to me. I was having a child in the form of an angel. I knew, just knew, my child was my salvation, my angel, my world.

I made many choices in that moment. I immediately stopped working at the bar and started working at a new restaurant as well as at the local gas station. I was prepared to do whatever it took to have a healthy life for my beautiful child. I found another place to rent because I didn't want any smoke around my baby or during my pregnancy. I would save as much money as I could and work those two jobs until I couldn't anymore.

I went to the doctor to make sure we were healthy, but still, I had not told Kane. After three months, I had the ultra sound and received pictures. I decided to send a picture, as well as a letter to Kane's parent's house, to let them know. I never received a response from that family and it weighed heavily on my heart, during my pregnancy, and then went away just like that.

My strength came to me as it always does within the confines of my own sadness. No one would be allowed to think of my child as a mistake or place the heavy burdens of stereotyping on his or her innocent heart. It was my baby and me together against the world.

My mother was excited and happy for me. She seemed to be reluctant to ever truly accept me, but, nevertheless our bond grew. My sister was a whole different story, she was super thrilled to be an aunt. She finally after five years embraced me as a sister should. We became close again during my pregnancy.

She would always say, "You're the best pregnant, Kerri." I took that as a compliment, never thinking there was an underlying pun or unspoken accusation. I graciously loved it when she was nice. Her friends I was always too shy, to be around. They were amazing, and a few of them weren't who I had thought they were. I guess it was just constantly being on guard that made me wary. I started to build a few friendships with them and I believe they felt the same way. Maybe all they had heard about me wasn't the truth or maybe they just liked me. I know I always craved acceptance from her friends, secretly wanting them to acknowledge me as a person.

I worked at my two jobs, never paying much attention to the frowns in town. Since I wasn't with anyone, was alone and pregnant by someone who did not live there, I was an outcast. It hurt me more than ever. That was when I started thinking that maybe I shouldn't raise my baby in a small town where everyone puts me down, or thinks ill of me, when they never took the time to know me, the me that was visible to the naked eye. I didn't want my child to grow up living with that or being an outcast before anyone ever knew him/her.

I started talking to my mother regularly, mentioning I would be moving back there to raise my baby. My mother seemed ecstatic. She started asking me to come back when I was six months along. I said I wouldn't do that until I went on maternity leave, as I still needed to work to support myself and my child. I had never heard my mother say she wanted me back there. It was a beautiful feeling, a feeling of acceptance that I have always craved. I was excited, I had a baby on the way, a family of my own. My mother was starting to really respect and love me. I worked and lived on my own; nothing could bring me down.

I never thought I'd cry leaving Provost, Alberta, but I did. I was about to embark on a whole new life-changing experience. I was eight and a half months pregnant when I stopped working and boarded that plane. No one came to say goodbye. It was just me and my new baby, I was ready with a whole new beginning planned.

Landing in Vancouver (Pregnant)

Perhaps even later in life, you will not realize at that exact time, but as you look back, you will see the cornerstones of your life, the turning points and also the learning points. As I look back now I see what shaped me, made me and broke me. If you asked me would I do things differently or want to change anything, I believe in my heart of hearts I was meant to go through what I did in order to share with others my knowledge. So, no, I would not change a thing, I just wish I had grown up a little faster to realize some of my mistakes.

I DID NOT know what would come when I walked off the plane, to finally see my mother again after all this time. I was a woman now, with my own baby on the way. I know, I expected her to treat me the same way she treats my older sister, welcoming the fact that she's her own woman at last and a mother. I had been speaking with my mother over the past few months about the huge move, a doctor for my baby's birth, accommodations until after my child was born. I was ready, I was responsible and had it all planned before I even left my small town to embark on a new path. I did not leave that small town without planning. I had everything in order from maternity leave to where I'd be residing and a doctor. It was all pre- arranged.

I was so happy and excited. I cried tears of happiness seeing my mom, as I also do with my sister, when I haven't seen her for a while. I was always gushy like that, joy seriously brought out, and still does, my onset of tears. I love goodness and to this day, call them my love tears.

I never expected the look on my mother's face once our hug was done. It was a look I had always hated growing up, a look that said I'm very serious about what I am about to tell you to do. My stomach lurched. I didn't like this at all.

It was one of those moments, which stayed with me for all time, a moment which I knew would shape me or hurt me.

My mother told me it would be a few moments until my luggage was brought to the carousel. She asked me to come sit in a nearby waiting room lounge of the airport. As we sat down, she asked me many questions about my plans. I thought that in this we should be all excited and embracing each other because we had been separated for so long. I was old enough now to know it just wasn't going to happen, and our time as daughter and parent were over, but we were still family and family should be united as far as I am concerned.

She looked at me with a pensive stare, a look, which was serious, as if I was still a young girl that she could victimize. It was quite weird really, she said, "Well, Kerri, you are healthy, the baby is healthy and I'd like to offer you a deal, a deal that you only have a few weeks to accept.

"I believe you are too young to have a baby. I believe you still have a lot of growing to do before you're a mature adult, as well as a parent!"

I was stunned, shocked and so silent that she continued as if I was okay with what she was saying. I hid again within myself the way I had learnt as a child, while others degraded or belittled me or even hit me. I took it all in, so I could come up with excuses for it later. She went on to say that she had already talked to her family and they are willing for me to go to England and live there for a year. She offered to pay for whatever course I wanted to take as well as *$25,000* for my child. Under the condition that when I returned or if I ever returned at all (as I might build my life out there) that when or if I ever came back, I would only know my child as a sibling. He or she would never **UNDER ANY CIRCUMSTANCE** know I was his or her mother. She would raise that child as her own, in a good home with proper parents, as I wasn't ready to be one.

My mother had no idea that she took all my months of planning, all my self- worth, she demolished and destroyed my heart that day. I was excited and happy about my homecoming and the lengthy process of planning with my mother, not just because I needed to stay somewhere and have someone around in case I went into labor, but because we were all going to be a finally united at last..

The woman who had become a mother to me again, within the last six months, who had acted as if she wanted me again, and was excited to see me and be part of my life, a mother who had never really wanted to be my mother, had another agenda. She had even talked to God knows who, in our extended family (how utterly humiliating) and had taken everything that meant the world to me, all my hopes, my dreams and once again ripped my heart out from under me. What seemed like belittling to others was a nightmare to me. My fears haunting me once again from years before, I was no good.

It echoed in my head, my legs were weak, I couldn't breathe. She didn't even look at me. She didn't even acknowledge my eyes or body language. She just kept going as if her word was it, and she had already made up her mind. She continued, as if my silence was my answer, my heart was spilling around me. My tears came upon me, but when she noticed, she acted as if it didn't matter. She continued saying that she would be there during the delivery. I wouldn't see my baby so it wouldn't hurt me, and then she would put me on a plane to England. She said her doctor for many years supposedly was okay with this, or my mother would let her know, from what she tried explaining. This doctor was going to deliver my child!

The waves within my head blocked her out at that time. I couldn't hear her; I was going to pass out. She gave me a quick hug and said, "I will go get your bags. I don't want you lifting anything or harming yourself."(She meant my child, I'm sure).

Then she said, "I'll give you a few moments to think about it." As if, I was going to jump on the opportunity, just sell my child, and travel to England. She really didn't know me, did she!

First off, I had anxiety about being alone, to the point of huge panic attacks (not that I took anything). I hated going to places I didn't know, it made me feel alone and scared. I had friends around me at all times, as a crutch, so I wasn't desolate. I liked the familiar; I did not travel especially to a foreign country, where I knew not a soul!

My own insecurities rolling around in my mind, trying to make sense of this abrupt assault on my heart and soul, *(I had become closer with my sister and mother, or so I thought, during my pregnancy). It wounded me.*

This baby was my angel who was sent to me by my God, whatever higher power that was. I was so sure of that, my baby was my whole world. I had solely focused on him or her as if nothing in the world mattered from the time I knew I was pregnant to now. I had plans for a future with my child and me. I had slaved fourteen hour shifts, until I was eight and a half months pregnant to prepare myself for my child. I already had bought so many items for my baby, and was looking forward to buying his or her bedroom suite for when he/she was born.

My baby was and still is my world, my future. I had even shared my visions of how I felt that he or she was my angel with my mother. Even to the extent of being truly blessed. I even planned becoming a beautician and going to college to get my degree as my mother had, perhaps owning my own studio one day, as she had once done as well. It was a huge part of my going back to BC with so many more opportunities in Vancouver.

I didn't care so much that Kane and his family never acknowledged my child. They were who they were, it never bothered me. I wasn't upset or sad, it just meant my baby was mine. I sometimes hoped that one day, we would be playing in the front yard on a sunny day and Kane would drive by and see us, see his child. My dreams were such as those. I did not want the stigma of meanness or stereotyping around my child to taint him or her. I just wanted that everlasting love and companionship that was the family life I craved.

My mother in that moment had shown me that she never wanted me; she only wanted the gift I could give her. That no matter how well I did, or how much adversity I'd overcome growing up on my own, she would never, ever want me or respect me. She tricked me, used me, also belittled me with her rash behavior, scheming and planning. To her I was still a child, her mistake, and she never loved me, or she wouldn't have offered me such a horrendous business opportunity as that. She squashed me at that moment, she completely took all that self-esteem I had built up within myself over the last year and a half and threw it out the door.

What was sick about that was that she had planned it; she actually planned trying to buy my child from me. Her daughter was nothing short of a breeder to her, nothing more. If I had ever wanted to have my child adopted, wouldn't I have mentioned it? I was planning to start my own family. I planned every part of my pregnancy. I was excited, wholesome and happy. I was radiating with such purity.

My sister even complimented me numerous times, that I was amazing during my pregnancy. We were excited to have our children so close in age. My mother, whom I thought had finally accepted me as an adult and was excited for my child and me to move back, and for her to be a grandparent, had another agenda. That agenda was sick, horrible and mean. That agenda brought back the old feelings of worthlessness, being unwanted and abandonment in me. All she did was walk away, as if it was a normal thing to do.

She said one other thing, though, she didn't want me to talk about this in front of Sam. She wanted to keep my precious little sister from knowing about it, so she would just think she had a new brother or sister. That's why she brought it up privately at the airport. She also wanted me to sleep in the trailer in her driveway, not her million-dollar five-bedroom home, so I would have my own space. I felt sick.

Or was it to hide me and keep me away from my sister to have her own private family where I wasn't included. My head and heart were heavy, my head was spinning, my silent tears once again surfaced. She broke me more than she will ever know that day. All the strength I had gathered, the jokes I had taken in my small town during my pregnancy, all the hurt I had finally let go throughout my lonely teenage years were gone. She depleted me, my courage wavered, but my opinion and my answer were the same.

"NO! You are not buying my child from me. It is not and will not happen, Mother!" I had enough strength to immediately say, "No!" my anger towards her surfaced in those moments as I have never felt, it was like two metal pipes letting off sparks within my whole body. I kept them within me, allowing the vibrations to rivet throughout myself, as I often did to keep my emotions in check.

Even though I had told her No, she crushed me. She had planted that seed in my head that I was no good again. She played on my very soul in those moments when I was growing into a person and woman. I needed nurture, love and respect. From all the belittling remarks, to abandonment and physical abuse, I was shaped into the person I believed I was, ugly from the inside, alone and not good for anyone. I was just here for people to take out their anger, hate and own torment on.

I had thought I was better, whole and starting to believe in myself, and as an adult it was going to be better. That innuendo hurt me in more ways than anyone will know. I wanted my mom to love and respect me. I wanted my mother to be my mother. My family to be a family.

We drove back to her place from the airport in silence. She still wanted me to think about it as I had three weeks before the birth of my child and her offer would still stand if I had a change of heart. The joy and preparation I had had on coming back home to BC, made my mother's offer kind of take the wind from my sails.

Being pregnant added strength and peacefulness to my mind and body. It was such a beautiful time for me and I wanted my mother to know this. As soon as I was alone after settling in, I gathered my strength and peacefully fell asleep with my precious child curled up in my womb. Yes, he or she was my angel. I often cried tears of happiness just thinking of when I would meet him or her, face to face. I was happy and blissful when it was just us. That was something, my mother nor anyone, could ever take away!

The answer to her offer stayed the same and she eventually got over it or so I thought. I contacted a few friends in BC and let them know I was back and to revitalize my soul and independence. I wish I had known the cycle I do now, that when I felt alone, degraded, I would reach out to the ones I thought liked and respected me. My idea of respect was very different then from what it is now.

They would take me out for a little bit here and there just to visit over coffee at our own famous Esquires coffee house we often frequented. My friends were happy and excited about my child. It was also nice seeing Zak. He was especially attentive to me during my last few weeks of pregnancy. We often talked about Kane and Zak said, "It's Kane's loss not to accept it". Zak would say to me having his daughter was the best thing that ever happened to him. We would often lie in the sun and fall asleep together, not snuggling, as I was huge. He would laugh that my thighs were bigger than his and hearing him say that didn't hurt me, because I knew he truly cared about me.

My Child

During a transitional period in one's life you become more stable, understanding and at peace with all around you. When you take a moment to truly look around you to see the change, you enjoy it and you make it possible to allow the change to transition. It is a moment in which you feel everything shift around you to accommodate it.

THE DAY MY contractions started, my mother treated me with exceptional care all during my labor. I was a frightened first-time mother and had heard enough horror stories and had seen pictures that scared me. As the second stage of my birthing came, I took full control and put myself in a zone. My beautiful baby boy was born after nine hours of labor. I cried tears of happiness. He was a little cone head. To me it was so cute, my little peanut.

I had already loved him but at that moment, my blue-eyed eight-and-a-half pound baby boy held my heart forever within his grasp. He was perfect, healthy and he was mine.

The delight on my mother's face was just as special. My little sister also fell in love, to her she had a new doll to play with. It was so nice to see my stepdad smile. It was a moment which I wish I could've kept in a frame. A moment, where no matter all the other drama or hurt in our lives, we were a family and my beautiful baby angel boy was born. My mom, dad and sister left shortly after and my road onto parenting and being a new mom began. I felt at peace and perfectly happy. I had the love of my life.

Zak showed up with flowers and stuffed animals. He truly took my breath away, with the natural way parenting came to him. He just scooped up baby, "Ashton", and crawled right into the bed alongside us. I was in my housecoat, my baby in his sleeper. It felt like a family. I believe that was when Zak once again fell for me, not because of me but because of my son. He was acting like a doting father to my new baby boy. It just fit and gave me hope that one day I would have that whole family I craved. The child within me would heal. To be accepted is one of the greatest feelings in the world. I had it in that very moment.

Once I brought my son home, to my mother's, she offered me the room, directly upstairs from her room. It was nice and made me feel so much better, than being outside in a trailer, feeling that emptiness. I liked being around people, but during the last few weeks of pregnancy I had slept most of the time anyhow, so I hadn't mind much. It still hurt, very much so.

My little munchkin was such a great eater. One night, soon after we were settled, he woke up in the middle of the night, he cried as I was adjusting myself to breastfeed him. My mother came storming into the room and grabbed him as if I was doing something wrong. I asked her to hand him to me and she reluctantly did so. He instantly latched on. She watched for a moment, but I could feel her degrading me with her eyes. As she wearily left, I heard her make a comment that I needed to get formula, so that she could feed him. I couldn't understand at the time why such a comment hurt but it did. I knew it made me feel inadequate as a mother, my baby was only two weeks old.

The next morning, as Ashton and I went downstairs, my mother said it again. She was heading out to Costco and would be grabbing some, so sometimes she could feed my son, as well as everyone else could too. She crushed me as though I was a child. I wish I had been more in tune with the signs, or not so sensitive, or such a pleaser to my family, so their Innuendos wouldn't hurt so much, or even stronger so it didn't bring me down. I needed to be that strong woman I knew I could be, but I wasn't. I believed in the good of things and elements and people, I trusted to easily. My insecurities about being in that home, at my mother and stepdad's, were starting to wane on me.

That day later in the afternoon, I was lying with my baby on my chest in the sun room with silent tears rolling down my face as I gazed upon him, wondering why his father didn't want him, or why people didn't want me. I felt little and low, my tears wouldn't stop. I couldn't imagine him suffering my same feelings one day. He was a gift and beautiful, my son, my baby boy just so precious. I felt more than most, because of the feelings I had, as a child. It was overwhelming, the thought that my son, would one day, feel the same from his dad, or anyone else for that matter broke me.

When my mother came home, she came into the room and saw my tears. She allowed me to snuggle into her chest, as I wept and truly spoke the words that were within my heart. She let me cry, as she hugged me. I felt as though she really loved and validated me. The moments when I received the slightest attention, I relished it, sucked them up like a dishrag. I needed it. As the tears were drying she said, "Let me help you Kerri, teach you how much easier bottle feeding is. That way you can rest and relax and still enjoy yourself a little, go out sometimes. You are turning nineteen in a week, let me help you." My mother was allowing me to be nurtured by her, she gave me a precious moment that day, Love.

Why didn't I see it? Why didn't I see at that MOMENT that it was a manipulation? Maybe it wasn't, as I look back it seems obvious, why was I blinded by the caring hand and soothing hug when my mother embraced me. I will never forget that day.

It was sunny, very sunny for early November. I started taking pictures of my son on the gorgeous couch in the sitting room. I did not feel a weight lifted from me, but a calming within my body from her touch and embrace. I felt loved. I knew she loved me and in her own way she did. Perhaps she never expressed it to me in the right way or the same way she did to the other girls, but I know in that moment she did. She often said to me, "You are the kindest and most caring of all the girls".

My mother had bought formula. I still wasn't keen on it, as I wanted my son to be healthy with breast milk, but I let her try. The look on her face as she held my son was adoration, she loved him. I didn't know about having to pump at regular intervals, even if you feed by bottle, no one told me. I wasn't close to my family doctor as she seemed to have judged me before she knew me. I never went to see her unless it was an absolute must.

That week I allowed him to be bottle-fed a few times, it seemed my son was fussier when feeding from me, as if he wasn't getting enough, so I would go get him a top-up bottle. Eventually my milk waned and wasn't enough as it was drying up. It devastated me. I had read so many books during my pregnancy; why did I allow a bottle. It irritated me. I was choked, and I was also seeing how my mother was dominating me with my child now.

On my birthday, which was quiet, just me and my family, I opened my present and it was a present all right, a very nice one actually now that I look back. But maybe in my heart of hearts I wanted something from my mother a little more intimate, as a woman, or maybe special just for me. From the scaring remarks on my arrival to the comments, it still hurt. That week was very trying for me, watching and seeing how she was over-riding me as a parent at every turn. My stepdad wasn't around much as he was running the company, so he would only hear from my mother. I received a rocking chair that made me blow up at my mother. I was hurt. I cried, it made me look as if I was an ungrateful, spoiled, rotten child. It wasn't just the rocking chair, it was so much more. When I tried to voice my opinion, it seemed to only make it worse. The power of my voice was nothing more than a whisper. My sadness was turning into anger, no one ever listened, but I looked bad.

I knew then what I was seeing, my mother was only about my son and no one would listen. I tried justifying it by telling myself that I heard things such as parents doing that with their grandchildren and children, as if it was normal, but I knew it wasn't.

No one would listen to me. I was angry, pissed off and when I voiced it aloud, I looked as if I were horribly rotten, instead of speaking and no one listening. I said again," that I thought my mother was trying to take over my son!" I phoned Zak to get me out of this house with my baby. It was a rash, ill-considered plan and it was too fast to soon.

My mother sat there as if she was the victim and said I needed help. She was consoled by *her* family, as she would often say. It was demeaning hearing her say that all the time, her family on the island: my aunts and uncles, grandparents. And her family: Mom, Tom and Sam, almost as if they weren't mine. I got the subliminal message louder and clearer. I had enough, I couldn't handle the innuendos anymore, the ridicules and degrading remarks. I was leaving!

What I didn't know then and only found out from my sister years later, was that my mother had lost two babies trying to conceive with" In-vitro" just before I came home. She had wanted so badly to have another child with my stepdad, but after my little sister she had her tubes tied. She took all kinds of hormones and was pregnant with twins, but lost them in her third month. She and my dad were then told there wasn't any way to have more children as whoever had tied my mother's tubes had butchered them so badly they were irreparable. What I was sensing, was my mother wanting my son. I wish I had known more or was enlightened. I would have understood better and been soothing and compassionate, but also more wary and self-assured. I would've understood more, my heart went out to her, when I heard that. I finally understood after the fact.

My mother's parting words the next day, were this, "You are a mother now, Kerri Lynn. Those are the presents you receive, normal parents love that stuff, be grateful. It's what you wanted! My offer still stands. I will be there for your son, always but you are no longer welcome here!" Her words cut me deeply. I was the one to be upset, but forgave just as fast, after a few minutes or a good rest. I didn't carry grudges, I loved people, and especially loved my mom. Why was she so brutal or careless with her words to me?

Those words echoed within me as I thought again, why can't anyone around us see what goes on, no one sees it, no one! My words within myself were my downfall, my insecurities were my enemy and my self-doubt was my mistake. If I had focused on how truly inspirational, loving and caring I was, I would have seen the light, the right path, instead I reached out and negative, evil grabbed hold of me. All these years had gone by and I was never unhappy, but I was alone and sad. I hurt when things were thrown at me, but I was never a mean careless individual, never would I purposely hurt or torment an individual in any malicious or vindictive way. I still had goodness in me. I had a light energy about me that allowed a lot to roll off me. I never knew that having no support group or uplifting people around me would affect me so much that I would eventually fall from the abuse. Especially the mental and emotional abuse that had finally got to me.

I am human and can only take so much. I never knew the importance of surrounding myself with positive people, people who would build me up and who cared enough to be there for me if something happened. If I had a proper doctor, who had noticed that I was borderline post-partum, or in the wrong environment I might have had some help. I was falling apart, my self-talk, my self-doubt and the years of begging for everyone to stop and just get to know the real me were pushing me into a deeper depression.

The knowledge that I didn't deserve to be hit and tormented was slowly killing me inside, memories were crushing me all at once. What I had gone through and overcome was what most 9/10-year-olds, and even 15-year-olds never go through. If I had had a real friend or even a family member who built me up, I know it would've been different. I never knew the path I was heading down even existed, so off I went with my son to the only person I knew who cared enough to take us in. Instead of taking a deep breath, or having a gentle hand upon my back, instead of looking around and noticing that in a year or so of being away people change. I went out on my own that day, with the idealistic eyes of a teenager as opposed to a new young adult, whose only guidance was and has ever been my intuition.

Perhaps what I knew from before, wasn't the same as what I was entering now. I went into the arms of the only friend I knew, the friend who cared, not realizing that his environment was different now. Perhaps Zak was the same, but his circle was different, the circle of friends that I had never known or ever met. They were on the side of the tracks I had never known even existed, the side I was too blind to see until it was almost too late for both me and my little angel.

I walked out that door with my baby in tow and into a black van where Zak was waiting and we drove away. I will never forget the uneasy uncomfortable feeling I had, as I had never really met any of Zak's friends before and whoever was driving, was a total weirdo. I didn't like it, but Zak said he could only come get me with this ride, as he was in the middle of something. We headed to his cousin's house, where he now resided. When we arrived there, I felt so much better. His aunt was a nice woman with two teenagers, a girl and a boy. Zak's cousin was running around in booty shorts singing with her girlfriend. At fourteen, she was a beautiful girl. I was welcomed with open arms; everyone instantly fell in love with my son.

As Zak made me comfortable with all our stuff in his room, everyone was cuddling and coddling my boy. He held me then and kissed me. He leaned in and said, "I have always loved you, Kerri."

I needed to feel loved in that moment, it was familiar. He loved my son, and he was a man, a young man perhaps, but a familiar friend. Everyone just assumed we were together and soon even we just fell into the routine, it felt great, and I never took it personally that he would take care of Ashton. He didn't make me feel on edge the way my mother did.

I tried to go on maternity leave, but in BC, it was different. I didn't have enough hours and I was in a different province, or perhaps it didn't count out here. I was worried about how we were going to survive. Zak introduced me to welfare. I applied and immediately was accepted, the only problem was that I needed a place to rent or they wouldn't give me a portion of the money. I was used to a lot more money than what I was going to get, but at least I would survive, with child tax as well as financial assistance. I asked his aunt if she could sign some paper they gave me for the rent thing and she said she can't because she's already on it. I was shocked, as I didn't know that. She lived in a nice place, with nice things, but I was never one to judge, I just noticed. Zak and I went out and looked for a place to rent together. I was ignorant about this whole welfare thing, as I've always worked. He had money as well, so it wasn't a huge hardship. I lost the good feeling I had in Alberta, before I came back to BC. I was exactly the opposite from that, I was unsure, uneasy and started needing Zak for more and more everyday things a normal mother would do. I felt like I wasn't a good mom, not that I would ever leave my baby, but when he cried I'd get Zak to hold him, as it would break my heart, and I would feel helpless crying too. I had all that mental garbage in my head that I was no good, worthless, perhaps I was a screw up as everyone said. I was frustrated. I started noticing that his aunt was up at all hours and the music never stopped.

Zak introduced me to more and more people who were older and shadier. I started noticing he had changed over the last few years. He was grungier but still clean, just different. He would leave at all hours and come home early in the mornings. He wasn't cheating on me, he was a petty criminal. It was becoming unbearable. We had to leave there, so I forced him with promises and gentleness that eventually we found another place. He always brought a light into any room, he had that way about him, always had. It's what drew me to him in the beginning picking me up at my girlfriend's a few years before. It was a comfortable feeling for me, knowing him, but not the him now made me weary.

We were back at his aunt's, packing, and in walked Kane's sister and Kane's Mother. My heart dropped and I was shaking in my knees, literally wobbling. I sat down on the couch and immediately reached for my son protectively snuggling him, my peanut, as they conversed with Zak in the kitchen. He had laughter in his voice that was enlightening. His sister was the first to approach and asked me to bring little Ashton into the bedroom, she wanted to meet him.

As we went in there, she gave me the hugest hug and said I already know this is my brother's son and she held him. She made me feel beautiful in the way she took me aside and hugged me. I hadn't felt that in the last few weeks. She was extra careful with him, googling him as I do. When Kane's mom walked in she just gazed at Ashton and reached for his tiny little hand, her eyes went wide. She said his little pinky finger is cricketed and then said he looks identical to Kane when he was a baby. Kane had the same cricketed baby finger. They were both exited.

I never knew his family that well, my first impression was really of a very discreet family who come and go as they please. They opened up to me then, a little, and said Zak had told them where I was, as well as they didn't like his family overly much. They gossiped a bit in a friendly manner, trying to draw me into their conversation about Kane saying that he has been fooling around with Zak's cousin. They didn't seem happy about something, I wasn't catching, but it had to do with Zak and Kane hanging out as there was always trouble. I picked up on something that must be ongoing, but never mentioned it (to my surprise, it never hurt me at all).

They asked if they could keep in touch with me, and couldn't wait to see and tell Kane that they had met his little boy, their nephew and grandson. I couldn't help myself for asking if they had received the ultrasound picture I sent them. His mom looked at me and said it's safe. I believe that was another moment that affected me, it felt good to finally be acknowledged by his family, but also a little weird that it was acceptable to them the way Kane had been, as they were like nonchalantly insinuating, It was a great joy that Ashton was born, but not a priority or a huge impact, just was what it was, a normal everyday occurrence. It was cold.

When they left, which wasn't more than half an hour, I belted Zak in the arm. I was choked in the sense that it completely left me unaware and shocked, then I wrapped my arms around him and said, "Thank You for doing that." I needed it more than he will ever know. Zak went on about Kane, how he doesn't deserve to be Ashtons dad. He was extremely upset at the way everyone acted. Then, Zak spent the time to ask me if I really loved him, to have a family, the musical dream of what I always wanted and the security of happily ever after. My young girl dreams, perhaps now as an adult they could be a reality.

I was overwhelmed by the devotion I saw in Zak's eyes and heart for Ashton. It was all very overwhelming how the plans I had to move down here had turned into all this negligence, hurt and pain. I was hollow on the inside, and continuously turned a blind eye to all I believed in. I just started going with it, accepting a life that had no structure or goals, whereas I thrive on structure and routine. I gave up on myself. I believe I had post-partum illness, but will never know for sure. As I look back now, I see a mixture of signs. I also see a girl, lost, among a crazy crowd, stuck in a situation because she had nowhere to turn, and the places she had were the places she realized were bringing her down. I also knew it was my fault for allowing the weakness to overcome me.

Streets of Corruption & Sickness

*The only thing you can do is accept the past, learn from it, and never
Try, to alter it in any way and solely use it as a base on which you
Slowly build your foundation, your character, as well as your
Individuality…..*

WE MOVED INTO a basement suite that was like a dungeon dark
and cold. It was a breaking point in my life. He was finally showing
exactly whom he was and had turned into while I had been in
Alberta. That carefree boy with light in his eyes was as mixed up as
I, but on a different level from me. He will always have that light, it's
within him, but that boy and young man I knew, was doing crystal
meth. He was no longer just a wild child, but messed up.

We were not a good team together, no longer the same people
we once were. I was down on myself, feeling little and starting to
believe all I had ever heard about myself throughout the years by
the people I loved most in the world. My self-doubt became my
weakness. I do know, that being with someone who introduced me
to a kind of life I never knew about and people who lived a different
way than we both had, wasn't good or healthy for either of us. I felt
as though I had no one, no other options, nor the self-esteem and
confidence I had always tried to enforce on myself, I no longer had
strength. I don't know what possessed me to do what I did. I have
no excuse for my behavior, not one.

I officially tried crystal meth with him. He taught me all I needed to know about it. He did it, he functioned, he was a part of me, so I tried it and it erased all the nights I had lain awake with tears rolling down my face, wondering why they hurt me like they did. Didn't they know their voices mattered? What could I do better other than what I've already done? That was where I made the biggest mistake I have ever known, becoming something and someone I never even knew. I had energy like I've never known. I was no longer that sad little girl or young woman. I was mean; I hated all that had been done to me. I saw it all in a haze and if I did meth, my mind was too busy to be sad. This all happened within a three-month period of leaving my mother's house, four months since leaving Alberta.

One day when I came home, two guys were at the door threatening Zak. They had a gun and the next thing I knew the house was flooded, the police were called and it was plain horrible. *I would found out years later what the true story was but for now,* my eyes wide, shocked and completely a mess, I knew I had to make a choice. If I wanted to continue to live like this, I was not having my baby boy subjected to this sick lifestyle that I found myself in, to me it was gross. I had no respect for any of it, and I wasn't too scared to say it. My son was too young to make that choice; therefore, I made a choice in the frame of mind I was in, to protect him and to save him. If I couldn't save myself, I would save him. I knew if I could do one thing in this awful world correctly, it was letting him grow up without the hurt I had or had seen, or what he was around.

People who met me liked me, but were wary of me, I cannot stress this enough. I wasn't me, I was angry, my sadness was anger, pain and suffering. I called my mother and stepdad. I explained what was going on and was honest to my inner core. There were no lies, only a painful truth. I was not being the healthy mother I envisioned. I was not a good mother by allowing my baby son to be around the horrors of this dark world in which I now found myself.

When they arrived, I looked at my mother and said, "Please watch my baby boy. I will not have him around any of this. It's not easy for me to ask you for this help, but I will not allow my child to be in this environment. If and only if, I get better hopefully very soon, I will be back for him. I love him and only him in this horribly, crazy sad world. My mother took my boy from me and said, "When you're ready, Kerri Lynn, he will be here waiting for you." She truly touched me in that moment, the look of concern in my mother's eyes was evident. She could see I wouldn't hesitate to hurt myself before I would ever hurt my child. I believe that was the moment she realized my own strength, and that scares her, for that reason isn't the right reason. She didn't cross me at that moment. I don't know why, but I believe she could sense I wasn't that little girl screaming for her mom to stop hitting her, "Please, Mommy, NO," or the little girl who wanted acceptance. I was a sad, lonely hurting person, who was doing the one thing every mother should do, not be a selfish individual and subject an innocent child to a world where they should not be. I could see past my own self-destructive path and still had the courage to ask my mother, one of those who had put these insecurities within me, for help. To save my own son took courage, and in that courage is the deepest gut pain a person can contain.

It left me devoid of all feeling; it left me sick inside. The only consolation I had was that my boy was safe, away from these dirty people, this bad crowd and in a better home, being loved by my mother who wanted and loved him more than anything. More than she loved me.

My only savior, was at a distance but safe. I hated myself, hated that I had finally succumbed to a weakness. Finally, after all those years I believed what the people who were supposed to love me said. I was nothing, ugly, I wasn't worth being around. I was nothing, nothing, and nothing. I believed it, and at least, they got the best part of me, my son, and let them be happy now because I'm gone. I wanted to die, and I started hating Zak. He disgusted me, for bringing me and my child around this environment. I was in a state of numbness and pain. My mother in that moment saw me hurt and helped my son, helped me to save him, offered him a good home. My mother helped me. All those thoughts swam around my delusional head.

In that dark corner, I found the courage to leave that life, that world and those people. In that painful state I saw all the years pass before me, reevaluating myself with a mind of utter chaos. Somewhere deep within myself I found the little light that flickered, and in that glow was my angel Ashton. In that flickering, glowing light, I found me, a whole new me and I rose, rose and rose up. My baby boy will never know how he gave me the courage to walk away from all that, the strength it took to walk away from his outward hand and to come back whole and me. I needed to hurt me, in order to find me.

This is very important what I am saying, because when I say this I mean it. I had to finally be the person I always had been told I was, in order to know it wasn't me. I had to do, what I did, in order to find me and to this day, fifteen years later, my son, I say sorry for falling on that path and I'm sorry I wasn't strong enough to walk away from a promised love until six months later.

I thank you, my son, for giving me the opportunity to know I was better than the voices that whispered to me, I am very sorry. "I love you, my guardian <u>angel</u>, and thank you for saving me, my son, my Ashton."

I went back for my boy and my mother wouldn't let me have him. She had fallen in love with my son, more than a grandmother/ grandson relationship and didn't want to let him go. It made me volatile and mean. He would be screaming, Mommy, Mommy and pulling my hair out at the door as my mother pushed me out. The nanny at the time, whispered endearments in my ear that what my mother was doing wasn't right. She would sneak me in, allow me in, just to see him and love him.

Finally in desperation, I called my stepdad. I have heard that many children have a grudge against their stepparents who suddenly entered their lives, but my stepdad was my only hope. He picked me up one day eleven months after that crazy moment when I asked my mother for help. He fed me McDonalds in the parking lot of a mall, as he spoke to me truly from his heart and I listened, really listened.

He spoke to me as a father to a young girl, someone who believed in me. He had the strength to influence my mother. He explained that it was courageous of me as a mother to recognize the signs of a lifestyle that a child shouldn't be in, and it took great courage to do what I did. He said most parents would never do that until their children were apprehended first. He allowed my tears to fall without the hug and consolation. He gave me cold hard facts and truths, and he also said how he could see the great love within me that others couldn't see. That made me ball even more, truths hurt, but truths also heal. He said he would help me. He said he has always loved me as his own child and when I was being mocked and ridiculed by my family, he noticed.

He said it was unfair but it wasn't the right time to intervene. The words that he loved me, echoed in my painfully heavy heart. In those moments, he healed the broken, no-good child within, and also allowed me to take responsibility for my actions. He said, "Work at being that mother I know you are, Kerri. You are a great mother. Your love for your child is absolute. I know this because I see it." He also said, "It's not going to be easy, a lot of frustration is involved. You finally gave everyone ammunition against you. It doesn't surprise me after all you've been through."

My stepdad shared his own past mistakes with me, including ending up in jail because of hanging out with the wrong crowd. But when he was in jail, he worked at a degree. He shared what he had been through, even though I might not remember it all happening when I was a child, it was why he went away. He had to own the mistakes he had made in order to accomplish all he has done. Now he owns a company and works hard for his family. He said we were a lot alike and he had faith in me. (I only found out recently in 2012 that my stepdad never knew my mother had beaten me with floorboards.) He said he would handle my mother. He allowed me to live, not in a trailer on the side of the house, but in their finished basement. He allowed me to hear my son's pitter-pattering feet running around upstairs as I healed. He imposed extreme rules as in: no going upstairs at all for a bit, no yelling at Mom, "Be respectful and just sleep, Kerri, heal." With that he gave me a choice to work at being who I am, and to become stronger for it, and learn never to give up on myself again.

My stepfather saved my life that day. He gave me hope because he believed in me. He touched on things about me and that I had never heard anyone speak on before. In that moment, my stepdad became not only my stepdad but my father. He would, as the years go by, become one of my best friends.

Those eleven months in that dark world took its toll. I would sleep outside behind my mother's house (after I handed my angel to mother to care for) facing where my son would be sleeping and stay up all night, waiting to see if his light went on in case he had a nightmare, or woke up missing me. I focused so hard on my inner self to send energy to my baby inside, so he could feel his mommy hadn't left him: on many nights I would see his little light go on, but no shadow of my mother going to him, as if he knew I was right beside him. Those nights watching my mother's house all alone in a beat-up car, just to be close to my son were healing me, giving me hope and what lead me to call my stepdad, and beg for a second chance.

I didn't just hang-out and do drugs in that crowd those months away, I would taunt myself and hurt myself by watching my son from a distance, often going days without food just to watch and make sure he was alright and well cared for, I needed to suffer and get as low as I did in order to rise above my surroundings.

Even though my mother had said that when I was ready my son would be there waiting, she never allowed it. She stopped me at every turn, to the point of false accusations and preventing me from taking my son: not even four months later(after handing him to her, I had tried to be back with my son, and tickets for us to leave back to Alberta, where I had a job and a home to go to with him). I wanted to be away from that stupid crowd I had met through my best friend/boyfriend Zak.

She held my baby boy, close to her bosom, as if she would never let go. In those days I would often scream at her that if social services were ever involved, I would've had my son back by now. Yes, I totally messed up, but I recognized it. I was angry, because I knew I would never be good enough for her. It was a tough battle. I asked for help before anyone or anything could get involved. I also stopped taking that horrific, mind-blowing drug within nine months, and had no cravings, as I never liked it. It disgusted me and grossed me out. Why couldn't I have my son back, other mothers would have, she would just use the same line she did when I got off that plane, "You're not ready, Kerri Lynn, to be a mother!"

It was a struggle. No matter what I did, it wouldn't work with her. I did everything I had to do, no matter what, working at a job, never talking to those people again, parenting courses (not one but many), down to cleaning her house and walking on eggshells to persuade her. I was a slave to my own mistake. Sure that talk with my stepdad helped, as did his gentle hand with my mother. Over the course of a few years of him going to my mother's on weekends and me during the week so, as she put it, I could have a life, it finally worked. She finally gave in, as there was nothing left for her to go on. I have to say thank you to my mother for that struggle because in that, as a mother and individual, I learned never, ever to make that mistake again. It gave me the strength I needed and the courage to fight for what I believed in.

I had to be honest with myself about all the mistakes I had made, as that is where I learned. Yes, for nine months out of my life I did do crystal meth, but never, ever will I touch it again. It is not worth the price you pay in the end. I still hear in passing of those same people doing the same things as they did back when we were barely out of high school and that is sad.

That year was transforming. Through it, I learned the difference between good and bad. Would I change what I did, how I feel? Never in a million years would I change that experience. I was meant to go through my own self-inflicted horror to gain the reality I always knew existed. I had to because if it wasn't then, it would have been something else. It helped me to see the dark side, in order to embrace the good. It helped me to be the mother I am today.

It was a stepping-stone to self-discovery, a stepping-stone to becoming the woman I am today. If you asked me if I have ever touched anything related to that after that nine months in my life, I can tell you No, I haven't nor would I. It is truly a sad and gross place to be, circumstances lead me there, but circumstances lead me home, too, and that experience didn't make me an addict. It was an experience, a learning curve, it gave me knowledge of a place I never wanted to be in again.

It is weird how life's moments can teach you how to help others. After that I turned around and helped other mothers get their children back and off the streets. It gave me the understanding of self-inflicted grief. It is a time that has enlightened me to another world. It made me more wise and knowledgeable. I may find it gross, dark and disgusting, but being who I am now, I can see past all that and see where some people get lost and also the good in people others may not normally see. I was able to find the little part of me that loves helping others.

It did have its affects, it took me almost three years to even drink half a cup of coffee, now I can't live without a coffee in the morning. My anxiety spiked within that first year, I conquered it all by myself with the power of the mind, self-talk, "That I am going to be okay, I'm not going to die." My anxiety had bouts of terror and claustrophobia. It has also helped me forgive more easily.

In that place where I was, I saw things, I wish I had never seen. It has helped me overcome that lonesome, desolate state I often went into as a child. It helped me overcome many fears and created a better understanding of life. It made me more aware of things, people and places around me and of my children. It prepared me for my future, created a certain web of protection, a layer of awareness I would never have known existed otherwise. I know it was my destiny to go through all that I have in order to save my children and me, to be that voice for the world. I know this because as many mistakes as I have made, each one I learnt from and didn't repeat. Each one has been a lesson. I am only human and had to find my place in the world by slowly understanding that we are not all equal, we are all unique.

I would be fiercely loyal to my friends, as to me they were the family I never had. It helped me to let go of that street mentality to lead a healthy life and to be understanding but also not to stoop to that level ever again. It has helped me to guide my own children with a firm but caring hand and to guide others in a helpful way. My knowledge is my power.

I had to mention that moment of weakness with drugs as it leads to me becoming the victim of another circumstance later in my twenties. I will never do street drugs again. If I even tried smoking a joint of pot, I would end up in the hospital with a severe anxiety attack. I just can't do it, my mind is much too strong for drugs. I would seriously drive myself mad. I believe that and I also can laugh at myself for that.

It also lead me to finding my father, my stepdad, my mentor and soon to be one of my, best friends in this world. . It gained me a reality of what I really wanted, who I wanted to be. Life takes its turns for its own reasons.

Shortly after that, in my early twenties, I found my family doctor, who would have such a profound impact on my life and that of my children. I started looking around me and saw that I did have people who cared. I did have good, positive, amazing people in my life who cared. It gave me hope and built my self-esteem to the roof, and started a soft glow of belief within myself. I may never have felt pretty, but I did feel good inside.

Life as a Normal Young 21 yr-old

If you have one person who believes in you, you can conquer anything. If you believe in yourself you can move mountains. Then you'd be surprised who you find who has always been in your life but sat back and saw the truth of other people's abuse. You find that "aunty" you always wanted, that dad you never had and if you're lucky, you find the friend who becomes your family, or that "doctor" who builds you up and believes in you. Throughout every experience that may otherwise seem bad or negative, you will find a blessing., so never give-up..........

DURING THOSE YEARS, I had a few jobs as well as working at my stepdad's company, as a secretary. It was enjoyable to be around him. He knows life and is a person you can actually talk with, have those intellectual conversations with, a person who has lived life outside the box.

My mother and stepdad's relationship was failing and I was able to apply comfort where it was needed. I became my mother's friend. She opened up to me and expressed the bit of trouble my little sister was getting into, even asking me for advice. She also said she was going to get a divorce. I didn't like that at all, as I believed those two were soul mates. I still believed in forever and I always will, in my mind I still believe in love.

Sam's grade 12 year, was an exemplary year for everyone. I had to watch my mother's huge home for three months, as she was in Australia with Sam, because my sister was homesick and needed her. Tom, my stepfather, had moved out. It was a great feeling to be trusted like that by my family. I always knew BC was my home, as three years had already gone by since that time of suffering, old wounds do heal. I was finally being in my age group and doing the things other girls were doing at twenty-three. I was happy and loved my son more than anything else in the world. My son gave me a good fight, and hope: I won.

I was able to help people, and planned to go to city hall to propose a new way for mothers to get their children back. I had it all mapped out, written down. I had a goal in mind and wanted to talk to the right people to lay out my proposal. I had the knowledge and experience to share. I believed in my view that everyone just needed love, trust and a support person behind them in order to gain their children back, even their lives back. That was who I was, a caregiver and I believed anyone could do it.

My only downfall was that I trusted too easily and believed in people too much. I never realized that I was being taken advantage of and used by certain friends, either for a free ride as I had the car or simply for money because I paid for everything. At twenty-three I didn't look at those things, so I still had growing up to do, but I was happy and so was my son. We had a gorgeous house up the road from my mother's, as I worked and was able to afford it. I had a few roommates, here and there to help with rent, often falling for their sob stories, which were cute.

I knew I was more mature than other girls my own age because of all I had been through. I enjoyed conversing with older people because the intellectual level was there, with their kindness and wisdom. I graduated from Beauty Academy with a ninety-three percent mark, just under the highest honors. It was exceptionally amazing to have graduated as a student, in my eyes even as a mother and friend. I was finally in my glory days in my twenties, loved it. I never ran from my problems, I dealt with them, it made me strong. I could own my mistakes, in vivid color and embrace them.

Sometimes now, I caught my little sister Sam sneaking out to the bars. We were becoming close and I relished the fact that she liked me because I had always thought she didn't like me. It was awesome getting the call that my littlest Sam needed to be picked up, or the call that she needed help because girls were picking on her. I could understand because I had been there. It was spectacular being able to be the big sister finally. I was my own person and that shadow was gone.

Part 2

Meeting the Beast

People who have to rely on their instincts to live by tend to be more perceptive than others, it's a matter of survival, as I was learning to acquire.

WHEN I FIRST met Damien, it was a moment I shall never forget. I was in the bar having a drink, my friend at the time, Patricia, was working the section where the beer booth was located, so the girls and I thought we'd go down there and enjoy a few beverages. That's how the normal twenty-three-year-old feels, I presume, it's how I felt. I was leaning up against the bar thinking, "I'm so not in the mood for this tonight."

I was about to ditch out on everyone and in the middle of having a casual conversation with an old man who had a horse ranch, this member (Hells Angel) walked up behind me and pulled my hair, "Hey there, WHORE." I whipped around saying "What are you doing?"

The older guy said, "Hey, Damien, whatcha doing that for?" I looked over my shoulder and sure enough, there's this chubby guy, wearing his colors with a smiling face with green eyes and flamboyant attitude. They frequented the places I went, so nothing was surprising. They were all over the mainland bars, until 2010 when most clubs and restaurants came out with a new law, "Bar watch," as there were too many gang-related fights and violence. It had become unsafe for society.

I didn't know what to think and then this guy does it again, this time harder and ripped pieces of my hair out. I thought this man is messed up, he's getting off on this and laughing to boot. Finally, I'd had enough, the shock was over.

I said, "Hey mister. I don't care who you are or think you are! I don't know you, nor do I want to, so if there's a problem, let me know. I'm not a whore, I'm a person. You must be getting me mixed up with someone else!"

The guy looked directly at me, full complete eye contact. There was something very eerie about him. He had the gall to ignore me and look over to the person I was visiting and say, "Hey, she's coming with me!" as if whatever he said was golden, and people listened.

"WHAT," That's when I leaned over the bar, grabbed my purse and this full patch Hell's Angel (member) grabbed my hair again and pulled me down to the counter. It hurt and he was just looking at me, really looking at me. Suddenly, he let go. I didn't know what to think but I can say this, it scared me to the point that my knees were a little wobbly, so with as much nerve and courage as I could muster I just walked out, with my head held high. I didn't like it when people put me down, it hurt me perhaps more so than normal. I had no idea what to do but vacate. I was so embarrassed and had no idea what I had done.

Patricia was trying to get my attention, "KERRI, KERRI, where you going?" I just ignored her. She is the type of girl who thinks along the lines of, if a member even touched you, or talked to you it was so cool. Heart of gold this girl has, but she likes the scene of bad boys.

All the while, I heard this crazy laugh, with hoot roaring bikers and felt that they were all eyeballing me, as I turned my head to look over my shoulder, sure enough, they're smiling, beaming actually, as if what just happened was normal everyday fun. I was making a hasty exit as fast as my little butt could take me out that door onto the street where my beautiful black Camaro SS was parked. I jumped in and sat down, absolutely floored as to what I just did to fuel him like that and wondering who this guy was.

What a night; I knew, I had a feeling I didn't want to be out. I didn't like that claustrophobia feeling I had, it was hard to breathe. I noticed my anxiety, which hadn't surfaced in a while, slowly come in and felt a shift in my circumstances.

That was my first impression, my first ever laying eyes on him. I know you are all wondering, how he ended up as your husband. Well, as this progresses from love, lies, deceit, betrayal and pain, I will share my journey into the unknown, as my past comes back to haunt me.

I went to sleep that night thinking, "Wow, what was that all about? How embarrassing, did I look like a whore or a hooker?" I don't know, but if you are anything like me you do your best thinking at night and that night, I was hurt, my feelings completely crushed, angels were no big deal to me. I say this seriously, they are just people, and on the mainland they're everywhere. I've seen them out before many times. They party like the rest of us, in clubs, lounges or events like car shows and such. The only difference is, they're older and it might look funny if a fifty-year-old man was in a nightclub partying to retro, rave dance, hip hop music, getting his groove on, even to the point, the poor man would get picked on and put down, but when a Hell's Angel does it, it's normal. Everyone bows to them when they walk in. That was the one thing that to me that wasn't so cool or real. On the other hand, my true character is to accept everyone for who they are(it is what it is). I am one of those people who love everyone for their own individual strengths and weaknesses.

It hurt me when that happened, was a huge blow to my self-esteem, it gave me a complex that evening, and a few times after that. I inwardly hoped not to ever run into that man again. I sure as heck would not tell Patricia what happened, she would be all over that. That first time occurrence forever stayed in me.

My Own Personal Demons

I HAVE ALWAYS had a flare for style and an addiction to clothes. When I see a style that I feel stands out and would look good on me, I will usually get it or work at buying it when I have enough money. My clothes and my perfume always go with my mood. I loved to look nice, to have the right appearance, it was one of the things I enjoyed doing. I loved doing my own nails, but not so much getting a pedicure. Often at night, now I would hang out with my mom, just visit and enjoy an evening with her, Ashton and me. She liked me finally acting more my age and enjoying myself.

Growing up with my sister who had seemed fully developed, by the age of thirteen, I always felt like a small-chested girl, never quite the woman I wanted to be. I wanted a little more curve and had a huge complex about it, as I would get teased by her that I looked like a minnow fish, compared to her raging beauty.

Everyone loved her and all the boys wanted her as we grew up. I was always wishing I was prettier. I never felt beautiful, just never did. I was my own worst critic. If I had dressed better or had the curves, and didn't look like a tomboy, perhaps, maybe I'd get looked at, wanted or even properly loved, like my sister always seemed to be. I wanted so badly to have what she had, a devoted husband and family. I didn't realize at the time that sometimes appearances aren't always what they seem.

My past luck and experiences prevented me from even dating or getting serious with anyone. I should've been happier with myself, but I just wasn't, my complex played on me a lot. I was so focused on saving everyone else, and giving all I could by being that perfect person. I never had the time to work on my insecurities, my own personal judgments and self-talk. I never took the time to look within and heal those scars, or look at my past insecurities and address them. I should have found a way to feel beautiful on the inside, as people would often tell me I was. I just never really looked in the mirror and saw it, I thought my inner scars were visible to others; I had imperfections. I believed in the love I had all around me now as well as my forgiveness in people, for everyone and everything was enough. I should've realized there was more to healing than that. How could anyone truly love you if you never loved yourself? I needed to know me, believe in me, love me and be happy with me. I just wasn't as secure as I thought I was, the world, people, sounds and places I loved completely. I really believed I was happy and fulfilled. I should've learn't to look within myself sooner.

My dream when I was a girl, was to have that protecting knight in armor, — cowboy, businessman, or even a farmer, — sweep me off my feet and love me forever. My immature and naive self still thought along those lines, with a few variations. The man who could do that, had to love my son Ashton, as my stepfather loved me, like his own. I still had my dreams and hoped for the day when they would come true for us.

I had been single since Zak and a few years had gone by already. I went on a few dates, but never anything as a seriously devoted boyfriend, only friends. It took a lot for anyone to capture my attention, my trust was feeble, it wasn't worth the trouble. I believed it was that way for a reason, my intimate way for me to get to know myself as a young woman. I was taking time to get to know the world through otherwise, wiser, changed eyes and emotions to please my mother as well as family. I wanted to do things right but still somehow, the guys I picked always had that wild streak, bad boy image. To me I could see past their wild ways. My reasoning was that if I could be nice, kind and grow, so could they with the love and devotion I could give them. Not that I had tested that theory out yet. I really still saw good in everyone. It's me, and I was never letting go of me again. So instead of looking within, I looked within others, to me I thought I had grown up, plus it brought me joy.

Life is learning. I thought I was ready to start dating, seeing guys and having that time to myself. I believed I was ready, so I started dating. My mother was thrilled and so was our nanny, an amazing Filipino woman, who was dating as well through an internet site, Lava life, I believe. Email was becoming huge back then, and she and I would spend time together as she often watched my son for me. That woman started an email account for me and came up with the name, sugarbabysweetlove@hotmail.com. On a sunny day in my mother's office she did that for me. My mother who had split up with my stepfather again, was also on Lava life. She was thrilled for me to be dating as she believed I was ready. I never dated guys from the internet, mind you, but it was at that moment that I started thinking I was ready to date in general. My girlfriends had no problem picking up guys, dating and having fun so why couldn't I too? I would often ask them how they did it so naturally, and ask for advice about dating. *It was an exciting time in my life.*

Kane was seeing Ashton a little bit, not that he ever kept an ongoing relationship with his son. He just wasn't that type of dad. I thought it was because of the way he was when he was younger, the invisible man who just came and went, as if it was acceptable.

As time went on, it hurt my son and slowly started bothering me. Because Kane was rarely around, it was hard for Ashton to gain a bond.

Kane's other family, on the other hand, was always around. We were becoming closer because of their involvement. I would get upset at times, that it was hard on Ashton seeing them so much but never his own father. I was never upset at them, just the situation. I thought it would be better if they were not around because of the affect it was slowly having on my son's precious heart. I started separating myself from them, other than his one sister who was as family oriented as me. I could see it was hurting my son as he often asked me why his dad never showed up, and I would have to dry his tears. It was taking away a little of his self-esteem each day. I could see the pain in my son's eyes, the questions and I knew firsthand how that felt. I knew I couldn't keep on accepting the way Kane was, as if it was normal. Especially when we all found out that Kane had another son, who lived with him. When his other son wanted to see Ashton, all of a sudden, so did Kane. It was wrong, no matter which way you looked at it. I wasn't into impressing his family so much or accommodating them. I never tried to keep them away; I just set boundaries. I knew the affect it could have on a person and watched as it made my son feel inferior. It broke my heart.

Some mothers say it's hard to be a single mom raising her child or children, but to me it was a gift. I was in my glory. It helped my mother sometimes to feel less lonely having Ashton on the weekends. Then when I picked him up on Sundays, there was usually a nice supper laid out. It gave me the freedom to be my age, enjoy life, still work and maintain a home. *Everything in life is truly a learning curve*, some friends go and some remain, people change, you have children and you grow apart from some friends, but its okay, its life.

I knew I was an adult, I was okay and that inner child that had been so lonely wasn't so much anymore, the child had to grow up, and that child did.

During the nights, I was working at the club called "*On the Roxxs*," and the days that I worked at my father's office for extra income were great. Still single, I enjoyed my weekends.

I had a few girlfriends, who now are no longer my friends, as we have grown apart and our priorities are different. But I remember some of those late nights, drives, getting ready and having a blast singing at the top of our lungs as moments I shall always hold dear to my heart. I also remember a special time, when I was just fourteen walking across the field from school back in my father and sister's hometown with a school friend, who surprised me by liking me. We just enjoyed our silence, as feelings of uncertainty were gathered in our minds, because of hormones, growing and life. These moments we all have of youth, are special no matter what path, anyone of us takes. We remember them with the brilliant eyes of wonder.

I had enough of my old roommate, Patricia, and had to ask her to leave my house. She was still my friend, but I couldn't handle her late hours, and constant stream of different boyfriends. She was a very sad girl and things affected her a lot, from people's comments to their judgments about her. Her parents upset her, as she was constantly trying to please them. She was supposedly in college but when she gave up on that, it was hard on her and even hard for me, so to save a friendship it was better that she move out and go back to live with her parents to salvage what she could, which at this point hopefully was soon.

I like to be around strong people. Substance is important to me, as my strength had already been such a milestone in my life. I still attracted bad boys in a sense, just a different generic group as it was more the bar crowd life, the ones who owned homes, cars and businesses, the ones who had pasts but maturity.

I met another girl who fast became my friend during this time: One day I received a call from someone when he needed my help. She was in a hotel with a guy who I had helped out from time to time with food or when his mother, who was getting older, needed a ride to doctors and such. It was in my nature to be that way. I didn't associate with them, only just to be a little angel bearing gifts. Those people were from my past, they knew they could trust me. Those people respected me for breaking free and knew I could help provide food, clothes, sometimes money and even words of encouragement. I had long wanted to help society and let the government know that not everyone is as horrible as their circumstances indicate.

I always had money now that I was in my parent's good books. They spoiled me because I was doing so well, and I believe, to make up for all those lost years in my young girl/teenage life when I wasn't allowed around.

I received a call one day, on my way to work, that so and so didn't have food, could I bring some; of course I could, it was who I was. I remember clearly that day (as I put sandwiches, juice and chocolate bars into two little brown lunch bags at my mother's house), to take to him, as a quick stop on my way to work. I was dolled up to the nines and as I walked into the hotel room, in the grungiest part of the city. A place I never enjoyed even driving through......

I saw the most precious big blue eyes peeking at me from under the covers. This girl's head popped up, she must have been five foot nothing and looked as if she was fourteen years old. It bugged me to see this guy, who was nothing more than desperate, with her. It sickened me to think she was getting hurt and subjecting herself to this tormented life. I dropped the two bags on the counter and lectured them, as I usually do about that lifestyle, about getting clean and healthy. I looked at her, wrote down my number and told her that when she wanted to get away from all this, I would help her. Then I left, just as fast.

It's weird, now that I look back at how much I did for people, because I cared and could see the good in them when no one else could. It has been what drives me, as well as little downfalls, because it takes a lot for me to let them go. I introduce this girl, Stella, because she had a huge impact on me later on.

Two days later I received a call from her as she was standing on the side of the road. She had a son she no longer took care of as he was with her mother and she had nowhere to go; she needed and wanted help. I told her, if she really wanted help, she would have to catch a bus two cities away and then I would pick her up in town. No one from that world can ever know where I live or be close to my home because my son is with me. She seemed to understand that, being a mother herself. I didn't expect her to make it. If she did, I thought it would be in a few days or weeks, even a month. It also gave her the chance to back out.

Nope that little Stella called again two hours later and she was down the road. When I pulled up, I wrapped my arms around her and welcomed her to a whole new life. This girl touched my very heart and would soon become one of my closest friends in the whole world. She was a little me, when I was lost but she had strength that one, and I believed in her. To me she was only lost, she just needed to be loved and accepted. My heart wept for her, as I knew she must have had a similar experience to mine. It never dawned on me that I was four years ahead of her factually and mentally, or the fact that we had 2 different hearts, and once we got closer later on, that she did have a family that truly loved her, and sisters who worshipped her, unlike me.

That was who I was once, I had healed and had gotten better from my own self- inflicted pain. I was a caregiver. I looked for love in everything, from the beauty of the vast sky or the rushing waves and squeals of sea gulls, to the littlest hobo, grumpy old man, to the crazy teenager and drug-addicted person. I was a healer, and accepted them when no one else did. I provided food, shelter and friendship. It would drive my mother nuts, but I know it touched her. She didn't like it, but it was me, who I was, I believe that was when she started seeing the me, she never knew.

I didn't like to see anything or anyone hurt. Sometimes anger is pain, sadness is loneliness and laughter is a simple way to cover up an ashamed person. What I had to give, I would give. That was the kind of young woman I was becoming, who always was that way, but was able to share it now and be accepted. I remembered what it was like to be lost.

I believe people often thought my kindness was weakness and in a way it was. It also helped me to forgive things I shouldn't have, forgive and forget them, when I should've just forgiven, walked away and not looked back. I couldn't understand, if I could do it, why others couldn't. I believe my kindness not only helped others but also helped to heal me. I was changing. I can look back now and see the changes within myself, to a friend, a child, and to a mother. I was finally an adult allowing myself to slightly shine through, without so many critical, mean comments that had often surrounded me.

Stella slept at my house, that first week and ate like a man. She was so malnourished it was sad. She was a beauty. She made me laugh a lot with her twisted little personality. Eventually, I asked her how old she was; she was just turning twenty. It was kind of a relief to me that she was not a minor, so I wouldn't get into trouble. She was more my age, a few years younger but had seen some of the same things I did. She loved her little boy, and, I believed, also had the fight to gain him back.

We had a lot in common; her son was with her mother as well from the same city too. It was nice. I was just years ahead of her when it came to responsibilities and maturity. We became fast friends once she was back on her feet. She got a job and was able to visit her son. I remember her mom looking at me as if she was unsure of me, and asking how a girl such as I could own a nice car like that. It felt as if I was getting the third degree. I remember saying, "Just a spoiled rich girl." It kind of threw me for a loop, so I came up with the fastest answer I could and from that day forward we were friends, her mother and I.

Her mother was worried about her daughter still being around bad people, which is understandable. It hurt me that it was never mentioned how I helped her or rescued her. Stella made the biggest step by calling me. To me that was so much more than what I did, and pride is pride. If I wasn't so gullible and naive I would've realized we had things in common but at two different times in our lives, as well as two different hearts, and goals for our lives. Everything in my life was falling into place; I was truly happy. I had a life outside of being a mother, a job and girlfriends who were so different from the high school crowd dynamics.

One day while I was at work, I ran into that Damien guy again. Many Hell's Angels, ballers and different types frequented that bar. When you work in the nightlife, things don't surprise you much, as well as who are the patrons. In the lower mainland Hell's Angels are everywhere, you just get used to it. So, when Damien came into my work one night sitting down in the far corner with a friend, it wasn't surprising to hear all the girls there talking about him. I never mentioned that I had a run in with him, at all! It was still very fresh in my mind as it was humiliating for any person to treat me that way, a moment that stuck with me.

The girls were mentioning that he was the member getting married, or was already married. I hoped he wouldn't notice me or remember me. It would be quite embarrassing if he pulled that same stunt at my workplace. I would feel so ashamed.

I decided after an hour of him being there, I'd leave my section and get a closer look at this full patch member who hated me so much. I'd check to see if he recognized me, or was It a fleeting, random moment. As I strolled past, his eyes narrowed at me, for a moment too long. I smiled and then talked to the bartender for a few moments. He never approached me, humiliated me or grabbed me in any way.

It was a revelation to me, that perhaps he was having a wild night with his bros that previous evening long ago, just making fun and being crazy. It instantly made me feel better, that some huge Hell's Angel really didn't have it in for me. It's kind of scary for a girl to get treated that way. A more timid person would never have gone out again, but me, working in that nightlife industry, seeing Hell's Angels was inevitable. I had to associate and serve these guys. I kept working and soon after, he was gone. Even though he had narrowed his eyes at me, that didn't make me feel threatened just aware of him. (What sucked a little, was that he wasn't the greasy type of Hell's Angel biker like the stereotyped persona of the public thinks. I mean to say more and more Hell's Angels were younger and better dressed, even better looking).

People who frequented the bars where I lived, thought it was cool to hangout or know them. I was slowly becoming known, accepted and people liked me. I had grown up to be loyal and solid, that was part of who I was, I could be trusted. It actually made a person who didn't know better, feel a tad safer, (maybe because I was an influenced younger girl and the night life was taking its toll). I had already been invited out many nights to the afterhour's club, which the bikers owned. It was the hottest spot to be after the bar closed, to me they weren't so bad).

I was working in an awesome bar, I met every type of person who frequented it: ballers (growers), Twinkies (young girls just of age), regulars (people who have been in the bar scene way too long so that everyone knows their faces), bikers or want to be bikers, or real old school bikers (members or not) and average individuals' just out for a good time. This was the place everyone went on that lonely Tuesday night or any other day. It was known for Tuesdays, for sure, best night to go and the most pumping. Shoot, did I mention pimps and hookers because they went there too. Which is sad because these young girls (Twinkies) need to realize they don't know who they are going to end up with when they take a person home from the bar. Alcohol infusion does wonders to a person's perception and frame of mind. Being a waitress in that environment you get to know the who's who, and the what's what! Trust me, it isn't pretty watching half the goings on and as a waitress, bouncer or bartender. You have to know when to intervene and help a person or simply cut that person off. That year, from when I first met Mister Beast as I now call him, I met a lot of others too and realized the whole Hell's Angel thing or biker thing isn't so bad and scary, as they are not all like that. They are just average people looking for something to fill a void or living up to their personal weaknesses, strengths and persona.

Many months later, I invited my little Stella to come to work with me, as I didn't have my son on this night and was always wide awake after work in an environment of banging music and lights. A sort of euphoria sets in. Stella had just gotten her ID in the mail after losing it months back and my boss was letting me off early, on the condition that I stayed and partied in his club. We were having a blast, everyone loved her and she was a wild card relishing all the attention. We decided to go to the after-hours club where we were welcomed with open arms. The place was packed and we had a blast. The worries about the stories you hear about the places known as the HA afterhours were just that, stories. It was awesome and going there became a regular occurrence on the nights we went out together. We were a team, Stella and I, a bonding experience of true friendship and such fun.

We were hot, sexy and known as girls who weren't easy to get. We had our own persona and aura. We had a security with each other, Stella and I. Girls would get jealous of our bond, and we would just look at each other over their complaints and laugh. I would even sit with my mother laughing and telling her our stories, the next morning after I returned home. My mother had become my friend now and I loved it. My little sister just adored and loved Stella. Sam started being part of our elite group and was known as Baby Sister. Everyone was normal and happy.

Shortly after, my mother offered to pay for my breast augmentation. I was completely, shocked and excited, I do not deny it. I was so happy I cried. I felt as though my life had truly come full circle. Stella was worried about it, me I just couldn't wait. I was finally going to feel like a real woman.

Some women don't get breast augmentation, just for big boobs, some need to get it for medical reasons or because of being self-conscious. There are so many variables about having them done, that people shouldn't pass judgment quickly. I know the reason I wanted them so badly. I will share my truth. When I was with my boyfriend, Action, on the night I was trying to leave and things were getting out of hand, the mental abuse and comments were very harsh. Mental abuse will stick with a man or woman and even children throughout their lives. He yelled at me a few times that I was as flat as a boy and then ripped open my shirt, as I hadn't developed until in my much later teens and even then I was an A cup. He told me to look at myself, how I looked like a boy and he laughed at me tauntingly.

I already felt so inferior to my older sister, who had developed so fast when we were kids. Being the ugly tom boy sister had such an impact on me, that when people during that time often said I was beautiful, I knew I really wasn't. I did not feel the way I thought a young woman should, I was never quite sure of myself or my body. It was imprinted on my mind when I was young and it never really left. I hadn't addressed my true feelings, I had just covered them with an invisible Band-Aid and continued on. My reason for wanting them was to actually feel like a woman with curves, to be whole, to finally be beautiful like other people. My mother understood how I felt and when she offered, it was a gift like no other. I was so happy about her offer that I accepted with gratitude. I never realized still by this point it would make me feel great but would never take the hurt on the inside away, until I chose to look within to heal.

Being flat chested affected me, even having sex with the few men I did, I always wore a shirt. I was ashamed of my body, and my looks. I never felt pretty as people would often say. I felt like the ugly duckling I always was, even though I had gained some self-confidence throughout my young adult hood and strength from my own personal mistakes. I was still insecure to say the least. I still took to heart the comments people threw at me, having it embedded within me since I was a little girl. I thought finally I'm going to be pretty, I'm not going to look like a boy, with a flat chest. I was in my glory.

I had my consultation and within a week, I had my breast augmentation. I had my beautiful son, and finally felt like a women. Life was good with friends whom I thought cared about me as much as I did about them.

It was glorious when my mother accepted me, when she became my friend an unforeseen part of me excelled.

I can say knowing the people I did and embracing them as role models ended up shaping me into being the best I could be around them. I had grown from an unaccepted young girl, to an accepted young woman by certain crowds and people. They were my family as I often thought, they were my salvation too, I levitated to the lost people, the people who felt like me, whether they showed it or not. I mastered being that girl, when the love and acceptance I received, were only from the bad asses or smoker's corner type back in junior high. They are the people who truly got to know the Kerri I was. I never received that from my family, until I was past a lot of hurt, and you couldn't deny I was not only an adult but a person, as I changed from that lonely child, unwanted teenager to a young adult.

I knew I had to show the outcasts my love and help in any way I could. I needed to validate them. I stress this because most delinquent children are the black sheep of the family, as many families across the world have labeled them. We needed love too. We as children, teenagers, young adults or simply persons, laugh, cry and bleed like any other people. Trust me when I say this, it can affect even the strongest person in this world. Some people can pull through past all the constant ridicule and others just cannot. It can and will shape us forever.

I was kind caring Kerri, just now a person who knew her place, surroundings and people. I had grown so much, seen too much, felt too much, but also I was shaping into a person who was actually laughing being embraced and accepted. I was in my glory and truly loving all these outcasts who were just as I was, and who stood by the same principles as I stood for. I may not have wanted to live like them, but my eyes were wide open by now to seeing the truth, others could not.

My First Kiss with a Hell's Angel:

Now I just know, that if you give yourself the time to really get to know someone, perhaps you wouldn't pass judgment so quickly, and would allow opportunities to embrace the ones otherwise lost. You actually might find someone you like or respect.

I HAD FINALLY felt a place to fit in, a place where people were successful, owned businesses and had great homes. I no longer felt out of place, people valued and respected my opinion. I had a mother I could now brag about who was my friend. I was in my glory, no matter what I did, it was okay, and I was considered completely awesome, or so I thought. I didn't think that perhaps my friends were around me because I had money, a nice car, a nice home, or the fact that I knew a lot of untouchable people. The people I served in my nightclub slowly became my friends, bikers or not they were people to me. I never thought about their shadier sides. I just enjoyed the "Hunny," or "Hellos," the invitations and the sheer joy of acceptance.

I was invited out one night after work on one of my days off and we went to the afterhours. When I walked in, Damien was there, sitting at the poker table, being loud, and obnoxious. I had Stella with me, but as usual she was already bouncing around, saying hi to everyone.

My stomach did a flip, but I blew it off. I had other friends there so I thought I'd be okay. Now that I noticed up close, I could see an Ontario patch on Damien's leather Vest. I remember thinking," Ohh this is good. Perhaps this Hell's Angel who had it out for me, was from another province just visiting". I was talking with a prospect at the counter, minding my business when his eyes sought mine. He knew, he remembered, there wasn't a chance to exit. There wasn't a chance to grab my Stella, he was fast approaching me. He was watching and sending out a feeling of, "don't go anywhere. I will be addressing you, today, right NOW!" I knew I was finally going to know his intentions towards me. A year had gone by and we had run into each other twice. I could not avoid this "coming to heads" thing.

The song blaring across the black and white checkered floor of the afterhours was, *"Angels Forever, Forever Hell's Angels."*

The place took on a different glow, a roaring upbeat. The rocking song made people move, they moved to the sound and feel of the place, their lips puckered, as they rocked to this song and their bodies swayed. It was dominance over the patrons, it was dominance within these walls, you are a guest, we are boss, and you will party like us! It gave me a feeling of euphoria being allowed in, even a sense of power. The members were like dogs marking their territory, but, enjoying it with an essence of if you're here you're lucky! Everyone was laughing and having a blast, guys were winking at girls and girls were cooing. It was a blatant show of utter supremacy and sovereignty. In turn, it left people who weren't members or girls, a yielding weakness to their dominance.

I was caught in the middle, already had a few drinks, and caught off guard by him being there. Not that I was weak, I was being enthralled by his blatant show, *of knowing what I never.* The hate he had radiated that very first time when he pulled my hair out, was gone and in his mesmerizing eyes was a man with a plan, a man who knew everything I didn't.

He was right beside me now, and grabbed me to dance to the tune, no pain, no humiliation, just dancing green eyes, full body and that vest that can sway even the strongest of celibate women, as I was. He messed me up, twisted my mind, and was a pure and utter amusement to me, a wonder. He knew how to treat a girl or young woman, his hands were gentle, his tug no more than a pull. I was a goner, he captured me right then and there, gone was the hurt from before.

That first kiss brought me to my knees. It was like a rush of fire through my body that warmed me for days. The chemistry was undeniable. He recited words, from the sauciest romance novel into my ear. I couldn't deny the feelings that raged within me. There is something to be said for feeling safe, completely carefree, wicked and oh so beautiful. Only the most advanced romance writer could capture this feeling I had within my body, heart and mind.

It takes a unique person to capture my attention. An aphrodisiac of the mind is a complete and utter way to enslave my heart and my body as well. This man with the wild green eyes and body that rippled with fierce strength did that. It had been over four years since I last had an inkling of possessive love within me. Being in love is such a thrill, you either have that chemistry that is or isn't and this man who wrapped his arms around me, with his badass vest, soft lips and soothing words, got me and he got me bad.

I couldn't stop myself, I wanted more and that kiss was not enough. We took off out of the clubhouse afterhours escaping from the confines of rules, leapt into my car and tried to drive off.

Prospects, who have to take care of the members, tried to stop us. (Prospects are assigned care for the members to the point that if a gun goes off, they put themselves between the bullet and the member, but not the bullet and the wife or child). We were laughing, but completely tongue-tied. I can remember Damien trying to say between kisses, tugs and kisses, "Follow us then," to the prospects who were yelling at us to stop, and them running to jump into whatever vehicle was available as we sped off, ripping down the road, as fast as my Camaro could take us. We almost fell off the road many times that night, we couldn't keep our hands off each other. Our lips matched stroke with stroke, our hands pet for pet, body, heart and soul, we were on fire! .

We lost them, without even knowing it, or caring and made it into my house in Brooks Wood. From the car, to the front door, we were attached. In my bedroom, we stroked each other into the early hours of the morning and fell asleep holding onto each other, as if we had known each other a lifetime. "No, we didn't have sex that first night," we (perhaps just me) were truly and utterly fascinated with the energy that was between us and our kisses did more than any sex could've done. We were oblivious to anything else that evening. I know he felt it, because for me it was like a homecoming.

I woke up that morning, feeling more beautiful than I've ever felt. He woke me with his vibrating hand and those kisses. "My God, thank the heavens those lips were magnificent," whispered within my mind. As I opened my eyes, my dreamy state, shocked me to the core. I instantly felt, not ashamed, but not knowing. I looked over at the pole on my bed and saw a red, white, and black Hell's Angels vest. On my dresser was this killer, fat HA chain and pendant with a huge ruby in the center for the eye, winking at me through the early morning rays. I thought, "Shit, what have I done, but become another one of those girls all the guys talk about."

I had always been thought of like one of the guys. "I'm never going to live this down. "Went through my mind. I tried to get up and he pulled me back down, oh, so gently he kissed me full on the lips and said that was the best night of his life. I felt instantly shy, and embarrassed. I found myself melting into his lips once again, that's when reality hit me hard!!!

I yelled for my roommate, who was moving out shortly, (but I was having a hard time being firm on it), "Patricia, Patricia," I heard her laughing as she bounded into my room. I'm trying to keep it cool as he pushes me back down on the bed, in another show of dominance and, "Scream all you want for your friend." I tried to sit up. Her smile was from ear to ear, this was exactly why she liked being around me. She was influenced by anything that was badass, but to me they were just people. But him, he was out of this world, even for me.

She told us that there's been a truck outside running all night. Damien was smiling away with his arm tucked over me, "So the prospects found me did they? Well, girls, I'm going to let them know I'm alive." He got out of bed butt-ass naked and walked down the hallway. This didn't look good, I mean I had shorts on and a tank top.

I said, "Pat, we never slept together." She's laughing, "Holy, Kerri he's huge." I kicked her out of the room, since she wasn't talking about his package, she was talking about his body. She had a way about her, could always make you laugh, an innocence she had to let out, instead of always trying to be someone else all the time.

I kicked her out of the room as he came waltzing in. I'm thinking to myself does this man have any shame, like he just walks around like that all day. Wow, did this guy have an ego and confidence as I've never seen, either that or he makes it a regular thing with girls. I was starting to feel like such a floozy, the glow wearing off, just a little as he jumped in the shower, my insecurities setting in. I never wanted people to think badly about me, I had a complex, a huge one.

As he was coming out from cleaning up and getting refreshed, I was by the dresser admiring his fat gold chain, laughing and trying it on. Oblivious to my awkward embarrassment, with full smiles, he says, "Hey, hey there, Hunny, only members get to wear those," and he pulls me onto the bed to kiss me, as Patricia walks into the room.

She's laughing, "Hey the guys just said its Super Bowl Sunday at the clubhouse and I was invited, Kerri can you come with us?"

"Hope you don't mind if I catch a ride with you guys, Damien." When did she get on a first-name basis with him; that bothered me! He looked over at me and said, "No, she can't come, but sure YOU can come along."

I was kind of shocked, by his fast response, but either way I couldn't go. It was Sunday, family night and I had to pick up my baby boy, Ashton, from Nana's house.

Plus, I didn't see the big deal about the clubhouse. I've been a few times, it was just another place and on a Sunday, I'd rather be getting ready for the school week ahead.

She left the room to get ready and he pulled me towards him and said "Super Bowl parties aren't for girls like you, sweetie," then kissed me full on the Lips. It made me glow on the inside, he then whispered, "its hookers and blow, baby," My God, where was my head at? I thought that was a special thing for him to say, or was it just separating me from the rest of the girls; well it worked.

He said,"K baby, will text you later and had an awesome night."
He winked as he strolled out of the room, completely dressed and
looking like a man of substance with an air of authority as he left.
How did that man weasel his way into my heart? After my first
reaction how was it even possible? My thoughts were wishy washy,
continuously about that night. That very first night would play in
my head from time to time over the years, looking for that man who
indeed touched my heart.

Patricia, came bouncing in to ask how she looked, in a blue jean
suspender outfit, she looked casual but good. I tried to tell her not
to go, it just wasn't for her, but she looked at me and said, "Kerri, a
Member invited me, of course I'm going." I tried to warn her, but
as usual she was under the influence of the bad boy image. *It's the
only fault in her I ever really disliked.*

I was beaming after everyone left, you know that warm, fuzzy
feeling when you are first touched with the springs of lust/love. As
I got ready, I tidied up the house and made sure, Ashtons room was
perfect and headed over to my Mom's for Sunday dinner and to
pick up my peanut.

Little did I know, at that moment when I made the choice to not
only kiss him, but invite him over and spend the night, I had veered
onto a path that would take me down some of the most horrific
moments of my life. That day my life changed, that day I allowed
the Beast into my world and me into his.

The Roommate:

LATER THAT NIGHT as I was sitting downstairs at my mothers, playing toys with my son (Woody and Jessie). I had just finished an amazing dinner with my family, when I received a phone call from my roommate, Patricia(I often shut my phone off at dinner time, for the evening, as it's my son and me time). I remember thinking the girl really has bad timing, but I did want to hear about Damien, so I answered. What I didn't expect was to hear her crying, she was inconsolable. I tried to get her to calm down. I didn't know what to do.

She's always been very passive and cries at the drop of a hat. I say this because I truly believe all she has ever wanted in life was to be accepted. , she started going off to me about the party at the clubhouse, how she was doing shooters between girl's breasts, and that a member who supposedly invited her outside, made her do things she didn't want to. I had heard the horror stories, but never ever saw it, so to hear my roommate convulsing crying telling me this, my heart dropped for her. , I had just finished dinner with my family, it was no later than 5:00 or 6:00 p.m. and she was calling me, seriously in trouble and hysterical. I immediately went outside my mom's house, asking Pat to calm down and to tell me where she was, and what did this guy force on her?

I believe Patricia, felt better that she was talking to me. She said how a member she was having shooter drinks with took her outside and forced her to give him a blowjob. I couldn't believe it, I was shocked, and no one deserves that. Pat had always been an easy girl, to me later in life that truly put me off about her, but she never deserved that. I tried to tell her it wasn't the place to go on Super Bowl, from my newest understanding and that I told her not to go! I think she must have been mistaken for one of those girls, I couldn't understand how, as Patricia was in a very innocent suspender pant outfit when she left.. I asked her again, "Where are you, Hunny? She said, so and so just picked her up and she was going over to his house and then to her parents. I told her if she needed me to just call. I did not hear from Pat for two days. I tried to get hold of her, but as usual she was MIA (missing in action). I felt sorry for her, but when I did finally see her, she acted as if nothing had happened to her. When I asked if she would ever go there again, she said she would. I don't understand that, nor do I get it. I have never been able to wrap my head around it. Was it even true?

When I met Patricia, she was healthy and beautiful with a smile that could light up a room. She really pushed herself on me when we first met, and I had a spare room, so I allowed her to rent it from me and in a matter of days, she was living in my home. I remember thinking I should say No, I even tried to but she was persuasive. I've often had a hard time saying no to people, if they needed me.

I was just trying to overcome my anxiety issues, so I liked having a person around me at times. It worked out and helped me pay bills. But, as I lived with her, her true colors came out. She would be up all night at times and was also a very dirty person when it came to cleanliness. It drove me nuts. I had to speak with her on many occasions. Finally one day, I became totally pissed at her and put all the dirty dishes from the spaghetti she had made and never cleaned up, into her room. I also have this huge heart and hate to see people suffer. That has wound me into many little confrontations, putting up with other's behaviors and habits because all I want to do is help. Kindness isn't necessarily a weakness, but you do have to be cautious about who you help. As I matured, I realized sometimes it's best not to help people who don't want it or aren't ready. She was still very much a person to me. No matter her faults, I cared, she sort of wedged her way into my heart, for a while, until I realized I couldn't have that around me or my son.

I was reluctant to talk to Damien after the Pat incident, but I was also excited at the same time. To me, no two people are alike, and perhaps he didn't notice she needed help. I only heard from her and maybe just maybe it was not true. I've heard the horror stories about the clubhouse and didn't know what to think. Often finding an excuse for other's bad behaviors, I liked to think along the lines of individual great goodness of all characters.

Shortly after that initial call from Patricia, in came a text from Damien saying he's going to bed, he had a late night with me, but wanted us to go for dinner during the week sometime. I said sure and left it at that. I was weary of him after that call, and all the memories of before, how he acted, flooded in.

The glow wore off after a little bit, within the next few days, since I'm no longer looking at things with a lusty star-struck haze. I started thinking about how when he first approached me in the bar a year and half ago, how he had a wife shortly after that, and was he married now or was that idle gossip. I started thinking of his attitude and how he treated my friend, why he didn't help her, why didn't she go to him, what was the hidden message that I wasn't seeing? Needless to say I had my doubts, and definitely second thoughts.

Messages came in frequently from him all that week. I didn't want to look like I was just available whenever, so I said I couldn't go a few times. Then finally I agreed, and we were going to a movie. He would pick me up from my mom's house in Morgan Creek. I would have to drop my son off for the night, as it would be more convenient.

I caved and had such mixed emotions. I believe that's when I became nervous around him, never knowing what to expect. I started questioning everything, as I often did because of what I had already been through. Why is he so interested in me? I felt nervous and agitated, not myself at all. I was very reserved when we went out. I felt as though I was going to be hurt by this man, as I had such strong feelings for him that first night when we kissed.

Jitters, I had huge jitters. I had a lot of self-doubt thinking, he probably was a man whore with tonnes of chicks and a wife. I had already told my mother all about him, so it was no surprise that she wanted a glimpse of him when he picked me up. He rang her door-bell like a perfect gentleman and she answered right along with me. The first thing he said was, "HI, Mom!" (Are you serious filtered through my mind, I was floored.) He actually made her smile and off we went on our first date.

He was so nice to me, and kind, he opened the door for me and closed it. I was treated like a princess, but as much as he was a perfect gentleman, he had a certain air about him that made me just not be me. I was scared or even intimidated into not talking very much. I was quiet and never really spoke unless spoken to. I believe he genuinely liked that about me. I sure didn't have the glow I had that first night. It was different. At the end of the night I thought he would drive me home, but he didn't, he pulled up to his house and we went in.

I was anxious, not just a flutter in my stomach; I mean a retching, vomiting and shaking panic feeling. I didn't want to go in, it was my intuition, screaming warning bells. I didn't listen to them. He pulled me into his arms and held me, as if he didn't want to let go. He told me that Ukrainians make the perfect wives and he liked I was a Ukrainian, like his ex-wife. I almost choked. I guess that answered that. He almost carried me up the stairs by the front door and when we were inside, I was hit with the unexpected.

His house was very nice and clean, with white carpets and walls ornamented with pictures of animals as well as Hell's Angels photos. The only thing in his house that was off, was the flow of things. I like to walk from room to room in a house with the decor flowing from one to the next, matched in a way but not. I was and had been always very OCD about my home, that was my only qualm.

I had a sinking feeling as if, either I am falling hard for this bad boy/businessman, or I'm truly just having one of my moments of insecurity. My warning bells were dinging, this was all new to me, the lifestyle, the man and the predator. I had dated before, but always in my younger days, with people who were in their early twenties, not a grown man who was close to thirty-five.

He went into the kitchen and came out with a pickles, cheese platter and wine. The very big tough guy had style and class and a flare for domesticity. He was turning the charm on and I liked it, it made me feel safer. I didn't say much around him, I found myself tongue-tied. If I had been more perceptive, not about the way he kept his house, but about the fact that I wasn't being the person I had finally learnt how to be, I would've seen that I was falling into the cycle of the way I was raised. I was like that inner child who took it all in and had no say. I just did, watched, learned and was fascinated. As he turned the channels and dominated the atmosphere of his own domain, we snuggled and kissed (he kissed and snuggled) but nothing more happened. I knew something wasn't right, it was all too pristine and nice.

Until in the morning when he was looking at me as I was sleeping, and told me he's been watching me for a while and would like me to continue seeing him. It was awkward, this powerful man opening up to me, he liked me, I mean really liked me. I felt exhilarated and a happy glow of worth. I felt special, and I also saw the greatness in him.

I went home after that. I was well on my way to becoming the girlfriend of a notorious biker and I had no idea what his fascination for me was. In my heart of hearts, I knew I should not fall for him, but I slowly was. When his charm flows and his gentle side comes out, it would make anyone feel alive.

I was ignoring my instincts nagging in the back of my mind saying, "It won't last, all the girls want him, he will cheat." I wish I had paid closer attention to the other details, such as a man who obviously lived two different ways, as I had noticed.

When I walked into my mom's, she told me that he wasn't even good looking and he looked as if he had a blockhead. I found myself instantly defending him, it goes back to all the ridicule and putdowns. I never really trusted my family's opinions as I got older. As good as it was to be sort of accepted by them, the comments never went away, they all, every last one of them still made me the butt end of jokes. They would laugh at me in that cackle sort of way as if it was just a joke, "Kerri, lighten up." I still heard it frequently in my mind. I could laugh at myself for only so long. Then it would wear me down and I would be upset. They just didn't understand that it hurt. When I spoke up it was if I was wrong to be upset over what they thought was normal, as if I should take it, as if that's what I was there for, their amusement.

Was it that I was just growing used to all the slander, thinking life was so good with my family, when really I had just grown accustomed to it? I couldn't understand why she would say something like that. She said that something was off about him and that I should trust her gut instinct on this. My trust of my mother waned. I've trusted her before, with my heart and look at what she had done. I had forgiveness, but there was never any closure to that. Somehow all she had done was okay. She had never acknowledged her wrongdoing, even though I had to acknowledge mine. Acknowledging mine set me free somehow and made me even stronger. Me being a pleaser and just wanting to be loved, and accepted, I would often nod my head, follow their rules, laugh at myself and even say sorry for things I had never done, just to keep the peace and not be alone.

Loneliness was my worst enemy, it was my anxiety and half the reason I wanted to be constantly surrounded; loneliness truly was my weakness.

I noticed that once I started dating Damien, I had more friends than ever, doors opened for me everywhere I went. It was like being a socialite without the stardom. Friends I barely knew accommodated me and gave me presents from clothes to drinks, even to jewelry when I bumped into them. It's yours they would say, trying to please me. They also gave presents to my son Ashton, making a point of one Christmas when I opened the front door to discover mounds of presents for my son, anonymously, of course. (I later found out they were from all the people I had helped in that old world.) It was almost as if rules didn't apply to all of us in that crowd, because we were different, perhaps successful, but untouchable.

It was hard not to live in that moment, smile and be glorious. I found a sense of strength inside as if I was a tough girl, with a cricketed smile. If you asked me if I ever felt beautiful, my honest reply would have been, "When I was hiding behind make up and nice clothes or having my son lying in my arms, were the only times I actually felt that way. "Inside I still hadn't fully healed after all that had happened in my childhood and teenage years. I put an invisible Band-Aid on that never came off and acted as if all was perfect in my world. I believed all my scars on the inside, were visible for the world to see and perhaps mock.

When my Romeo, Damien would pick me up, he'd say, "Hey beautiful." It was one thing to hear it, but not once did I feel it. It was too good to be true, a man like that really loving or even liking me. In the back of my head, I wondered when the ball would drop. I believe it was my way of protecting myself, from him hurting my heart. He was all domination; he had no fear for his body or image. It was a trait of his which I was drawn to. He had no insecurities, he was not God, by any means, just self-assured and confident. It radiated off him. I was drawn to that. The girls who surrounded guys like that never bothered me, as it was programmed in my mind, that girls were just drawn to that type of man, because of his powerful nature and bad boy image. It was something you just get accustomed to. He truly was a man of substance. To me he was beautiful; his eyes were a dynamic force that drew me in every time I saw him. I was falling for him no matter the shield I put up. His world was becoming mine, as opposed to me just enjoying a night out once in a while and partying with that crowd. It was seeping in to the point that it was where I belonged and where I would only go.

Damien had sandy blond hair, with a 275 lb body, and his skin was an olive color with that hint of natural tan. His green vibrant eyes were slanted to cat eyes that could pierce anyone's soul. His mouth was soft with perfect white teeth and the hugest smile I had ever seen. His hands were like a bear paw that could make a big fist, but be gentle to the point of sensual. He was perfectly formed and his persona was that of hardcore bad boy, until behind closed doors he was a manly lover with the gentlest touches. That is how I saw my Beast. He was my perfect soul mate, it would make me deliriously happy just to be around him. My life was once again turning into that of a young woman full of a lusty infatuation with the first man who could truly touch my inner soul. We belonged together and matched as a man and woman match. The critics would say it, aka, friends and friends of friends, we were officially known as Beauty and the Beast.

He acted as though he truly cared for me, with his protective glances, and pulling me into the comfort of his chest when we were out, to the romantic soft gestures he would murmur in my ear at random, out or behind closed doors. He allowed me to be a woman with him.

First Trip

HE TOOK ME on a trip to meet his oldest child, as we did only a few other family things as well together. There I started to see past his persona and got the tiniest inkling of feelings, as if all he did was for show. I can't explain what I noticed but it wasn't nice, it was awkward. I watched how, when we were out of town visiting his family, they didn't seem to recognize him as a person, but that image of a Hell's Angel. It was weird to see the bowing down attitude everyone assumed around him. It wasn't what I expected when going on my first mini vacation for a weekend out of town to visit his daughter and his kin.

It never felt family-oriented at all. I was back to feeling confused, also in an unidentified way, not welcome there as I was there only to serve what he needed and be a statue among his family and friends. I had been brought, not to be introduced, but as a showpiece. It felt awkward because I loved children. I wanted to bond and be caring, do special things not sit there being completely unwelcome and uncomfortable.

When we got back, after leaving my son for the weekend at my mother's, I just held Ashton, and never saw Damien, aka Beast, for a week. It was as if I lost that star-struck gaze for him, and it was dulling. It was no longer, "I couldn't wait to see you," but "I'm busy, will try to see you on the weekend." I remember my mother picking up on it and making a comment along the lines of, "What happened, Kerri?" I just pretended nothing had happened and shrugged it off so as not to look as if I had made a mistake in front of my family, or give them ammunition. I just knew in that first trip, he wasn't my "Prince, in shining armor," or a family man at all. He wasn't it. I knew then, and from that point on I was sort of blowing him off a little.

I avoided him on every call for a week and a half straight. You have to understand he is ten years older than I am, and me brushing him off, he could tell, not that I was smart enough to figure that out yet, but he was onto me. He had to have known that I was a little repelled by our trip and unattached as well as pushing him away.

On a Friday evening, he called me up and said, "Hey, why don't you come down to the clubhouse to say Hi, Hunny, I miss you."

I told him I was just helping a friend out, about to make an excuse, and my friend, being the party girl, overheard me, saying "no", and she's in the background telling me she wants to go out. I knew I was stuck, he started laughing in his chuckle and said, "See you in a few, and bring her down."

I had anxiety issues during these times with overwhelming bouts of terror, loneliness, and panic attacks that rendered me useless. This girl gave me the comfort of having someone around, so my thoughts of no one helping me if I was dying weren't so crippling. I barely hung out with this girl at all. She just didn't have the Mommy in her, but would be accommodating to me when I didn't have anyone else around. I know it was wrong to use those girls as I did, but in the same sense, they were using me. It always made me feel badly, but it was the truth. She was a kindhearted person, who really deserved to be loved. I liked her, just didn't have any respect for her at all. Sometimes I noticed how she engrossed herself in romance novels as I did and it would spark sadness in me watching her, because I was that girl. It was one of the things we did together when she was around: make snacks and read together, just our books, my son and the simple pleasure of having the one person around who enjoyed something I truly loved doing, reading. I stuck up for her lots with Stella and everyone for that matter, because that girl had heart. No matter how off-track she was, selling her soul as she did, by allowing guys to use her when she gave her all, just for a taste of love, was almost degrading.(She was not a prostitute).

I wasn't into going out that night, at all, but we did. When we arrived, Damien was half loaded, shooting games of pool, enjoying himself. He immediately walked up to me and gave me a huge kiss, whispered in my ear, "You know the rules, no necking in public, Hunny, or I get a fine from the boys," and started howling. He sat me down at the front of the bar offering me any drink I wanted.

I don't know what It was, but I never drank it. It was placed in front of me, whatever he ordered. I was sort of growing out of the drinking on weekend stage, slowly becoming yielding and subservient to him more and more.

I would much rather enjoy a bottle of wine, but my little party girlfriend had already had a few drinks, slamming them back as she did and he was giving her weird-looking eyes and laughing at her in an attentive sort of way. That was a glimpse of Damien, I had always known was there.

I went to the bathroom, then outside and phoned my mother's house. As it was only early evening, I told my mom I wasn't really into having a weekend off and wanted to come over, sleepover at her house with my boy, and we'd figure it out in the morning, if Ashton wanted Nana time the next day, he could. She said, of course, as my mother was a little lonely during this time during her separation.

We sort of leaned on each other and became quite close. I don't know if she ever knew but she was perhaps my closest friend during these times.

I went back inside, and told Damien I had to go, and that my baby boy needed me. It was a false statement but not entirely untrue as my son always needed me. He had speculation in his eyes. It was then I saw for the first time a flare of deception in them, a panicky feeling welled up inside me, a feeling I knew all too well. I had the urge to run right home, but I sat down for a few more minutes to soothe him. He was onto me, he was mad. I will never forget that pensive, calculating stare as if he could see right through me, as he glanced to my drink and back to me. He just watched intently to see if he could get a reaction out of me, then he kissed me, I mean really kissed me, as if the rules of the clubhouse didn't matter. He melted my resistance in a genuine heartwarming, lip smacking sort of way.

He lingered and whispered, "I've missed you, Baby, don't push me away." Then he stopped, he had never called me baby. As he continued to watch me, he bellowed out loud in his well-known dominant voice, to all the prospects, "I'm walking my girl to her car. She's such a good mommy, she has to go make sure her boy is okay. Fill up her friend's drink, she's staying. One of you guys will drive her home later!" It was awkward, as I glanced at my friend, she ran up and hugged me saying, that I was so lucky to have someone who adores me like that and she'll call me in a couple days. "Give Lil Ashton a big kiss from auntie." I felt her animosity and jealousy, seeping through because I had a guy like that, who put on a show that looked as if he was completely enthralled with me. She didn't even know.

It was a surreal, unbelievable, fast moment, that's embedded in my mind, I was smart and could see past the biggest facades. I've lived life, its how I've survived, by watching and learning. I say this, it was the strongest intuition feeling I had so far, that something was off. I could taste it, feel it and even almost put my finger on it, just not say it, or even act on it. My silly *kindness and giving the benefit of the doubt* attitude often prevented me from jumping to conclusions and walking away.

It wasn't the drinks he'd had, it was his stare and the knowledge that he's lived the life too, much older. He had caught me making an excuse, and bellowed a perfect complimentary sentence and a statement to one and all, that I was his woman, going home for the night to take care of the boy, even though his own mechanisms were working on something else.

I knew in that moment as he walked me to my car, pecked me on the lips and shut the door as fast as he could, that he'd exaggerated in there, put on a show, he was choked. Not only that, I knew something was going to happen, I had a sneaking suspicion of more yet to come. This night was not over for me.

I visited with my mother for a bit, then my son and I snuggled as he fell asleep in my arms, there was no place I'd rather have been. I was lying there looking at him, just so happy and content. He truly was my inspirational angel.

When I woke up the next morning all refreshed and looked at my cell phone there were over twenty missed calls and text messages. It was crazy. I phoned back as it was early morning, no later than 8:30 a.m., and he answered saying he was just getting back to his place, and had a great night. He was still partying, not slurring his words, but definitely still up from the night before and music was blaring into the phone. I remember thinking I'm so not into this, it's not the way I want to start my sunny beautiful day. I blew him off and hung up quickly.

I ignored a few more messages and went about my day. I will never forget later getting a message from my girlfriend, at around the supper time hour, saying she's so sorry, so sorry he fed her all these lies. She hopes I will talk to her in person that she really needed to say whatever it was in person.

My heart, or was it my stomach, plummeted to the ground, met-aphorically speaking, my mother watching me, as my phone was ringing again, over and over, probably ten times before I answered. It was a prospect saying I needed to get down there and pick up Damien, he needed to see me.

Awkward to say the least, but heart breaking because somehow, and some way, I had just received the most ironic message from my girlfriend begging forgiveness and acting as if a life-altering event had taken place, somehow I was in the middle of it. It was a sick moment of clarity without hearing the words I knew needed to be heard.

My mother gave me the opportunity to go for a little bit, and she'd see me later and hugged me. She seemed to be doing more and more of that lately, hugging me, since I had started dating him. She had no idea the strength she gave me with the power of her touch.

I knew my instincts were screaming the truth behind my hurt heart. No one had to tell me, I already knew what had happened. I knew the type of girl my friend was, and with Damien I knew what guys like that must be surrounded by or perhaps were like. It's a known fact that girlfriends have to deal with, but you actually really never have to deal with cheating and suck it up. You have to know its wrong, it should never be acceptable for a man to be able to do that. I was asked to be at the clubhouse within the half hour, as if it was a demand, no option just a demand, an appointment time, he knew I was ignoring his calls. So he had someone else phone for him. Sly.

As I approached the clubhouse, the gates opened as if he'd been waiting for me and watching the cameras. He came walking up and jumped in my father's truck I happened to be driving. He asked if I wanted to see a movie , I said," No, Thank-you". Then he asked if I could drive him home as his vehicle was there. As I look back now and replay that most vital moment when I was actually falling for a person and knew the trust had somehow been severed, I knew I was wiser this time and more aware of the effects of a bad relationship. I was waiting but I needed the truth, had to hear it, in order to come to the proper, responsible decision. Not jump to conclusions.

"We could go have a relaxing night at my house," he spouted in a tone of exhaustion. I was boggled. I had had no intention of even going anywhere an hour ago. Now, I was across a city because of a prospect's request, tricked into being a chauffeur while my heart was breaking around me. He was acting oblivious to me. I knew something had happened between him and my friend. I could tell by her.

message, by the hundred calls throughout the evening and day from him. I was floored as to how a guy could play so many manipulative, domineering games and be so uncaring. I silently drove to his house as he had his head laid back with his eyes closed. He wouldn't look at me, but obviously he had the prospect call so I would listen and obey. The true nature of his character and heart were being displayed throughout our drive. I did not question myself, or my thoughts. I was smarter and wiser. I was not a typical girl who would question when she had doubts with a guy. I had already seen so much in my short life that I knew to trust my gut intuition as well as my mind. I felt sure as sure can be that he had done the unthinkable, but what I couldn't understand was this crass behavior of such coldness.

As we approached his house and pulled in, I will never ever forget as he got out, came around to open my door and as we walked inside he said, "Your friend just left." I didn't get it. The whole situation and his demeanor were off. As I sat down on the couch briefly, he sauntered off to the kitchen. He said loudly enough for me to hear, "Don't worry, I didn't fuck your friend, gave her a bath, played with her a little, then had her leave." Just like that he said it, no word of crap, utterly heartless and mean.

I was stunned, shocked, humiliated and silent. He was in another room when he just blatantly said that, as if it was nothing. It was cold, so cold and said in a matter of fact way. I was aching inside as my silent tears rolled down my face. His ignorant crass way of hurting me as if it was normal and acceptable was gross. I was a deer caught in the headlights with a smashed heart, stunned mind and the knots within my stomach were turning into sickness as it often did when something hit me with a force of evil.

My need to leave was strong, but crippling. As he continued on in his kitchen, I reached for my purse. The stairs downstairs to his door were directly under me and I moved to leave as quietly as possible so as not to alarm him or have any confrontation. As soon as I got up, he walked in or was watching somehow from a distance.

He looked at me, the tears on my face and turned immediately into that bashful person, "Awe Baby, Baby, Hunny. I only played with the little man in the boat," then laughed.

I almost puked, really almost puked. I started panicking inside. There was something sick going on here, this isn't normal. I wanted to leave right then, but couldn't. He held me by my shoulders in a gentle manner, looking at my reaction, feeding off it or something.

He sat me back down with a gentle push and landed beside me. He could see the terror setting in, panic and then finally somehow he saw the tears rolling down my face as I quivered inside, or maybe he chose to notice. He became all sensitive as if a trigger went off in him. He said, "Hunny, Baby, I never knew you wanted to be exclusive. I had no idea, why didn't you say anything. Hunny, why didn't you ask me to be all yours? Awe, Baby, don't cry, I never knew that would bother you, you have to ask me out for me to know."

I was so stunned by his demeanor that my silent tears flowed without me knowing it. He was a very sick person to be able to say that, even act like that. I've met some weirdo's in my day, but never have I ever seen such a brazen act of selfishness.

I don't know how I spoke between all those terrible emotions but I did. My voice cracked as I said to him kindly, "I want to go home, please." He just held me in his big arms as he rubbed my back gently, smoothing my hair, and kissed the top of my head. He whispered how he cared about me so much, there was no way I could go home like this, "Relax, Hunny, next time tell me," echoing in my head.

I was not so messed up that I couldn't see what he'd just done. He had just completely blown my mind. My tears dried immediately, just like that, but I had to get out of there. He wasn't letting me go, so as docile as I could be, with my survival nature, I played the way he wanted, while my mind carefully calculated his. I let him hug me gently and as I relaxed more and more he fell asleep. I waited until the early morning hours and then gently told him, I have to go. He kissed me and said, "I'm glad we worked that out, Hunny, have a good day." I left and as I drove to my mother's, I knew inside without a doubt that I could never see him again. I knew there was something seriously wrong with this man, I had almost fallen hopelessly for. It was my moment to walk away. I would never allow another man to dictate my destiny, affect my life and that of my son. I had too much to lose, so with as much bravery as I could muster, and my self-worth, what I would and would not tolerate, my true strength prevailed. I did just that. I walked away and deleted him out of my life, gangster, Hell's Angel or whomever, I was not going there, nor did I want to. I was becoming my own "Woman of Substance".

I was not that girl who was upset with her friend, because I felt sorrier for her than anything. There was no making excuses for him and no girl inside me thinking it was my fault. My eyes were wide open. I felt a sudden release of accomplishment that comes with success. I knew without a doubt, the outcome of being with someone like that, just like in that moment at his house with his demeanor and carelessness. I knew it wasn't me, that it was not my fault and that this was that man's true character. I had to repeat that because my story is to shed light to help anyone who may need it.

I never knew much beyond the fact that perhaps it's just what Angel's do. I mean it might just come naturally to give themselves freely like that. They have their own fan base of girls and group-ies, its inevitable with the whole image and persona of that world. But with him it was different and I knew it, in the way he acted when I left that night and when I picked him up the next day, it was premeditated.

The only thing I didn't realize was why he would do that, why he acted like that, and how can he be so kind, caring, gentle almost beautiful one minute and then so cold, evil and brutal the next. I had no idea if it was how he tried to get back at me for pushing him away during the previous week after our trip, or was it a sick way to see how far he could push me and what I would tolerate. I did know one thing that was definite in my mind; I knew he liked hurting me. I had seen the bemusement in his eyes with my reaction a few times now.

There was no way I was letting my mother catch wind of my hurt. I never knew when it would result in an embrace or would be used against me. I wanted nothing more in the world than a hug from her and acknowledgement, advice or anything. I believed in my heart of hearts I was lucky to have gotten away with just the mental scarring, but I was allowing it to continue to affect my life.

I tried to let go of him in a nice way instead of ignoring or being rude. I simply said I needed space to focus on my son and home. It worked for a while, but he had a fascination with me. I was sure of it, but the, *what ifs* and *maybes* played often in my weaker moments.

He would leave songs on my answering machine and messages. It would actually make my heart thump a little louder and put smiles on my face; my friends laughed. I never heard from my one friend who did that with him for a while, not for years anyway as not many of my other friends liked her. I did secretly, knowing she just needed love. I knew one day I'd hear from her. I still didn't blame her, but what little respect I had for her was gone, I needed space. It was wrong and that was that.

Growing into a Woman

Every time someone cared about me it gave me strength, and a will to survive, a hope that someday there would be love for me out there, in that big world, and that love would last forever.

TIMES WERE CHANGING. I was growing more into that woman I wanted to be. I wanted more out of life. I quit working in the bar industry and solely focused on raising my son, and exerting my rights as a parent. I had had enough of my little boy telling me his Nana keeps trying to get him to call her Mama Bear, as that was a huge violation.

I was upset and talked to my stepfather more and more about things. He pointed out to me that I had to quit paying the way for all my friends. I still have years ahead of me, to learn to remain as kind as I am, but not to get taken advantage of so much. Stella and I were still best friends but even she was growing. The biker phase was wearing off and we did not go out often anymore, not that we didn't once in a while, but we were more focused on other things.

On a lonely evening with no children, I received a random message from Damien again, a song. I loved the music and it gave off amazing waves of feeling, bringing back moments otherwise forgotten. He touched me, in a way no other really had, so on that lonely night I phoned him. He was as happy to hear from me as I was to hear from him. It was on going like that for a year or so. Many things had changed, people grow or so I thought.

I was once again putting in a few hours at my stepfather's company and visiting Damien on lunch hours as he was just over the bridge, a ten minute drive. One day I walked in and he had laid rose petals all the way up the stairs, down the hallway and into his room, where he was lying in bed.

It was a sunny, beautifully green day and he had utterly touched my very heart. He made me feel invaluable and passionate. He made me feel like a woman. The once star-struck gaze and infatuation I had with him was being replaced by a womanly need, a forever thought, time heals as I believed and people grow in character, age and substance. There he made me a promise of not lust, but love, he wanted to be an item. I foolishly and too quickly agreed, lying in his arms, kissing and snuggling. I didn't make it back to work that day, I was consumed by desire, love and forever.

It was easy for a girl like me, who craved the forever after and promises of a man I thought I knew. I had been strong enough a year previously to walk away from him when he broke my trust. It wasn't just that though, it was the perverse way he addressed it, the frightening feeling I had in the pit of my stomach. Why didn't that thought cross my mind lying there agreeing to a second chance, even though to him it was really a first chance. I didn't doubt his words of promise; however, I did doubt his fidelity, but I believe in people, it's a gift I have. I see the good, when I feel it, I hold onto it with a firm grasp. When I open my heart to a man, I stay there. I'm not a floosy looking for loving between the sheets of other men, until I find it. I'm the sort of woman who likes the comfortable feeling of the same touch and person. Now that I look back, I was even like that in my teenage years and the time when I wasn't with Zak and then ended up with him after my son was born. The familiar felt safer than the unknown. Once my heart was open it didn't turn off like a switch, it stayed open with hope, promise or optimism.

His promises were what I needed to hear. It was an intoxicating desire that swept into my soul and a piece I was always missing between a man and woman.

This time we did things more along the lines of events to attend or movies and love oriented, as opposed to afterhours and parties. I had briefly introduced my son to him the last time, but never allowed it to blossom. I was not a mother who introduced my son to my dates. However, this time I allowed it a little more, only a little.

I agreed to go with him once again to see his daughter for her birthday. She lived three hours out of town. We would only be gone a day as it was two days before New Year's, a huge event for club guys. I did not bring my son, as I chose to allow my mother to watch him. It wasn't much different from the last time, except that my guard was up and I chose to stay in the hotel while he visited. I read, relaxed and actually enjoyed a day off.

I thought he'd bring his daughter back, but he didn't, saying he just wanted the time for us. It was blissful, so blissful that my glow, glowed and my zing zinged.

As we pulled into town, I was excited to be home with my Ashton. One overnight away from him would drive me crazy. My son went with me everywhere, with friends, to appointments. My baby boy was my other half, but something within me kept him away from Damien. It wasn't that he was a bad father, he loved his other children to the point of tears when he talked about them living so far away.

Ashton and his other child were only six months apart in age. Damien was immediately attracted to my son, an attraction that simply filled the void of missing his own child, I thought. Something within me made me reluctant to allow a full introduction that he was Mommy's new boyfriend. I kept that special. I wanted whoever I married to be that special someone for my son so I rarely took him around Damien. He never met anyone after the Zak incident. It just wasn't going to happen. I protected him as my right as his mother not to allow certain people or events around him. I never liked leaving him for any period of time. He was my existence and if I was away for a day, all I wanted was to go home.

Damien had other plans. He drove right past my exit and on to his house. I never liked when he did those *pulling his rank maneuvers*. I hated it. I still was that very shy girl/woman around him. I was more gentle around him and timid, never, ever myself. However, I would look at him and raise my eyebrows in a shocked sort of way as he'd pull his domineering way. He would just laugh purposefully knowing what he was doing. As we pulled up to his house, he swept me into his arms and said, "I only want a few more hours with you, Hunny." Then he said, "I will see you at the clubhouse for New Year's, right?"

I never realized I was invited. It was still unclear how the Hell's Angel thing worked. That was when in a perverse way, he enlightened me. It came as a shock to hear this, but on he went to inform me about how it worked. He was so happy to share it with me he said "Baby," *as if there was nothing wrong with any of it.* "Functions such as these are" wife nights, all the wives go, or girlfriends, other than the typical weekend though. Fridays are girlfriend nights and Saturdays are wife nights at the clubhouse." Needless to say, I was floored. My face expressed my shock, and he started howling as if what he had told me and the look on my face had just melted him.

He grabbed me and threw me on the bed. We were fully dressed having just come back from our trip, and he kissed me in his roguish way. I was utterly speechless as my mind evaluated these ideas and tried to come to terms with what he had said. I tried, how I tried, I was flabbergasted. He started murmuring in my ear, "Baby, you know your mine, my number one girl, only members can lay claim to one girl that no one can touch or date or even go near. Baby you're my girl." He kissed me then with a possession that knocked the wind out of me.

The grip he held onto me with was strong to the point of hurting. It was a moment, a choice in my life, I had to decide which way to go, if I could. His kiss, Ohh his kiss, although his grip and forceful-ness hurt, it was a claiming, thrilling bad boy kiss that knocked the socks off me. I am not going to fabricate it, it was a huge turn-on, but once the moment was gone and his presence wasn't around, the tingling would wear off. The time of truth would come along with reluctance and awareness as his words played in my mind, as they always did. As I drove home my mind worked hard at processing my feelings.

I had so much going on in my head, it was nothing short of wishy-washy and a choice. I didn't want to go out for New Year's. I was the type that liked to bring New Year's in with my son, kiss him at midnight, a stay-at-home and relaxing sort of night.

My best friend, Stella, was the one I turned to during this time. She was planning on staying home too, or pulling a dress-up-1980s night with her sisters, and to be with her family. Only when we could get our moms to watch the boys would we go out. I looked at her family and saw such a bond of sister hood that I would be envious, not in a deceptive way, but a yearning way. I wished I had a family bond that was as close as that. Later, Stella told me, that she's the black sheep and they all put her down and she says they're not as close as they appear. But I knew it wasn't like mine. They loved her, were always there for her, and did things families did. She couldn't see how my family was, I don't believe she ever did understand it. Her family cared, stuck by her, it was her choice to leave, and never my choice to leave mine.

I explained that I was invited out for New Year's at the clubhouse with Damien and really wanted her there with me. Call it a gut intuition, but I didn't want to be there alone. We made plans that I'd pick her up the next night. Everyone loved little midget, she was wild. I believed it was because she was so tiny, that when she had a few drinks it hit her harder and that was always my excuse for her behavior. She was never afraid to get loving from guys, whereas I couldn't do that unless I knew the person. Years later I asked her how she did that, as it was becoming an issue with me not allowing the feeling of touch, or allowing anyone for that matter, any man to even kiss me. I would tell her later what Beast had said. I just needed to be home with my son. I missed him, my mind was full of indecision.

The love I received from the presence of my son was unbelievable, we often slept together and whispered things such as he holds the keys to my heart, and that we fit like a puzzle. He gave me purity and a clear head, my little button of unconditional love.

I asked my mother to watch my son for the evening, as she often said yes, if I was out with Damien. She said it in a reluctant way this time. It wasn't until much later into our relationship that I confided in my mother about the goings on. That night stands out more than anything that she had said so far with something she said then, it stuck with me. "I wonder why his ex-wife lives so far away, Kerri, there has to be a reason." I don't believe she liked the fact that we were dating again, after the whole incident of the year before. She didn't like it at all, but respected my decision. She was worrying me, and I'm sure I was starting to worry her.

Around this time she was becoming sadder. I could see the longing in her eyes for my stepdad, but the stubborn nature of her character only acknowledged that it was all him and never her, and wouldn't allow it. I felt sorry for my mother and my heart wept for her. I tried to open her heart again. I wanted her to be happy and loved. She went on to say, "Kerri, I need you to beware of him. I'm not fooled like everyone else, his ex-wife left for a reason." It was there she placed a notion in my head. He was very brutal in the way he said things. Yes, he had hurt me, crushed my heart even by betraying my trust as I believed *that who you share your body with should be sacred.*

She had no idea what he had said last night to me, but it played on my mind. Does that mean he has other girlfriends right now, was he doing it again and just told me, is this really who I want to be with? I want to have more children, is it even safe?

Ashton had often asked when he's going to have a little brother or sister. I want happily ever after. I am ready. Am I prolonging it by being with this Hell's Angel? The seed of doubt was planted and that dang incident last year weighed heavily inside me. I don't believe I ever got over the broken trust, but the butterflies he made me feel were beautiful. Now, he got my mother to start asking me, if it's all right to have Ashton, or what did I think? He gave me the euphoria of power within my own family, which was strength I had never had, my opinion finally mattered. I was no longer that girl they accused me of being, but one they respected (the constant barbs at me and laughing comments would never go away, I would still be the butt end of jokes, it was and will always be like that, but now they even thought I was pretty and looked nice, it would throw me back at times being so openly complimented by them).

I picked up Stella on New Year's Eve. We did a huge burnout and it was crazy. We chatted, laughed and sang at the top of our lungs. When we were halfway there, we decided to stop at a pub and have a quick drink and a visit before we went to the clubhouse. We were growing out of the biker scene as we saw it, and liked to mingle with people our own age as opposed to the older patch guys and the girls who would constantly be around them.

At the Pub we talked about what Damien had said. I had never known Stella to have a true opinion and voice with me. I believe I dominated her a lot, because I had saved her. She was starting to understand that it was her strength that saved herself. I may have helped with an outstretched hand, but she did it. Being back with her son and her family had made her grow tremendously.

She was serious as she leaned over the table and said something I will never forget it. "Kerri, I have never seen you EVER act like yourself around him, you don't even laugh. You sit there like a statue, you're not you, Hunny. He is cool to have fun with, but he's not for you at all. It's their way of life. He will always cheat; it's in him and I don't think you should be with him at all." I believed her, she gave me a serious gentle punch, to open my eyes as she said "Let's go have fun, wooo- hooo New Year's," Her serious moment had passed as most of the intelligent conversations did with her. I truly heard what she said. It was already gnawing at me, that truth. He was not something I could live with. I was not myself.

As we arrived at the clubhouse, things were banging off the hook. The bouncers were prospects, the hottest cars from Maserati's to

Mercedes to jacked-up trucks lit the road. Diamonds were glittering off people's wrists, hands and ears, the fattest diamonds and gold that you'd see even on movie stars. It was bling, baby, and it was the life. Money in wads stuck out of everyone's pockets with the ladies sporting theirs with designer bags and rocks on their fingers the size of five carats. Insane, but normal and I had seen it before. The night had an aura about it as limos were pulling up and everyone was hugging and yelling, "Bro," and banging their drinks on the table. As we walked right into the house, it was hooting and hollering and all smiles and loves.

A lifestyle that anyone could get wrapped up in for a time. You could feel the love in the air with everyone's sense of belonging and in a person's mind who was new to it all, but there were skeletons and closed doors behind every false smile. When someone yelled, "Damien your girl's here," he looked right at me with a smile that was beautiful, but when he came over and kissed me, he was looking at Stella with a mischievous look, putting on the show, "Hi, there," would become his famous words. I don't know if he was happy I brought her, this was a first time for me at a function. I was uneasy and had learnt long ago to trust my instincts.

A few hours went by while everyone was having a blast and midnight was close, when another limo pulled up. He was too busy bopping around, being himself to care much about me. Stella and I were thinking of leaving after midnight and going somewhere more fun and exciting, when in walked this girl, tiny and blond (not beautiful) in a sparkling top that glittered. Damien was on her like glue and when she walked in, she stood right beside him. Stella and I commented on it. I could see I was invisible as I had been half the night to him. I needed to see this clarity, a brazen truth, like a slap in the face.

As the countdown for midnight began, the clock struck twelve, and he wrapped himself around the girl in the winking glittery top, and kissed her full on the lips as he would have me. Then he hugged a few bros and made his way towards me, to settle a kiss on my lips. He noticed my shrug off and his eyes narrowed dangerously. It was a horrible moment, in which I looked to Stella for help. She jumped up and screamed, "Happy New Year" and hugged him. She was fun that way, and right on it. She often sensed the panic in my eyes and knew exactly what to do. It diverted his attention and off he went to mingle.

As the night continued, he ignored me in a blatant way that everyone knew. The energy in the clubhouse changed, it was daunting and dangerous. All I wanted to do was leave. I looked but couldn't find Stella. I had a horrible feeling. I had already diverted one chick from trying to fight me and was looking at this in a whole new light, as I felt a tap on the shoulder from Beast. He said, "Hey, you should leave. Your friend's outside." As I went outside there was my Stella, bloody, black and blue and my heart dropped as I helped her to my car. She was a tough little thing, and went on to laugh, saying that she had told the girl who tried to grab me, not to ever touch me!

When Stella had gone to the bathroom, she was approached from behind by guys, and punched and then kicked in the head. She had that nervous laugh as she told the story and I quickly started my car to get out of there. As we came to the gates, a prospect leaned in and said to me, "She was trying to get you for fifteen minutes," and a simple, "Sorry. " He opened the gates and we drove through, as a dawning came over us.

I drove in silence until we got far enough away for me to pull over. I was in no shape to drive, but there was nothing going to stop me from getting us to safety. She cried then, really cried as I cleaned her up, our make up running down both our faces. I couldn't hold back, my poor girl, how could this have happened?

We burst out laughing a short time later as we looked around and saw that I had parked in a ditch, not an accident but out of sight, away from the road, away from them or him, to hide. We laughed so hard we had to pee. When we jumped back in the car, good for Stella's character, she grabbed our New Year's Hats and put them on our heads. We were both done with clubhouses, bikers and everything. That was a clear indication that we didn't belong.

We laughed for hours as we drove 30 km an hour across the city. We had just taken the turn off the highway, when I noticed police lights. Stella quickly grabbed perfume. We were still partially inebriated and she said, "We don't have gum; open your mouth," and she sprayed perfume in my mouth to cover up the scent. I was choking as I pulled over. As the police officer approached the car, I already had the window down. We were hysterical because we had just sprayed alcoholic perfume in my mouth.

He asked us to get out of the car. He was smiling looking at us, and said, "Looks like you two had quite the night." Stella and I burst out laughing again because of her already forming black eyes, our party hats and make up smeared down our faces from tears. The police officer couldn't hold back his own laugh as he said, "Yes, girls, I have had my lights on for over twenty minutes. I couldn't call in a high-speed chase because you girls were only going 30 km an hour and with my window down I could hear your guy's horrible singing."

We laughed some more and asked for a ride home, even though we had almost made it back to my apartment. He said we were not getting any tickets, nothing, because it looked like it was already a really hard night. The tow truck came to tow my car home and he offered us a ride. As we jumped in the back of his car, he cranked the music for us and allowed us to smoke with windows down. The whole thing that cops are goofs, wasn't exactly true, they are human like the rest of us. It was a momentous moment for us, as he offered us advice when he was leaving. He said something along the lines of, "I sure hope you guys learnt whatever you needed to tonight. " We laughed at him and said, "More than you know!"

When we woke up the next morning, so hung over, we went over the night's events. We cried some more tears, and laughed our heads off about the policeman. We would recite that story over and over to others throughout the years. It was a moment of chance, change and growth. It's an experience in life to learn from and grow.

Stella and I packed up all our "support clothes" and put them in bags. We dropped them all off at the Salvation Army. We would never wear that stuff again. I felt horrible, for her to have to go home to her mother's and explain what happened. We vowed we would plan a new, New Year's in a few days at a place where no bikers go and with people our own age. We would celebrate in a good way, with new people and make new beginnings.

That was a moment when I made a choice. I didn't want a man who could carelessly cheat and be okay with it. I wanted a place where I could go and feel safe, as I could never be with him. It did not hurt me that day to say goodbye in my heart. He had caused my friend to be hurt. I don't know how I know, I just do. He took a mother, a person, to a party where she could've been killed and had been hurt.

Once again, no matter how much love he had pretended to show to me throughout those short few months, he would never change. He was okay with being who he was, and he did not have the heart I did when it came to love. I couldn't have imagined at that time, being with him and allowing another man to touch me. I was his and to him he was everyone's. He was a man that had no sense of security or vigilance or even forever, when it came to being with someone. It was goodbye to already a long chapter in my life and hello to the good boys and the good life. Hell's Angels and Ballers were not what I was interested in.

Letting Go

People don't want to remember or block out certain moments because they're not yet strong enough, or emotionally ready to acknowledge it….all they need is time…..

WHAT HAPPENED THAT New Year's really affected me. I realized that no matter who I knew in that lifestyle of Angels, it was mean and deceitful. Who I had thought were my friends, weren't or so it seemed. Seeing my Stella, during the days after that, with black eyes was hard on me. I just wanted to wrap my arms around her and wish the bruising away. She was a tough girl on the outside and she never acted as if it bothered her, but on the inside I knew it did. Just like I knew that it wasn't right for her son to see that. As I look back now and replay the events that happened with my eyes wide open, I realize, she was defending me. She should have been safe with Damien watching over us, but he never cared and I had no say.

I will never know if he provoked that altercation in his premeditated way. Inside I feel that he did. She should have been safe, as I should have. I was invited by a man who whispered I love you in my ear and we had only just gotten back from visiting his child the day before. Didn't any of that mean a thing, did it mean anything, at all. If I had taken him to bond with my son, he would've been safe. It was a sickening realization that I never held up to his standards, so in turn, I was almost jumped and my friend was curb-stomped by men outside. All he said was, "Your friend's outside," turned and walked away. It bothered me. How he could be so crass, so ignorant as if my friend wasn't hurt or I never mattered.

For days I licked my inside wounds with the knowledge he would never be the man I wished him to be. I surrounded myself with cleaning products to polish every inch of my house, soft music to heal inwardly, as well as the laughter and puzzles with my stunning son. It was exactly four days since the incident, when Stella came over and as our sons played, we conversed on recent events, and laughed at how pathetic that life was. We had a way with us that would make even the outside people gigggle on how we re-enacted events, as if they were skits on a television show. It was our way to make fun of the stupid stuff that seemed to happen. We not only laughed so hard as to pull a few muscles in our backs, as we lay upon the floor in heaps of laughter that bellowed, yes we were quite mad.

As the laughter faded, we came up with a plan to re-do New Year's, with the right people, good people, the ones who never wore vests. It was then we decided to phone our parents and ask them to babysit, which they did. As we were getting ready that evening, we had no idea where to go, as all the places we did go, they attended. It was huge back then bars, and bikers. They were in every night-club, but a few.

So we picked one down the road a city away, a glow-stick hip-hop hopping nightclub to go to. We had never been there and decided it was a start toward meeting people who mattered. It was also hard to cover Stella's black eyes but I did my best, as she consoled me that the black lights would hide it all.

We jumped into my car and off we went. As we pulled up, there was a line-up all the way around the building. We had never stood in line-ups before. It was always *go past the line up in the bar*. People knew me as well as Stella now, so when we looked at each other, we laughed, passed eye contact like watch this, right up to the bouncer's at the front door as if we owned the place. Sure enough, due to our looks, style and class, we were in. It was glorious to see the people our age, hear the music we listened to, and be in a safe environment, it was different but oh so right.

As we were getting a little tipsy, Stella started doing her I'm friends with everyone routine, and before we knew it, we had twenty people, men and women around us all having a blast. Then up walks my old manager, my boss from On the Roxxs, the one I had such a crush on when I worked there. I was beaming, as he wrapped a huge hug around me and introduced me to his friend.

Chase was at least six feet tall with green hazel eyes and dark hair. He had perfect teeth and with the whole Nike outfit that screamed "clean and wow" look, pretty boy. He always wore dress shirts and black slacks at work, so to see him like that, and perhaps the booze I had drank, definitely turned me on. I believe I started having a crush on him, when at the end of every night where I used to work, he would go up to the DJ booth and talk into the mike about how much he loved his girlfriend, who worked at the same place. It touched me right to my inner core. I've never heard anyone declare their love so openly. She would roll her eyes and he would laugh, not to mention, I've always liked dark brown hair types of guys, so being with Damien previously and his sandy blond hair was something new for me.

We got to talking and I asked if he was still with his girlfriend since they had recently shut down, *"On the Roxxs"* a nightclub where they were working. He said, "No Way. She's with someone new," and that he worked where we were now. Stella finally clued in after her tray of shooters, that she was dared to do by some guy.

She was becoming a mess, but I could read her without ever talking to her, her senses were still reeling as her eyes zoned in on Chase. No, Stella, do not embarrass me. She just laughed and went right up to Chase and said, as she pointed her little finger in his chest, "Don't you hurt my friend. I have seen enough of that," laughing as she pointed out her black eyes. That insinuated she had stuck up for me with someone.

Chase started laughing and introduced her to his friend. No sooner had that happened, he wrapped his arms around me as if we were together. He openly showed affection, that touched me as I was just in a relationship where there were rules about that. It just fit, absolutely perfectly, he was nice, amazing, kind and had a true heart of gold, with the funniest personality. It was such a feeling of warmth to have someone display affection publicly. I relished in it and the difference of how I had felt with DAMIEN.

It was everything I longed for, the feeling of security and perhaps the buzz I had, but my romantic nature got the better of me. For most of the night, he acted as if I was his, even to the point of when ordering a drink at the bar, he put his arms on either side of me as we waited, for all the world to see he adored me. It was then he whispered the name he would forever call me in my ear *Fancy face*. He, Chase had me at hello, this re-enacted New Year's was a blessing and the fates aligned. There wasn't one feeling of doubt, just a sense of belonging. I was proud to be with him.

Stella was dancing like crazy and was getting out of hand. Being as small as she was, his friend picked her up and we walked out of the bar. His friend drove my car, as I jumped in with Chase.

Along the ride back to his friend's place, Chase kissed me. His kiss was nothing like Damien's, it was hard to the touch, but his feeling and the security were far better than that. His snuggle: was a snuggle of caring, kindness and to me it was far better than a lusty man who preyed on girls. We hung out at his friend's, and lay on the couch together in between helping Stella in the bathroom being sick. His friend was especially attentive to Stella, so I was able to visit with Chase. Having my liquid courage I told him how I had the hugest crush on him working at On the Roxxs. He just laughed and said he always thought I was just the prettiest girl there. He wanted to take me out sometime. We exchanged numbers and I knew he liked me. It just fit almost as if two lost souls found each other.

I even openly told him about my son and my life. The look on his face was that of admiration and he immediately changed asking me out to he would like to take both of us out sometime. At that moment I knew I had just found my family man of worth. It was that fluttery feeling of assurance that left me grinning well into the next day, wondering when he'd text. It was a New Year's to be remembered, a good one, with good people. The power of suggestion and thought go a long way.

Our romance started immediately. It was clarity for us, that we both wanted the same things in life. He went out of town shortly after that first night, which was the best thing to happen, because we were able to talk for hours on the phone each night about our hopes and dreams. We missed each other a lot those days while he was gone, and formed a bond that was undeniable. While I was reluctant to introduce Ashton to Beast, I was not reluctant at all to introduce him to Chase who was amazing around children. It made me proud to have him around my family. I felt so special, like I was number one in all things in his life. The bond he formed with my son was no less extraordinary. We were immediately smitten and on the same page in all we wanted in life. I felt as though all I had been looking for in life fit with him. He was the fairytale husband I always wanted and needed.

Chase said he had no family, until I realized it was by his choice. I found strength in his words and was able to give him the gift of family, by allowing him to become close with my son and I. That man was my perfect fit, in all things provided other than his kiss. That kiss from those bad boys were my downfall, they gave me the sense of *theirs* but never the sense of *forever*. I had a forever in all that I had ever wanted in Chase. Our conversations, companionship, friendship and our dreams united, formed our commitment. My family loved him and so did my son.

Damien, constantly left songs on my voicemail and tried to contact me, but I avoided him. He was the farthest thing from my mind. I believe that is what drove him to become a little possessive. I will never know, nor did I want to I was done with that, it wasn't me, the fake feeling of belonging, always second, third or fourth best. The cheating and games were a sickness to me. To be part of that lifestyle you have to allow those things, swallow it like a pill and take it. I wonder why all those ladies who stay in that life look so haggard in the prime years of their forties. It's because of what they tolerated and continued to accept, it takes away their spirit slowly. It is a disease within your soul that kills you, eventually one day, and the part of you that was once there is gone, forever.

Chase knew about Damien and it drove him nuts. I had no lies from him, I truly loved him and believed in us. We moved in to together within three months and it was a huge step, a step we both wanted. Shortly after that, one night, he proposed to me at a restaurant with my son there. He did everything to perfection, even asked my stepfather for permission.

What made me say, *yes,* was how he held every dream I ever had in his hand and was slowly making them come true. He loved my son as his own. He was truly a beautiful person with a heart of gold. I loved him, I thought, with every fiber of my being. I still had a lot of insecurities within myself that had not healed. I never had a chance to find me yet. I doubted promises he made to me, because of other's past promises that were never kept. I wouldn't realize until later what those things meant as I do now, they would eventually become a downfall in our life.

He wanted a baby of his own, I started feeling claustrophobic with him, would pick things apart about him, that were normal everyday things, such as snoring, it drove me nuts. I couldn't be with someone where they had to sleep on the couch there whole life, that wasn't fair, or the kissing while we made love. I don't say we made love lightly, I mean it, he was tender when he needed to be, he never left me feeling hurt or disgraced, he left me feeling whole and complete, but how could I be with someone who couldn't kiss me soundly, who couldn't slowly sensually kiss me. It would drive me crazy bonkers. I would tell him or try to teach him. I didn't realize I was taking a part of him away by saying that, we would have our tiffs, but that didn't mean I didn't love him. I believe I planted that seed of self-doubt and jealousy within him. I would find him comparing himself to that man, Damien, all the time, when the one thing that meant the world to me was that he wasn't Beast nor did I want him to be. I loved him for himself! We were delusional in our dreams, or perhaps not yet ready, or it was all just too fast.

He would be out more times than not. My older sister accused me all the time with her usual belittling remarks, "I would become a crack-head if I was ever with you, too, Kerri." It hurt me to hear that, as if I was the downfall of everyone. He never liked the way my family treated me at all, He became detached from them because of it. He saw what I always knew was there, but him saying those things about my family made me defensive.

One day we were out at the movies with Ashton and came home to find roses and a note from Damien, not on the doorstep but right on our bed. It read something along the lines of, "Hi, Baby. I'm home xoxoxoxoox." It killed Chase. He was instantly upset and left to stay at his friend's house. I tried explaining it wasn't me, I didn't do that, but he wouldn't listen. He would go and air out our dirty laundry to all who would listen. He had the right to get it off his chest, but that just drove us further apart.

I called Stella and she came to stay with me. My anxiety hit a peak then. It was as if everyone I love leaves me. It made me feel panicked and alone, very alone with bouts of terror. Chase never really liked Stella, often said, "She's a trouble-maker," that I should open my eyes and quit spending all our money to help others. I thought of that, as if he was trying to change me, instead of that he was defending me, which I should have known. Our bond was slowly becoming fragile. I couldn't keep myself from thinking that as fast as we found each other, is as fast as were losing each other. It was a very rocky time and the slightest thing would set one of us off. The one thing he would be upset about was Ashton. He loved him but I couldn't understand, if that was true, why did he keep leaving?

That broke us to the point of destruction and the wedge became a gaping hole, until one day when we finally moved to different houses. I lost the engagement ring he'd given me, because of an immature fight we had. Wherever it was thrown in his truck, and I swore he still had it!

He came by my place with his friend, while I was out picking Ashton up from school. We came home to find him loading all our new furniture into his truck. I snapped, couldn't believe he would do that. It was ridiculous how he could only think of himself, what about Ashton or me. It was the end as far as I was concerned; we were finished. His character was weak to me, intolerable, as well as no way to live at all.

We spent a little while apart after that, but as with any break-up it only lasts a while before you miss what you had. It's the comical error of belief in people that you can recapture what you once had on false hopes and promises of a better life or beginning. It was my fault, now that I look back, that during that break-up I went to see Damien, even shared a few kisses that I'd been craving, kisses that were more along the lines of hello and good-bye, not dumb to the fact that I could never have him as a family man.

I felt a little more confident around Damien, now that I had come to terms with the fact that I would never be with him and didn't love him. I never knew the mechanism of Beast's mind or how it worked which was my bad. I should have realized back then, that me explaining about being in love with another man, and introducing him to my son as well as our engagement would enrage Beast. Not that he acted like it did at all, just chuckled and said, "Now you know better, Hunny." He acted all nonchalant. Inside I was still nursing my broken heart and dreams of what if it's my fault with Chase, perhaps even looking for clarification.

I missed Chase in that month we spent away from each other, so when he showed up at my house claiming the same, it felt right and perfect. I relished in the fact that we were going to work it out, that he missed my son like crazy, all the whispers of promises we once had came pouring back. I remember as if it was yesterday......

It was a sunny day as we were parked outside of Ashtons school. He was looking at me with the sun glaring in his eyes. Eyes that were full of love, hint of green and brown, they were beautiful to me. It was a moment of understanding, that perhaps the silly petty problems that slowly seeped under my skin about snoring and kissing were my own issues to work out, because to me he was the perfect family man. I was so happy we were getting back together, that day. We picked up Ashton and had the most perfect family day ever, until the evening when he borrowed my car to go meet a friend somewhere. I had no idea that that would be the last time I ever kissed him or held him, the last time I would ever hear I love you.

Yes, I can portray this as a happily ever after all my fault scenario but, there were other issues that bothered me with him. He would drink, always wanting to go to bars. It would drive me nuts. I hated it and slowly disliked one of his friends, because of it, who indeed was the more responsible one as I would later find out. I also would find messages from numerous girls on the days we would fight, blaming myself for that because of Damien's messages and placing that insecurity in him or the simple fact that he was a little possessive. I didn't blame him for that, I blamed myself because that was the way I was, always taking responsibility for other's actions.

He hated Stella, would say how she's trouble and that he couldn't stand her around me, that she would use me. Perhaps he was right, but she was my best friend and my love doesn't just go away. I hang on until every last emotion of feeling is gone. I hated giving up or letting go. It made me feel empty and hollow. I loved him and to me, if we really were getting married or having a family, we would have to take the good with the bad.

I needed to grow up and quit pushing people away. I was growing older, as I could take responsibility for my actions and own them, not only to the people I had wronged but also to myself, it's part of growing as a person. I believed that the only way to change a problem was, not by justifying my actions but by owning them and learning from them, as I was now doing. Power is in truth, to yourself as well as others.

It was a moment in my heart, I knew I never wanted to be with anyone but Chase. How could you replace a person who had now, finally after all these years, been a proper role model for my son, who accepted my family and never believed a word they said in ignorance about me, who defended me to all the world, who loved me for me.

When he went out that night to his supposed meeting, when in fact he went to the bar and never came home, I was frantic that something had happened to him. He drove away in my brand-new Mustang convertible. I started calling him like crazy, leaving messages, until on the next try I called a friend to make sure he was okay. I had a sinking feeling in my stomach as his friend picked up.

It was close to 8:00 a.m., rainy and foggy. He said, "He never wants to see you again. This is where your car is. He has been beaten up pretty bad." The heart I had left, was only fragments, splintered into a million pieces.

I couldn't understand what had happened. Why wouldn't he want to see me; is he dying, hurt or in pain? I panicked, woke my mother up and dropped Ashton off in haste, driving his black ford F150, ripping down the road. My heart was breaking, crying, not knowing what was going on. I got on the phone again, "Where is he, where is he?"

The only response I ever received, was, "He doesn't ever want to see you again. He is at his house. Your car with the keys is across the street. Come pick it up and leave him alone."

I don't know what possessed me to stop and get flowers, an orange spring bouquet, the biggest I could find, at a local convenience store with a card that said, "I love you, Baby." I drove on and arrived within an hour of that first call. As I pulled up outside his house, I noticed my car, still running, with blood on the seat. My heart did a trillion flops as I ran up his driveway forgetting about the flowers, and right into his house where he stood, broken, shattered, bleeding, swollen, so beat-up, his face was almost unrecognizable.

He tried to run away from me, from room to room. He wouldn't look at me. I begged him, "Please, darling, tell me what happened? What did I do, why is this my fault." I was at home, why are you pushing me away? If you lost both your legs, I'd still be with you. What happened please stop-running, Chase, baby you don't have to run from me, I love you, no matter what".

I had thought he was just embarrassed at being hurt, perhaps looking as bad as he did. My beautiful motherly nurturing side, never prepared me for what spewed out of him in that moment.

He turned on me so fast, in a slur he said in the most hateful voice I had ever heard, "You lying, cheating whore, I fucking hate you. Stay away from me and don't ever come near me again." He grabbed me as he rubbed his bloody face down my cheek and in the most despicable lowest voice he could muster, he shattered me. My knees gave out as I crumpled to the ground, trying to breathe, my head wasn't wrapping around his innuendos, wasn't grasping the situation. He spoke venomously, "Do you like what YOUR boyfriend did to me? Do you like it, you *deceitful BITCH. GET OUT,* go home to your *HELL's ANGEL.*" I got up on my knees begging for him to listen, "I was at home. I don't know what you're talking about, please stop and listen. I didn't do anything, I would never date a Hell's Angel. I don't want to. We have been over this and over this. Please." I begged until I couldn't beg anymore.

"GET OUT," was all I heard as he chased me to my car, in his truck were the flowers where I had left them. I sat with tears boiling down my cheeks. Fifteen minutes later, defeated and all alone, I slowly drove away without a clue as to how in the world this could've happened. Chase had a missing front tooth and his eyes needed stitches. Somehow, I was to blame.

I went to my mothers where I collapsed in her arms and cried. She held me that day as the implication of what had happened slowly came in. No one would talk to me. I left messages for days on Chase' machine, to no avail, he didn't love me at all. I was crushed.

Weeks went by and still I tried. I couldn't visit with anyone, and pushed everyone away. I would lie in my room with candles burning and tears rolling down my face and sobs racking my body. Everywhere made me claustrophobic, so I found a new home, a beautiful condo on the beach and tried moving, hoping he would come over and surprise me with *I love you, Baby and I'm sorry*, but nothing. The messages I left him were begging him to see the truth, hear me and tell me what happened. I was left with nothing but that I was a cheating whore, my fault echoing in my broken mind.

I was scared to know the truth, but deep in my gut I knew Damien had done it. I hated him for whatever had happened, I never really knew, thinking perhaps it was one of Damien's people, or something, or maybe it was someone entirely different and perhaps had nothing to do with me whatsoever. But I was getting the blame. I couldn't face the truth that we were over, just like that, not a word but over, with nothing. It killed me.

About three weeks later, I received a message from Damien asking me to come see him, "I need you to meet me. I'm getting messages from people telling me that you're harassing someone, clitoris's." That's what Damien had nicknamed the guy I was engaged to.

I was enraged, upset and horrified. They never knew each other as far as I knew. How dare Chase or whoever, ask Damien of all people to speak to me about my fiancé. Who was he to get involved? I was trying and begging him to love me, and come home. I felt a mixture of humiliation and betrayal, by a man who had promised me the world and who supposedly loved my son and I above all else. Chase was a man who possessively coveted me, how could he just leave like that. I thought he was so much more of a person than that. I would often say to my family, even if I gained 150lbs, Chase would still love me. I believed that, because that is how I truly thought my Chase felt, as I did.

How could he just walk away like that? Isn't commitment supposed to be about working through problems? I was hurt, confused, betrayed with a loneliness of sorrow. I went and met Damien at his local strip bar later that evening to get answers and as I walked in, I was shocked.

I couldn't understand how someone could just shut someone off like that, my feelings of devoted attachment to Chase could never allow me to do that. I was hurting inside like I had never done before. It was not knowing and also not doing anything but staying at home waiting for him. I was so confused and hurt it was sickening. As I walked into the bar, I was shocked that a prospect escorted me directly to where Damien was sitting, smiling and calm. An uneasy silence filled me inside as I sat down.

He pulled me towards him and in front of everyone, at least six people, he kissed the top of my head and said in his flamboyant, boasting voice, "Look everyone, what I have won, my Baby is back, my girl!" Everyone laughed. When I say they laughed, they bellowed with laughter as if they knew something I didn't.

I looked up at him speechless, tears pooling in my eyes as he handed me $5,000 in in fifty-dollar bills, and said, "Here you go, Hunny, for anything he had of yours. No-one hurts my girl." Motionless, I sat there, numb and stunned into silence. I stared at the money as if I was a joke, a piece of nothing ripped through me.

He then pulled me into a hug, which was protective as he whispered, "Don't worry, Baby, I would never give you up, you're too special and beautiful for that. I would never do that to you, you're mine, Baby. I will always keep you safe."

I had so much sadness rolling inside as I sat there in his arms, as he held me, tears welling up in my eyes with every word he spoke. He was whispering in my ear and kissing the top of my head as if he was my hero, everyone looked somewhat awkward. I then heard the true story of what had happened the night I lost my fiancé, the night my life changed forever.

> "It was supposedly a meeting my fiancé went to, instead he went to a local bar (once again) Cheers, a place where they had just done renovations. He was drinking with his buddies, I guess having a good time. It was midnight when Damien had received the call that the guy he was looking for was partying in this bar. Damien was sleeping, from what I heard, and he quickly got dressed, put on his rings and drove like a bat out of hell down to this night club. When he walked in, he had the bouncers (supposedly) block all the doors so this guy Damien was looking for couldn't get out. As he approached the area Chase was in, he leaned up against the bar and ordered a drink and watched Chase for a while, who was being belligerent and loud, acting all cool. It was once Damien had watched him and said his "hellos" that he approached this weasel as he put it, "Clitoris," the nickname Damien had given him,

grabbed him by the shirt and punched him in the face. That was when Chase started saying, "I'm not with her. I'm not with her," begging for Damien to release him. Damien started punching him, again and again as he said for everyone to hear, "Don't ever take from a child. Don't ever go near MY GIRL Again. She's MINE!" and that's when he supposedly gave him one last staggering blow and walked out as people shook his hands..."

I was mortified by how he told the story to his buddies, as they all laughed their heads off. I sat there stunned. I was utterly shocked to the core. Damien then looked down at me and said, "See, Baby, I stuck up for you and Ashton. He never wanted you and he was hanging off the bar like a loser. You don't want that around." Then he said to his friends after he had helped Chase up, that he told him that he only had a certain amount of time to come up with money for all the items he had taken out of our home. It was when he dropped off the money that Chase started showing him all the messages I had left him, trying to show Damien it was me begging for him, not him wanting to see me.

I was so humiliated that Chase showed Damien those heartwarming, loving and begging messages, something so private, something I had kept so sacred, it hurt to the point of a sad anger. It made me feel as though he never loved me, and that if I had stayed with him, he never would've fought for me, or fought for us. Even under other circumstances, if something really bad had happened to us, like a burglar, or cancer or anything. I felt as though, for a man who loved me, he never did, just never did. As I was fighting for him and his worth, at every corner turn and endeavor, he was not holding the love I shared for him, betraying me.

I was torn between *hurt* and *anger, sadness* and *betrayal, humiliation* and *deceit*. It was an overwhelming feeling, seeing that $5,000 sitting on the table still, as I didn't want to touch it. It was all I was worth; pay me off to get me away from him.

The guys who heard the story, then said what a loser wimp he was and that they would never do that to their girlfriends. That only reinforced the way I was feeling. Between all the times I had fought for my family to accept me, my friends to understand me, my boyfriends to always love and adore me, I was a completely crushed broken-hearted person, not just as a woman in love but in the whole as a person. That moment, that situation took a piece out of me, it shaped me and in a way broke my otherwise strong spirit of righteousness.

The guys all laughed as Damien told them I was engaged to that "creep." I could do better, he made out like he was my hero, and showed me what a man he was, he made himself out to be some mercenary opportunist.

I was stunned and silent as I let it all creep into my heart, body and mind. It crushed me how Chase could just give up on me, as I was waiting at home for him and he was at a meeting. I hated Damien for hurting him. How could he purposely destroy someone with the utter force of brutality, how could he twist it with enthusiasm? My thoughts were devastating. How could he have humiliated Chase like that? Spinning, I thought of my own worthless self. How could Chase ignore me, when I begged him for weeks and weeks? How could Chase show the man he knew haunted me, the man he knew I didn't want to be with, a man who could hurt me, how could he show Damien the messages I had sent, daily, begging for him to come home. It was the ultimate betrayal in my eyes, a disloyalty, and a cowardly thing to do.

My already crushed heart was weak, my self-worth gone. I knew then because of a man, that I had tried to stay away from, as I could see the corruption of a life I didn't want, also that what Chase and I had was over. I knew hearing the story from Damien, him knowing my secret messages and wedging himself into our private life; that I could never be with Chase again. I knew my trust was severed with Chase. I knew whatever I was holding onto in my hurt and sorrow-filled evenings lit with candles, was over.

I wanted to leave. I could only handle so much. Beast just held onto me, saying, "I won you, Baby, you're mine. I hope you're all done running around!" He said that he gave me time to be young, see the grass on the other side, and that I belong with him now. He would supposedly never do that to me; he felt like such a man.

With nowhere to go, nowhere to hide and being so hurt, it's hard to explain the rollercoaster I felt. To see someone care that deeply about me and knowing how wrong the whole situation was, I began to feel trapped. It was a manipulating mind game of the worst order. Because he was able to prove how weak-minded Chase was, that even after three weeks of ignoring me and me begging him to come home to figure things out, that when he met Damien, he even showed him the messages. There was no missing me, there was no fight for me, even on a night's rest, a week's sleep and a month of work. Chase had no drive to even try to see me, try to contact me, nothing.

While I was licking my broken heart, a man came along saying he would love me, saying he wouldn't give up. Watching the guys who said they wouldn't roll over while another man did that to their woman, was a revelation that perhaps Damien was right, I should give him a chance. I was stuck with him, deflated and I just leaned into his arms and let his love engulf me.

Damien said it hurt him to hear me so sad, that he'd drive me home, and someone would drive my car. I never had the guts to decline, nor did I want to. I was numb, hurt and confused. I lost a piece of myself that day, I lost the idea of knowing what I wanted in a man.

As we climbed into the truck, he changed his laughing demeanor to a man of control, explaining that he's ten years older than I am and it was time for me to quit leaving messages for Chase. Then he pulled me right onto his lap as he drove directly to my new place without even asking for directions. I snuggled right into his big arms and chest, but not before I thought, "I guess he got heard my address from the messages," and tried my hardest to forget about Chase.

Damien was right. What was I thinking begging for someone to love me, when I had a real man holding me and willing to stand up for me as a single mother? It was an impressive way to relinquish my hurt. I knew, I never wanted anyone to ever get hurt on my account again. I blamed me, it was all my fault and in the end Chase was humiliated. I forgot all about the tarnished relationship I had with Chase, the happening so soon, commitment and also the drinking all the time with him. I forgot any of the bad stuff and as normal people do when they miss someone they love so much, only thought of the good and the what ifs. I knew I couldn't leave him another message, it would come back to me, or hurt him. I was devastated with no place to go, but sulk in my own self -pity. I knew loving two different men, total opposites would come back on me. I may have been completely committed to Chase, but often thought of my Beasts sensual lips. I blamed myself from that day forward.

It was a night off from my baby boy, as I invited Beast into my house. He sat with me in my new condo and just watched me in such a beautiful way. He complimented everything about me from the decorating of my home, to the way I was as a mother, compared to other single mothers he had seen. He enjoyed the fact that I was

Ukraine, a care giving woman who always puts out food, for guests and "Cooks the best," as he often put it.

He was a man of substance when it came to politeness. He knew how to be whatever person he had to be, in whatever situation. I loved that about him, instead of thinking how can a person have a smile on his face when something so horrible has happened, I thought of it as such a wonderful trait he had. There, my friends, was my mistake, there was where he was my adversary in life, and there he had the upper hand, because that mind mentality was nothing to be proud of. If I was smarter or wiser it should have been the indicator that made me run.

It was when he was done building me up, he grabbed me as I sauntered by and said to me, in the most serious loving voice I had ever heard, "Why did you love him, or think you loved him? He doesn't deserve you, he was a coward." I was honest to a tee that day. I believe Beast finally gained a little more than trophy material out of me, for I found my voice and in a quiet manner I told him the following message.

"It was awful and disrespectful to me as a woman, what you did that New Year's. You blatantly ignored me, kissed another girl, and allowed my friend to be hurt. I am done with that lifestyle; I can't be with someone who wants to share their love all over the place. It hurt me once with my friend, and Damien you did it again with sparkly shirt girl." Then he laughed and tugged me closer as I continued. I believe, he truly cared in that moment, *"I loved him because he was the other half of you, I will never have, Damien. He is the family man who shares his love for me to everyone, and sticks up for me with my family. We were going to get married and have a baby brother or sister for Ashton."* I finally cried, really cried then for a lost love, a painful break up, and for a man who will never be faithful for all of it. But most of all I cried because I was another disappointment to my family and my son Ashton."

Beast held me like no other, I can't explain it, he held me unlike Chase ever could have. Which was why, I often thought of Beast even while I was with Chase. It was my fault for caring about two totally different men, knowing it could never be. The music on my messages did not help. No one could compare to the sensual Beast, the loving Beast behind his patch, his lips truly matched mine. From his fingertips to his knees, he had the man body to my woman one.

As I continued to tell Damien why I cared so deeply for Chase and the sobs subsided, I opened up to him for the first time ever. I told him, I was ready for the simplicity of life united with someone, a home and family of my own. My dreams were finally becoming a reality. That was why, what happened to Chase left me feeling so alone. I was a hurt woman who lost her family man, whom I did value and truly care about when it came to how amazingly devoted he seemed to be to my son and I.

Damien then spoke as he carried me to my room and laid me on the bed, "When I got the call, Baby, that someone I was looking for was at the bar, I thought it was someone else. Then I sat back and watched him, how he acted, he was all over these girls, acting like a tough guy. He was a loser, Baby, he wasn't good enough for you or Ashton. I stuck up for you. I wouldn't have done anything once I knew it wasn't the guy I was looking for, but, Baby, he was an idiot. He deserved it."

He kissed me, as he looked at me he whispered, as he often did between his kisses to me, "I can be that family man, Baby, you just weren't ready. You had to live it up and see what you would miss first. That's why I let you see for yourself the grass isn't greener on the other side. I care about Ashton, too, Baby, he is the son I don't have out here. I've been missing my son being so far away. I will be the man you want, I am that man you want, I want you to mark this date on the calendar. We will have a family. I *am* the one you need as your man. I love you my crazy woman, I love you." He swept me right into his heart in that moment. I will never forget when he truly said he loved me. He was as gentle as he could be. He swept me right from the brink of sadness, into a womanly *bliss*.

He made me feel as though I was worth the moon and the stars. Little did he know, he had had me at, "I love you, Baby, I can be your family man." We made love that night, as never before. He stayed many nights after that and he moved into my city. He was officially my boyfriend and I his girl, once again. He gave me a piece I was missing, to be treated as though I was worth everything. He gave me self-esteem and a promised dream. I loved him with every fiber of my being, he was finally not just that bad boy hard ass, he was all of it rolled into one, but my family man as well. I gave him my Beast another chance.

Under a month later, he came home to tell me Chase was with a stripper and they were having a baby, he thought I should know. Isn't that ironic? It was as if he wanted a reaction from me, to see if I cared, I never showed him any, but my heart broke all over again inside, privately. It was my confirmation that Chase never did care that much. It hurt.

It also gave me a sense of feeling a lot better and needing Damien more. I was able to give Damien my full love now, not just a piece. My full heart, I handed to him for his honesty and integrity. It hurt hearing the truth but I was now strong enough to deal with it.

My friendship with Stella was drifting further apart, as she was with someone, as was I. She had met a guy and was sort of drifting on the lines of bad again. I refused to have that around my son, or perhaps I just was starting to see what others had said to me over the years. I was focusing on college as a legal secretary and was accomplishing my own goals. I just wanted to surround myself with more goal-oriented people and parents. It was simply juggling Ashton, school and home. I never went out much except with Damien to certain family Hell's Angels functions that were important events.

It was normal, me being tucked away. I know Stella wasn't happy I was with Damien, she didn't like it, or the way he treated me. I was blind to it at that point in our relationship. She said I just listened and never spoke. I wasn't me and she couldn't be around it. My friendship was brittle with her, the circumstances as I saw it, were I had better things to do than be silly. I knew my loyalty, I don't believe she knew hers, she would figure it out.

I had a new roommate who was another single mom trying to get her kids back. She was a laid back genuine person, with a heart of gold. She accepted Damien. I don't know if she was an everyday roommate, more that when she wasn't at her mother's with her children, she was at my place. That was another insecurity I had yet to overcome, the feeling of being alone, my own self-anxiety was still very much within me. It gave me assurance when she was around. In return for rescuing her, she helped me.

Beast and I didn't live together yet, but he was only a few blocks away. I liked my space with just my son and me, and a few times a week my new roomie, Joan. I valued Joan's opinion on many things. She was a real go-getter and worker. She had the life skills to become successful and never threw herself around like Stella, more grounded. I knew she was a good mother right off at the start when I saw her that day, in the early morning walking past me at the gas station as I was filling up. I knew her from when I was fourteen briefly, and it had been years since we had last seen each other. I honked my horn and we said our hellos and went for a drive where we opened up to each other on our life events. That day I asked her if she'd like to stay with me and work on getting back her kids and family. I believed in the lost soul, she didn't deserve what life had thrown her way.

My sister and I were no longer close as she hated Damien, her latest reason for not wanting a relationship with me. My mother was supportive but would always tell me to watch out, she didn't trust him. She honestly believed there was a reason his wife lived far away. In the back of my head, I always wondered if they were still together when he flew out there once a month, as it was the only child of his I had never met. I was not asked to go with him even though most of my family lived out that way. That was an inkling of wonder, always there in the back of my head, so I believed when my mother was saying that, I was trying to avoid the truth in his already controlling ways. I was just getting sick of everyone picking me apart, with the way I was around him and how they felt.

Revelation

People in general feed off what others say and how they act. It's human nature, peoples voices carry a lot of weight, whether we like it or not. If a teacher speaks about another child in a class all the time, about how a certain child constantly needs help, other children in that class will start realizing it and thinking that child isn't as smart as they are and needs help too. Then as groups are formed that child will be left out, feeling more alone then ever.....

I KNEW SOMETHING was going on with my body, I felt different, more relaxed, more aware.. I went home one day to Joan sitting on the couch. She was about to leave to go to her parents for a few days. I asked her to stay a few minutes while I went into the bathroom and took a pregnancy test. This time I didn't scream. I was quiet. I went back out to the living room and I asked Joan, "Do you see a line?" She smiled, she beamed, she was grinning as she often did to voice her opinion. I asked, "Are you sure?" She said, "Yes," and jumped up and down with me. I was having a baby, just what Ashton was wishing for, a gift to us both. I was so excited, and so happy.

It was the right time in my life, older, wiser and well into my college degree. I was happy and couldn't wait to pick my son up from school. As I look back now, I wonder why I felt nervous about telling Beast. I know now, but then, it was almost awkward. I had lost my voice with him, I started in that moment really noticing how bad it was. I couldn't even call him, I didn't have the guts. It was becoming almost unbearable to be around him, or perhaps that was my hormones. I was going to tell my son, but wait until after the doctor's to tell Damien.

I was officially two months pregnant, or perhaps a little further. I was so happy and excited, Ashton had been wishing for a baby brother/ sister for so long and me, I was positively glowing and surer of myself than ever before. I knew from the moment I found out there would be adversity but I could inwardly deal with it. To me my family was complete.

Damien had told me, "Mark this date on the calendar, Baby," and sure enough it happened. I was slowly becoming more excited to tell him. We went out for supper that night a week after my third test and my doctor had confirmed it. I was nervous, completely unsure how to tell him as to me he was unapproachable. I still hadn't found my voice with him at all. Ashton was coloring as I scooped up enough nerve, and said in a timid but sure voice, "I have a surprise. I went to the doctor's and well we are having a baby." I thought he'd cheer, kiss my hand or announce it, in his boisterous voice. Instead he went very quiet and looked at me above his glass of orange juice and ginger ale. He looked towards Ashton and said, "Hey son, do you think your mom's baby is even mine?" In a mocking tone.

I was horrified. I felt as if I was going to lose my supper all over the table.

Ashton was a smart eight-year-old. He looked at me and I saw his face drop, he was sad. Ashton was as excited to tell Damien as I was. I couldn't believe he had just done that. My son was right there.

What he had said in front of my little son was appalling, disgusting and rude. What he did to me was utter humiliation. I couldn't even stomach him, it was gross. I packed up my son's coloring, grabbed my purse, and then asked Damien to drop us off at home. I felt sick. He just laughed and paid the bill, he knew exactly what he had just done. It was like reliving that moment with the friend incident, as if he liked to see me in pain.

My regret was instant. I was thinking of ways to eliminate the pregnancy, for the briefest of seconds, or even how to get him out of my life and that of my son's at the same time. I truly never thought in a million years, he would act like that or lash out towards me in front of Ashton, and degrade us in such a way. It was mentally abusive. I was now very aware of the affect that the mental and emotional words toward a human being could have. It was evident he had no respect for me whatsoever. My world did a 180 degree turn around and I had no idea what to do. I needed time to think. I knew I had to work through this. Ashton and I were stronger than ever, I wasn't losing the gift I had to share.

Happily ever after wasn't going to happen to us if I stayed with that jerk, was always in my mind, but I could never say it to him. I was thankful Ashton and I had our own condo over-looking the ocean in White Rock. He was mortified by the way Damien had spoken, as silent as he could be on our way home. Damien just dumped us off without a word and drove away.

It was a sickness in him, of that I was sure and I was only coming to realize it. I remember holding my son, promising him we could do this, and making an excuse for Damien's behavior. My son was innocent and I protected him against that lifestyle. He was a gentle soul who didn't deserve that crass behavior. There I gathered my strength and decided it was better after that to no longer allow that man around my son! We would discuss things eventually but right now I had a decision to make. In my heart, the decision was already made, now I just had everyone else to deal with, as I hadn't told anyone but my Son and Joan, and, of course, Stella.

I needed to be honest with Ashton, as well as myself. I had made a promise long ago that as his mother, I would be honest, kind, understanding and always put him first above all else. It also allowed me to accept the things I've done, that I cannot change, but can learn from. I believed in truth. In that sense it helped me grow into the mother I am, who does put her children above all else, no matter what. I stayed in at home that week with my son, no school nothing just us. I asked him what he wanted, a brother or a sister and if he was happy. I could tell he was lonely at times being the only child. I felt that he wanted a little brother and was excited. He never really acknowledged that a dad had to be around and to me that was half the battle. He truly was sunshine, my boy and he gave me purpose. I knew no matter what, I could have my baby and do it on my own I wasn't the type of woman who needed a man to pave her way, independence had become a part of me. I was not going to take away my son's dreams, as well as mine.

I had one diploma already and another on the way. I didn't have to worry about partying or anything because I just never did that anymore at all. I had grown out of that long ago as it was never really what I wanted. I was also more stable now than ever. My condo was gorgeous with all new furniture. I was set and my decision was made. I was going to be a mother. If he wanted to act like that he could keep away from us. I was excited now to tell the family, share our news.

It sure wasn't what I was expecting. I knew they wouldn't be happy, but the threats and comments were horribly wrong. My little sister who had just turned nineteen, had come into her opinionated self where the truth behind the impact everyone had made on her over the years, by their insinuations about me, and black listing me in the family. All the years of belittling remarks had helped her form the opinion of me as worthless and good for nothing in her mind. She said I should get rid of it and never have a child and that she would have nothing to do with my child when it was born!

Those snide remarks hurt like nothing else. I believe that was when I began distancing myself from her. It was brutal how she could be so careless with the way she spoke to people. She did it to everyone around her. She believed she knew everything in the world. It was then I told her that she might be very bright and smart in books, but she had a whole lot to learn when it came to life. Many times I'd seen her belittle our mother and I would defend my mother from the brutality of her words. She once said to my stepdad, who had now become one of my best friends and my guide in many things, that she would hang herself if he and mother ever got back together! To me, Such big words from a girl who during her lifespan had everything handed to her, all the options my other sister and I never had. She was a very lucky little woman in our eyes, that was just an example of the careless spoiled way she acted.

My mother was hesitant, not because of me but because of whom the dad was. She pushed me to contact his ex-wife. I thought that would be abnormal and never did. My stepdad was the only one other than my older sister who was happy, as we would once again have children around the same time. It gave her the sense of building our families together at a distance. She was the one who, I believe, in her own way stood up for me. She hated Damien and always had, she said he gave her a bad feeling. I thought it was because of the patch on his back which was understandable.

My best friend, Stella, believed in my baby and me. I also had, Joan, so my support system was good enough and everyone who told me not to have my baby was black listed to me. It was time to expand my little family and quit caring what the family thought of me. I knew who I was and they never took the time to get to know me. I was far kinder than they even could grasp. I never yelled or screamed at my children. I never stereotyped people as others do. I believed in the power of forgiveness and good. I would not subject my child or children to any more scrutiny, no matter what.

I was not prepared for the unusual phone call I received from Ashton's father's side of the family, it shocked me. The call came in that they had heard I was having a baby with a Hell's Angel, also, "If I had the baby they would have nothing to do with me or Ashton!"

I was shocked because it was from the one of Kane's sisters that was always there. It left a hurt mark and somewhat of a scar, then she carelessly hung up.

I couldn't understand why she was being like that. I thought we were on good terms. How did she know? My mind lingered and stewed on that for a while.

Mixed emotions from so many was hard on me, but as it did in childhood, it gave me strength when I knew I was finally breaking away from what they all wanted, finally being me and who I am, doing what I know within me is right. My baby was a gift not just to me this time, but to my son. I excelled.

I was trying to separate myself from Damien, with a baby on the way, but I was willing to give it one last chance to salvage the relationship. I accepted his invitation to go to Mexico and meet him there. I had never travelled so far, was apprehensive and had always stayed within the confines of the elements I knew and trusted. I hated the way my anxiety crippled me. It was time to grow and conquer my own self and spread my horizons. Everyone I knew travelled, why I couldn't I. It would be amazing to see this land called Mexico that everyone loved, and to have one on one time with the father-to-be of the little baby in my tummy. I wanted to know why he could say such an ignorant statement like that in front of my son.

The preparations for this trip were unbelievable. I hadn't left my son, now eight years old, for as long as a week before since he was a baby. It was a long time for me. With my roommate and my mother caring for him I was able to go. I didn't like leaving him, it gave me an emptiness only a mother can feel.

On the day I was leaving, I received a frantic phone call from Kane, whom I hadn't heard from in months, as was his usual behavior. He had finally heard the news about my pregnancy, my trip, and who I was dating. He begged me to meet him that day," Life or death Kerri, please, I beg you, meet me. I can't talk on the phone." He gave me a crossroads address, not a house to meet him at, but outside, which was extremely weird as that's just not normal. That's a moment in which you stop what you're doing and go, as I did.

I wasn't scared or worried, just thought he needed help. I didn't know what was going on, but my curiosity was peaked, invisible man was going to meet me. I was going to give him crap for standing up Ashton lately so many times.

As I arrived at the location he gave me, it was busy, bustling with traffic, a place visible to everyone. I was driving my stepfather's work truck, a white ford F350. I sat there for no longer than two minutes. Kane pulled up very close to visit face to face through the driver's windows of our vehicles. He immediately asked if," I was driving that Hell's Angels truck"!

I told him, "No," a little weirded out he just said that. Kane relaxed and then he came undone as I had never seen him do before. He had always been calm, cool and collected. He was scared, frightened even.

Kane told me that Hell's Angels have been part of his life for a long time, as far back as he can remember. He said how some Hell's Angels, or one he knows, has ten children and about how he knew I was pregnant by one. Panic- stricken then, he looked at me and said, "Kerri, please, I beg you. Do not have that child. Do not hurt Ashton my son. You have no idea what is going to happen. This is not good. I beg you Kerri, do not do that, to you or him or Me." He cried, my Kane.

After all these years the infamous, discreet, and invisible Kane was shaking so hard he was crying. He had told me something about himself that he was otherwise hiding or being very quiet about. He had acknowledged his son. I saw the love for Ashton pour out of him. I wanted to get out of the car and hold him, but he was too close for me to get out because our vehicles were side by side with the doors almost touching.

He was begging me with a panic in his voice. I told him I couldn't get rid of my baby, Kane, but that doesn't mean I'm going to be with Damien. I said his name then and Kane started looking around in panic. He was scared for himself but also for us, then in a very quiet voice, he said to me, "Kerri, do you remember when you first had our son, you were with Zak," my gut flipped. "Do you remember your house being flooded, how you left? Well that day two guys went to your house when you weren't there with guns. They were looking for me and Zak" My heart was stopping, my insides rolling, my past being relived.

He was finally telling me what my instincts had always told me, but I never knew. I did not have a clue why everything was as it was. My eyes started watering remembering that horrific moment when I handed my son to my mother, because inside I knew something bad had happened while I was out.

"This guy ripped me off. I asked Zak, my best friend, to help me Kerri. In the end we landed in a whole mess of trouble. We had to pay money to these people, Kerri. I ran one guy over, just trying to get away, Kerri. YOU need to listen to me. I was kidnapped, Kerri, tied up, bella clavaed, my ear ripped half off, and thrown out of a moving vehicle on highway 10, after I made the last payment I supposedly owed !" As he looked around, in a panicked state as the unrelenting tears poured from me, he said, "That guy, Kerri, is Damien!"

"NOOOOOOOOOOO, oh Kane, Nooooooo", I couldn't comprehend the devastating truth, I couldn't do this, in my state I did my best to see the good, I did my best to just take it in, and understand.

My world crashed into a million pieces at that moment. My world spun, I couldn't breathe. Kane had shocked me and left me speechless. I had no idea what to do. "I am supposed to go to Mexico today, KANE, to meet him. We're trying to work it out. I'm past three months Kane, I am having my baby." Trying to grasp onto anything.

I yelled at him, "Why didn't you guys tell me, why did you allow all that happened to happen, why did you allow me to hand over my son", pouring tears of long forgotten memories ran down my face ,"why didn't you guys tell me?" Between my utter horror and my reluctant mind, I tried to make sense of what he had said.

He said everything is okay now. He had help and it was dealt with years ago. "I'm sorry, I never knew at the time, I just kept it hidden, it was never to come out. I knew I had to tell you now, but I couldn't let you have this baby, *without knowing*." He finally whispered, and asked me not to go, begged me even, then just like that he drove off.

I didn't know how to process any of this, in my mind was a doubt so profound I couldn't place it. I had that heart of compassion, also a realization maybe just maybe everything would be all right. It has been eight years, if Damien knew, I would have known, right? I went home then, numb with the information I had just received. It was a secret, a secret that had been left hidden for years. That secret explained why Kane and Zak are no longer friends, as well as a reason why my world as I knew it back then had affected me so profoundly. I had a mother's instinct and without ever knowing this, placed my son in my mother's care for that year and also the fact that I was a total screw up and wouldn't allow my own selfish behavior and that life around my angel.

Life was better now. Years have gone by, people grow up and they change, but the biggest question was, why was I hearing it now?

As I hugged my son, I told him I would see him in a few days. I boarded that plane after a hug to my mother who drove me to the airport, her looking at me with speculation in her eyes. She could see something was bothering me, a mothers instinct knows, she just hugged me and told me to enjoy myself and have fun. I was nervous, flying, going to another country where I had heard people were abducted and I was going alone to meet him there. Yep, panic was in my every step. My mind was still reeling with the information that had been bombed on me only mere hours before I left. I never told a soul. It was to fresh and painful, it was now my secret to hold, passed onto me.

Mexico 2005

AS I ARRIVED, I never saw Damien. He wasn't at the terminal as I waited for the bags that came on the carousal, then I rolled the two heavy bags outside. I was hurt that he wasn't there, but as I approached the door leading to outside, he was waiting on the steps. He gave me a hug then he turned around and walked outside, leaving me three months pregnant rolling the two bags with no help. Welcome to Mexico with Damien.

I was horrified at his behavior and immediately disliked being in Mexico with him. I struggled, then finally the cab driver noticed me and helped. At that moment, I wanted to turn around and go home. I knew things weren't good or going to be good.

When we arrived at his condo in Cancun, he again made me carry the bags upstairs. It was a humiliating moment. I felt him continuously being upset because I wasn't fast enough, impatiently holding the door open to this run-down place he called his" Melrose Place."

I started becoming weary. I already knew his behavior, the way he was. I hated it and I could tell he felt my uneasiness in being there and purposely left me at that moment saying, "I have to go to the gym, be back in an hour." He walked out with no kiss, no welcome, no nothing just an unpleasant feeling of the chore he had picking me up, and me being there. It was another of his traits on the way he treated me.

I was scared to be there, as there wasn't a phone or anything I could use. I felt trapped in a country of which I had no idea whether or not I could call the police for help. That is weird the way that sounds, a solid girl such as I was, who would never call police, who would do everything else other than that, even to help other people first, and that myself I would think of calling police for help. I was out of my element with no voice and a man who treated me as though I were a burden. He never even kissed me when I arrived and dumped me off as if I was trash, in my panicked state. I tried to get to know the place and walked around. There was no food in the condo and I was starving. There was also a colored picture of a monkey, signed by a girl with love. I thought it was cute, standing out on the table in front of me. It reminded me of my son and my homesickness set in.

I tried to fall asleep waiting for him to get back, but could not. Hours went by and when he came in he just nonchalantly walked past me and jumped in the shower, letting me know not to allow water to get into my mouth because of parasites. I had already been informed of that by my mother, but thanked him as politely as I could, sitting on the edge of his bed, looking for any sort of communication or acknowledgement. He walked out of the shower and kissed me with his wet face. I was appalled. I didn't want to get sick with my unborn baby and tried to turn my face. He stopped and said, "WOW, great welcome!" he laid down and fell asleep as if for punishment.

I tried to sleep that night, I really did, but was wound so tightly I was in knots, and scared. He treated me as if I was non-existent. I tried to go down the street in the morning to find a store to get a calling card, yearning to already go home. As I returned, he was by a pool, with a couple girls. He was splashing in the water with them, visiting, happy and smiling.

I went upstairs and tried my best to be happy. I put on a game face as I went to lay by the pool in the hot sun. The girls were there still and said, "Hi," to me. One was super nice and immediately made me feel welcome. I actually felt a lot better knowing they were close, even though in my head. I remembered the name on the monkey picture was signed by her with love. I was at the point at which I believe I just didn't care. I knew after so many different behaviors, I couldn't be with him anymore. It wasn't healthy, so I was grateful they were around. I believe that was when I relaxed a bit and just went along with things, accepting the things I couldn't change.

I was counting down the days until I would be home and I knew in my heart that it was Ashton, Baby and me against the world. I was excited, never a doubt I wouldn't have my blessing. I was not going to be with Damien. I didn't even like him anymore, after the way he had carelessly treated me now too many times. I was done, but was still going to enjoy myself on this trip. I was determined and with that in mind, I was more content.

He saw me being happy and immediately said it was time to go to a meeting and I was coming, so get dressed. One of the girls looked at me with wide eyes. I believe she noticed the way he treated me. She told me if I needed her, she was there.

There was no more guessing. I thought it ironic and knew within myself it was just me he couldn't stand to be around. I never did anything to him such as talked back or being rude, nothing. I listened, as my friends would say at home. I would act as if I was non-existent around him. I started realizing the truth of their words.

Sometimes all it takes is to be out of your element, have a few truths thrown at you and you see the world unblended as it is.

I went with him to his meeting. He held my hand and introduced me to a white Mexican man, who had relocated from wherever to Cancun. Damien then told me to go lie down and tan as he visited. I was no longer convenient for him. That hurt, and the man he was with was shady. I didn't like the feel of whatever he was up to.

I asked for a drink of pop with no ice on the advice of mom from the waiter as well as something to eat. I was starving and Beast had yet to offer food. I had my own money as I always have, and ordered lots, my baby needed to eat. I was so full I fell asleep in the sun, as I hadn't slept the night before being so nervous.

I was perhaps in the sun for an hour when I heard Beast say, "GET UP, you're burning, Jesus!" You have to hear my voice as I mimic how he says it, so mean and loud, like getting a strip torn off you. I was a lobster, I never knew any better.

I was horrified because my appearance was shattered with a blistering face, and going to off as he put it.. I was devastated, hurt, he never helped me, or even looked at me as he took me back to the Condo. He kept saying in a tone that was blatant and rude, "WOW YOUR RED!" with a slight turn of his mouth.

I stayed in and soaked my face with vitamin E. It wasn't as bad as I had thought it was, from the sound of his voice and the way he said it. When I looked in the mirror at the Condo I was shocked to find yes, I was Red, pink but not peeling with my face falling off like he had said, embarrassed none-the-less and self-conscious. I stayed in or was going to stay in until the redness died down at least.

He was going out again, so I asked if he could grab a pizza on the way back from the gym that night, as it was close to 11:00 p.m. when he was leaving and I hadn't eaten all day again other than around lunch time. He just walked out the door without a word. I had no idea if I was getting any or not.

When he arrived back, he put the pizza down and went into the room to have a shower. I was taking a bite to eat when he freaked on me.

"You can't say Thank You for that? You selfish Bitch." I was shocked. I nearly choked. I never felt I did anything, he was only back maybe five minutes. Of course, I was thankful. I burst into tears. "Please, stop Damien, I am thankful" He then went on in the most undignified manner, "You are an ungrateful Bitch and can fucking sleep in the other room, you pig!" He made a bunch squeals like a pig, real squeals as he walked into the other room.

Quickly, as fast as I could, I grabbed my bag from his room and went to lay down in the spare room, terrified and alone, sadly weeping as quietly as I could. He then walked out as girls were screaming for him to jump in the taxi from four floors below. He squealed once more like a pig and slammed the door. I had never felt so degraded in my life.

I felt safer once I heard him jump into whatever vehicle they were in and drive off. I couldn't eat after that, even though my stomach was rumbling. I felt gross and I cried myself to sleep that night, yearning to go home so badly. I wanted my mom. I never heard him come in that night or morning. When I woke up I was too worried to go in the other room, so I stayed in the spare room, terrified and starving. A few hours later, I didn't even know if he was back so I crept out of the door with my purse and walked as fast as I could to the store, where I bought chips, juice and whatever else I could quickly eat. I also bought some more stuff for if I ever became hungry again as well as a phone card to call home.

I didn't have to walk far to a payphone. I tried calling my house but there was no answer. Then I called my mom's and she answered. I was on the phone no more than two minutes when he started walking towards me. I must have set off alarms in my mother because she started asking what was wrong. I knew he could hear me now so I spoke about what we had done so far, what we had seen was amazing and how it was so hot. She noticed the change in my voice instantly. I will never forget because she said," He's right there, isn't he?" I kept speaking, trying to hold back tears but I couldn't anymore. Hearing love in my mother's voice, so far away, I wept.

He came up then and said, so my mom could hear, "Baby, don't cry, it's just you got sunburnt. Hi, Mom, don't worry I'm taking care of your beautiful daughter, were going out for dinner tonight." He was looking at me, trying to rub my back, acting all consoling. It was the first time I ever heard him try to cover up his wrong doings to someone else in my family. As I tried to talk between sobs, my mother said these words into the phone, "You call me, Kerri Lynn, if you need me, at a distance away from him. He doesn't have me fooled, everyone is fine here and your son loves you so much."

She gave my heart a feeling of safety and survival in that moment to endure the rest of this trip. My mother knew what I needed to hear. My mother, no matter all the bad that had happened, was my mother in that instant and as I hung up I said, "I love you," that was it.

I couldn't talk now between trying to hold back more sobs and tears of hurt, as he was trying to be so loving beside me. I was never fooled by him, I saw the changes, noticed the harshness of his tone, the putdowns and the manipulation. I saw it in him and it hurt, it hurt to know someone I actually loved, could be so hostile to me and when I was pregnant with his child to boot.

When I turned to him, with my still pink face, he changed. "Let's just relax. I could feel you didn't want to be here. Come on, we will go for dinner. I will show you Cancun. We'll get ready later". Just like that, like a switch. I reluctantly walked back up the stairs to that horrible condo, as he tried to kiss me and hold me. I didn't want to lay down but he pushed me into his arms. As we lay there, he fell asleep. My eyes were wide open, his kiss or few kisses, he tried to share only made me try to keep the sunglasses from falling off my face. I didn't want him to see my eyes, the hurt and what my eyes could reveal. I no longer thought of him as I had. I tried to get up only to have him embrace me tighter.

He acted so attentive that afternoon, not in a loving way but watchful. As nightfall approached he took me to Tony Roma's. I was looking forward to Canadian food, but when it came time to order all I did was get a salad with chicken. I could still hear the squealing in my head. I've never stopped hearing it. He looked at me after the woman took the order, watchful.

I went on this trip to meet him, to salvage a relationship for the sake of our child. I had to argue with everyone it seemed, for my baby's very life. I was rocked to the core on all I had learned, the knowledge of the past was still echoing in my mind from a few days prior. He had treated me as nothing more than an inconvenience since I had arrived.

I was sad and miserable, pregnant and alone in a country where it felt as though I was unsafe, with no protection. I was confused as to how someone like him could be one way and then another in such an extreme fashion, when I've been nothing but loyal, faithful and committed. I couldn't handle any more of the slander and meanness. I needed answers for the sake of my baby and my little son, and our future. I found a sense of courage and wondered which way to approach things, as always.

In that moment, in a mousey voice, I asked him, "Do you know who the father of my son is Damien?" So simple, very quiet and nice, I probed him to see if he knew, I needed to know. As a casual conversation.

His response as his eyes flared, I will never forget, was the sickness that thrives when evil is born.

"Of course, I do baby. I've always known! I've had pictures of you from private investigators since years ago, when I lay with a catheter in me for three months, from that truck running me over! KANE is Ashton's father, the guy who ran me over! The guy who owes me hundreds of thousands of dollars! I swore one day I would take whatever meant the most in this world to him, because I couldn't get anything, from insurance *or call the cops*!" he said in a wicked, quiet domineering voice as his eyes flashed with pure hatred.

His green eyes danced with the confirmation that I now knew. With anticipation, he waited for a reaction. He sickened me, in that moment and my knees were too shaky to stand. I felt as if he was going to kill me. I knew in that instant that I was going to die. I had to get out of there. I had to get home to Canada. I could do no more, the knowledge was within me. It hurt me, a blow that left me rocked to the core, a truth that can never be undone. A circle that had come full circle, a circle I had only known existed for two days. A mishap I had nothing to do with eight years before. I had the answer as to why he treated me as he did.

He hated me. I was nothing more than a useful tool in his sick perverse game. "What you don't understand, *Kerri*, is I do love you, and now you are going to have my baby." It echoed within me, the feeling of being trapped. I don't know which was worse, the realization of what he had just said kicking in, or the look on his face.

He may have planned the sickest thing in the world, but I won, I looked for that blessing, I often sought. I did win, was all I could think. I had the best part of all of this: I have my baby, my baby, my poor little baby. I repeated to myself within my mind over and over, my baby is my baby, my other half to my heart, this time good is going to be my blessing.

My survival skills set in. All I had to do was get my passport, get to the airport,' GET Home'. It was all I had to do. I was aching and scared inside. He had me in another country, with the mind and capacity to kill me. I felt like it was get out or die!

In that moment I knew, I had to get away from him, and play my cards right. He saw me wanting to bolt and cancelled the order. He asked me to walk nicely outside. He leaned into me and said if you want to leave go, find your own way home. I'm done with you! As if this was a cat and mouse game to him, for his amusement.

All alone in the middle of Cancun I bolted. I jumped in a cab, gave them the address to the condo to grab my passport and what money I had left. It was getting dark as we got there. I bolted up the stairs after I asked the cab driver to wait. One of the girls noticed and asked me if I needed help. I was crying, lost and she was willing to help me, and to get in the cab with me to the airport.

That was when Damien arrived in his cab as I was about to leave loading my bags. He started freaking out, if it had not been for those girls there, he would've hurt me. I know that as well as I know my own name. He had never hit me, but he was ready to. It was a blow to his pride that I could just walk away like that, leave. He never understood why because he didn't think he had done anything to warrant that behavior. I realized it was just who he was.

That girl calmed him down and said, "It's not safe for her, to go off at night with a cab driver like that, let me go with her." He must have wanted to look like the good guy, justify what had happened, who knows but he allowed it. I know now why he acts that way, years later, I know why. As we were driving to the airport, I will never forget seeing Damien in another cab full of women as he stared into mine along the road with the most demonic look.

She held onto me as I cried. This girl was another angel that walks this earth without ever knowing it . I paid the cab and as she hugged me, she whispered into my ear, "Please stay safe." And drove away. I was alone now, desolate, at an airport in the middle of Cancun that looked all but deserted.

I was still on survival mode, as I picked up the phone at the airport and called home. I called my roommate and woke her up. I was crying begging for her to help me, she being as amazing as she was, called my family and explained all that had happened. The terrifying thought of being in a country, with no one, or no help was

. . . .

I looked around and realized there really was no one there, it didn't seem right. I came across a janitor of some sort who couldn't speak English and he called a security guard. I didn't expect that the help I received from a security guard would be in the form of five or six younger guys who came around a corner looking at me as if I were a piece of meat. I was scared as I had heard many stories about Mexico and they played in my mind. It could have been my over-active imagination this time because of all I had just learned, the hurt and betrayal, of being part of the sick games of some of the most important people in my short life. I was terrified. I called the operator as they approached, begging to be connected to my mom. I needed reassurance that they knew someone was hearing what was going on. I stayed on that phone as I was connected, pretending someone was already on the line, as these guys came closer with huge smiles as if they were laughing at me. I was petrified. I thought I was going to be a sport for them, raped or kidnapped.

I started crying, like really crying, clutching the phone begging for help. My mother came on the phone soon after the one guard started talking to me, smiling. I didn't want them to smile, I wanted concern in their eyes. Gut-wrenching fear now enveloped me and racked my body.

They all surrounded me as if my tears were a joke. I didn't know this country. I was frantically looking around for any other foreign passenger I could ask for help. The security guard was telling me that I was in the wrong building, barely understandable. I had to go across a field to the other airport. That was where I should be. As I looked outside, I saw darkness and the long grass which he pointed to for me to cross. I freaked out because my insides were knotting and I started hyper ventilating, and they were all still smiling. I thought for sure they were going to rape me, kill me or abduct me. He picked up his walkie talkie and started talking in his language about me. I collapsed in that moment as I clutched the phone and begged my mother to please do something, anything. My mother was panicked, screaming at my stepfather as he was on his phone trying to get hold of the Mexican airport. They were both doing their best to calm me down (everyone on all separate phones).

I was still being watched, but now finally one of them was looking at me with concern, not a reassuring word, just a little different from before, as if I had help and they couldn't attack me. I described the men to my mother in case I was never found. The security guy told me its five minutes to walk to the other airport. My mother said, "Drop the phone, keep the door open and if I hear a scream, I will call as many police as I can. Hunny, be strong, in that other airport there will be people."

I thought for sure the cab driver who brought me to this airport had set me up to be abducted, and I was going to die. I had to be strong and do this. I walked slowly to the door with this guard and as I approached it, he opened the door. I ran back to the phone, now the guard was starting to see the panic. I couldn't let go of my mother. The thought of never seeing my son again overwhelmed me. I begged them to call a cab to take me to other airport. They either didn't understand me or didn't want to. In an instant, I whispered in the phone, "Mom, if you don't hear from me in five minutes, call whoever you can to find me, please, and mom thank-you if I never told you how much it meant to me that you took my beautiful baby son in when I needed help, tell him I love him".

I acted for a few minutes as calm as I could be and clutched my bag. I didn't care about the other one at all, I just wanted something to get me home, passport and ID. I ran out that door as fast as I could, terror rolling up my legs, bunching my belly. I ran through that field and across the street. At one point I heard rustling as if something was following me. Up this street I saw lights, lights, a cart and a man driving a few carts. He looked at me with no smile but instantly beyond him I could see the lights of the other airport. I ran and it seemed to be almost as deserted as the first one. I still had to make it through this dark path to get close to the steps.

When I made it, the relief I felt was instant, until I looked around and didn't see anyone, no people in the place. I started banging on a door, as I saw a head peek up from the floor as if someone was sleeping. I looked up, saw a woman janitor walking down the corridor and slowly I saw more and more movement. Because of the state I was in, I had only tried the one door. When it was locked, I panicked again, unaware that there was a line of other doors that were open. The gentleman in a tired state came over and pointed to the other doors. As I was allowed entrance into this airport, my relief after all I had been through made me burst into tears. The man, who was not Mexican, took one look at me and hugged me, he made me feel safe.

I called my mother again. The overwhelming panic in her voice and concern made me ball my eyes out. She was just about to call the embassy for me. The man who hugged me was now out of sight. I told my mom everything, and I mean everything. She had my roommate on alert and my stepdad. They were going to get me home. She had to let me go to use the phone and try online to get me on the first flight out! As I hung up, I was ordered to call my roommate and stay on the phone with her while everything was sorted out, everyone was terrified for me.

I promised once I was home, safe, to never ever trust Damien again. He put me in a very dangerous position. Probably 3 hours of talking, crying and relentlessly balling my eyes out, I hung up the phone with everyone and also with the promise to call back in a few minutes.

'I found the gentleman who had opened the door and sat beside him. He asked what was wrong. I told him all I could and burst out crying at the revelations. That man would stay in my life for years. He changed his flight to Italy for the next one just to keep me safe until my flight arrived five hours later to get me home. He could catch one directly after mine, he was yet another true hero in my life, another person who opened my eyes to a kind and caring world.

As our flights arrived, he walked me to my plane, right up to the door and hugged me. We exchanged emails and kept in touch for a few years. He owned a winery in Italy and was such a good man.

My relief was replaced with a fatigue that racked my body. I was pregnant, tired to the point of exhaustion and finally on my way home. I arrived, without any sleep on the plane, six hours later. My mind was still too busy processing things to settle down enough to feel safe. I just wanted to land on the soil I grew up on, the land I call home.

My mother and roommate were there to hold me as I collapsed in their arms. I had never felt so happy to be home in my life. I asked them not to bring Ashton, as I didn't want him to see my terror, pain or the haggard state I was in. I needed to rest and I did for sixteen hours before I awoke in my own condo, overlooking the ocean and hearing my beautiful son playing in the living room. My body ached. I thought I was losing the baby for a few moments until it subsided. That experience was life altering for me as well as everyone around me.

To think all I wanted was to have a family, make things work with Damien and give him the benefit of the doubt, which almost cost me my life. That wasn't how I wanted to live or put my son or anyone around me through again.

I was by now officially the true meaning of red as a lobster when I woke up. We all laughed at my red face and it was okay to laugh at my face with everyone because it wasn't mockery or ignorance, it was the laughter of those around me who loved me. The strength and the silent knowledge for once that Kerri didn't need to hear any ridicule because they had almost lost me. I had a kinder smile and acceptance from my mother, a stepfather who was and had always been one best friend, strength as well as guidance, and a sister from afar who once again became a sister to me. No one told me not to have my child after that. They just knew that baby, Ashton and I, the three of us were a family. I felt as though they finally acknowledged

I was my own woman and was strong enough to handle the worst as well as the best of things. I had been through enough.

I begged my mother to please keep it a secret from my real sisters and real father on what had happened. I was ashamed of it all. She agreed and that was when I truly started trusting her again. She stepped away from trying to control me and finally looked at me as a woman, a person and at my courage. She was slowly becoming my mother again, not that friend but my mother.

I was proud to be me, an awesome mother, great friend, as well as a kind-hearted person. I was tired of all the nonsense of my youth, the pain of love and betrayal. At that point, I lived and breathed for my children as well as my home.

I even started having Bible study, once a week with a few women from church, it was uplifting and revitalizing. I wasn't following God, I was just allowing my surroundings to be filled with peaceful serenity and good people. I became part of the community more and more and valued the talks I had with elderly women and people in general. I loved life, had no respect for the other side of it, the crass brutal side where everyone knows your name and they all talk about it, good or bad. It wasn't for me. I had tried to save so many only to get hurt in the end. I was once again growing, not just in the belly, but as a person.

I tried my best not to think about what had transpired between Damien and Kane, or Ashton and I as their victims. I tried never to see it that way and believed I created my own path. It wasn't until a few years later that I acknowledged or faced it, but I did know there were blessings to be found. I pushed it away out of my mind in order to be strong as a mother. I focused solely on being that and the best I could be instead of facing all I had found out. Perhaps I didn't have the strength to acknowledge or face it at that time.

I knew I never wanted to be with Damien again. I ignored his messages a week after he came back from Mexico, asking if I made it back safely. I simply hit delete. He had his own life and I had mine or so I thought. I just assumed it was over and never clued into that I was stuck with him. I just thought it was a mutual understanding that we weren't together, because now that I knew the truth I just thought it was over, the pain had been dealt.

Usually when you're with someone you're with them. I was no longer with him or seeing him at all. I would hear through the grapevine that his was the party house and he was dating all sorts of girls. I was okay with that and believed that at a distance perhaps we could be parents one day.

I tried over those few months of pregnancy to build that separate life without him. Only on three occasions did I leave messages. Once (4 months later), when I found out I was having a boy, I left a message on his machine. He even phoned from whatever country he was in at the time, happily quoting, "I put a stem on that apple, did I," hooting and hollering into my message system. Then another time, right before I was due on Thanksgiving, he phoned to say happy Thanksgiving and asked if I was cooking my wonderful food. Me being who I am offered him a plate. I remember Stella glaring at me as I was on the phone saying that. Instead of allowing him into my home, I decided to take him one and so I did with Stella. I sat there for only half an hour at his place down the road, pregnant as could be, and was introduced to all the little girls running around with booty shorts and the guys he had living there as well, his cousins I believe.

It was humiliating to see. Stella and I left there thinking, wow, he sure has gone downhill. I was so lucky to be away from that.(Stella had a lot to say back then, she constantly told me how rotten he treated me, I agreed whole heartedly, I just inwardly wished she spoke with more class). I truly didn't really care anymore about Damien as I had better things to do. It was neither here nor there for me.

Then the last time was when I had a phone call to meet him, because I was going to go into labor soon and he invited me to a lunch. Stella who was going to be my birthing coach and was my best friend came with me, as I couldn't be alone with him. This time he truly disgusted me. He invited us to lunch, but as we arrived, he was already eating. He offered Stella something to eat, but not me. In front of all his friends and Stella, he gulped down food, without a care in the world. I was pregnant and hungry sitting across from him, it was appalling. He then commented, "Pregnant women are fat." It was sick. As he went off to explain and introduce me to someone, he tag teamed, as he put it. Stella and I just got up and left. We were both disgusted with him. It felt gross to be around that, and I hung my head in shame at his brazen comment. All the while him watching to see my expression.

As Stella and I drove home that day, she once again had me laughing at him, really laughing at how gross that lifestyle was and how one girl there was so into it. We couldn't get over that lunch. Many times to release the strangeness of situations we would laugh about it, and make jokes or imitate it. It was a release of pent-up emotions and the humiliation of the situation. It was a way, to put it on the back burner, instead of addressing it.

I had no idea I was fooling myself, thinking we were finally at the point of perhaps a parenting friendship. I will forever regret that mistake. I should have put up more boundaries, or been stronger, even addressed the whole situation, instead of continuously coming up with excuses for him or everyone for that matter.

For Damien, it was just his lifestyle. I could visualize the good of the situation: maybe now those two guys, Kane and Damien, could finally be friends and Kane would not hide from him. There were two children involved now, two innocent beautiful boys. I chose to believe in the power of good, not the dark side. I wanted everyone to be happy. When I went out to buy something for myself, I'd buy the person with me something. It's who I was, if I shined why couldn't they. My thought process was always on the brighter side of people, places or things, or simply giving back what I had been given, **LIFE.**

Birth & After

Sometimes in Life all you need is love

MY WATER BROKE late one evening and I went to the hospital, but I didn't go immediately into birth. They sent me home and after six hours, I went back sure that something was wrong. They had to induce me. At one point the nurse walked out saying, "This is wrong. We have reached our maximum inducement, she needs a caesarean. Where is the anesthesiologist?" He/She were nowhere to be found. I could have been painting my nails for all the inducement was doing as a matter of fact, Stella and I were playing cards, rummy.

Then all of a sudden, in one contraction thirty-two minutes long, after an injection of morphine directly into my arm because I was begging for help and crawling up the bed, my beautiful son, Sable-was born, eight lbs, five ounces. He was a truly beautiful little gift from our prayers. I loved him immediately, my newest precious son (baby Bam, Bam). The way my baby came into this world was the way he was coming out, I was blessed with a baby boy, after two days of non-labor.

My baby son had somehow in his panic pushed my pelvic bone out of place. I never felt it then, but as soon as the morphine wore off, I did. It was so painful I couldn't even move an inch. I had to relearn how to walk, from a wheel chair to a walker. It was not shattered, which my heart goes out to anyone in that situation, but it just had to go back into place. It took physiotherapy as well as time to heal. I lay on a couch for a month or more. My son in his panic, stuck in the birth canal, came out with his little hand first.

My baby boy, my heart filled us up with such love, in an instant, he was the other half to my heart, and the piece I was missing, and never knew, until that moment, with Ashton owning the other side. As a mother, I was complete, we adored him.

Stella and my mother were both there for me, during that time. I guess my mother phoned Damien, explaining there were complications. She knew more than I did at that time. I was in such excruciating pain and from what I understand, she put him in a panic. He was in Edmonton with his other son. She told him they might have to choose between the baby or me. He rushed in a panic to catch the plane and get back in time.

I now know he finally had told his ex-wife, as well as other son he was going to be a dad. As he arrived at the hospital a mere three hours later he, was introduced to his newest little boy, Sable.. His eyes were immediately full of love. I saw it, he had a bag full of stuffed animals and a video camera as well as a camera to take pictures. He was once again acting like a father. He looked concerned when he walked in, but when he saw his son, he had not a care in the world for anyone else. If you asked if it hurt me, well it did only to the point of humiliation when he told me to take a picture. As I did, he started getting upset at me that I couldn't record with the video camera and it wasn't at the right angle. "Get off the bed. "

I could barely walk as the morphine was wearing off and I was shaking uncontrollably. He was mean to me, very mean. He even scared the nurses. They asked me when he left if I was okay. It was the first inkling others outside our circle had of noticing how he treated me, but it didn't open my eyes then, it just saddened me and took away such a precious moment, because of my incapability's, in his eyes.

I asked him if he wanted to drive us home from the hospital, just to include him and be nice. He said "ya" and to call him, then left. I never called him as I was in the hospital for six days.

They had to put my son in an incubator because, during the many hours that had passed within my womb, he had swallowed amniotic fluid and needed antibiotics. It was definitely hard waking up that next day not being able to move. The pain was unbearable and knowing my baby was down the hall hurt me more than you can imagine. I broke down as my hormones from pregnancy were dropping.

I would not allow post-partum illness to set in this time. I was stronger and surer of myself, *knowledge shall set me free*. When my mother first held baby Sable she was wearing blue, which made it look as if my baby was turning blue. I freaked, "Get my baby away from her." I felt horrible afterward. I believe underlying issues lay within those moments, which I was able to address long after the fact.

It was a joy when I was allowed to go home. As I was just getting comfortable with the newest member of my little family, in walked my real dad and my sister from Alberta to welcome baby Sable into the family. My heart was so filled with love in that moment knowing they cared enough to drive all that way. It was incredible and I loved the surprise.

Damien never once came back to see baby Sable, so I just thought he was busy, really didn't want anything tainting my new son. I felt like the cleanliness wasn't up to par and I didn't want that environment around my children. To me it wasn't a priority, my family was and I relished their praise as well as love. It was then I named my son Sable-Thomas, after my stepfather who had helped me so much in my life as well as the pregnancy. It was my gift to him for all the support I had received over the years, my gift to make him truly a blooded family tie to us three, Ashton, Sable and me. My mother was touched. The other side of the family not so much as they always thought I was too gushy.

These moments were such a transition for me. I was fragile at heart, but at peace within. My babies/children were my world.

I leaned a little too much on my roommate who was moving soon. Now that my baby was here, she was ready to fully be a mother to her own children. I believe she was ready long before and I held her back, I know I did. My faults always lay behind my need to be around someone, anyone, due to my anxiety that had built up. She was my other half and I begged her many times to stay one more night, please. It was unfair, but my own insecurities were coming out. I was more than capable of being alone it was just that initial moment when I felt that void.

Anxiety is a crippling form of over-whelming personal issues, or it was to me. I had to retrain my mind to say over and over I am not going to die, I have to be strong. She helped me greatly during those first two months. She truly was my family, in my heart. My children loved her, but her place in our life was over. She had other things to accomplish in her own life, as did I in mine.

She was special to us. I started noticing Stella showing her jealous side whenever my roommate was around and would get me going on picking her apart. I always knew Stella had a greyer side as people would often tell me she used me and was no good, but to me she was my little world. I hated it when people put other people down.

She definitely stirred the pot with us. I later realized as time went by and my roommate moved out, Stella had indeed wedged her way in there and manipulated the situation horribly because we were no longer friends. My eyes were starting to notice the vindictive side of Stella.

Damien started coming around a little more. One day he fell asleep on my couch, after me feeding him. I moved him into the other room because I was having my weekly Bible study with my ladies, who were super excited to visit baby. Damien must have woken up, because he walked out in the middle of it. When he noticed the ladies, he introduced himself and one of the ladies in her 60s said, "You must be the Dad, our sweet Kerri's husband?" I had never said I was married, just having a baby. Perhaps, because my home was that of an interior decorator's design or very homey, it was a presumption that I was married. Oh, I don't know, but he looked over at them as he sauntered away, very ignorantly and said, "Yeah, right! I'm not her husband, but sure hope I'm his dad," ha-ha-ha as he chuckled at the look of mortification on their faces.

I was humiliated and devastated, they were my ladies. I had grown to adore them and my own private time enjoying their presence and caring nature. I loved them and was ridiculed by Stella and everyone that they were Jehovah's Witnesses. But to me they were ladies who needed to be heard, as I did. They had such a great energy about them that truly lifted my spirits.

I was embarrassed to the core. They looked at me and didn't share the same nervous laugh I did, as I tried to shrug it off and continue. They had to leave, even though we were only half an hour in, it hurt. I made a meek excuse for his rashness and we said our goodbyes. Usually we would arrange a time for the following week, but never. They said they would call me and give me a little time, that we would resume our weekly meetings in due time, so I could enjoy more time with the baby. I shut the door and leaned against it to breathe, knowing he had just affected another beautiful thing in my life and I had allowed it.

I did not understand the consequences of mental manipulation or negative self-talk, but slowly and surely he was making me feel worthless. I had only one dream left in my heart that I would recite daily. It was to be the best mother possible, have an amazing family and that I could finally break the cycle from my own separated, depressing family. My dream was always to be loved and show my children the best possible lovely life ever, happily ever after so to speak. My visions of a prince in shining armor had been revised. I had all I needed. I wondered if what my grandmother had said about me reading all those romance novels had gotten into my head. It was sad to see, envision myself never truly having real love. I had not wanted children from all different dads and was not the type of girl who even accepted that. My two precious sons, I knew were enough for me, two halves of my heart, my babies they were, always would be. That was something no one could ever take from me and was where my one strength lay. I was slowly separating myself from my friends, as they just weren't like me. They couldn't understand that they were second in my life. They would often call me names like selfish and ignorant or it's all about me, when in fact it was just all about my boys, what was best for them.

It was then I separated from Stella, as she had clung onto my old roommate and once again pushed someone out of my life. I saw the Stella everyone had told me about, but I never cared much then about it. It felt good just to be me with my two sons. I didn't realize that by separating myself from Stella, I had lost the strength and knowledge of what she had always reminded me about my time with Damien. She had said that I wasn't me when I was with him and told me to stay away from him. Because she had stirred up so much with my previous roommate, I just immaturely thought she was doing the same with him, still upset with her lies and tactics to Joan, my mistake. I just really wasn't interested in resuming a relationship with Damien, at all.

My silly, lovely heart of gold always looked to the brighter side of things and situations. I would often justify certain behaviors in people, in general, to find their light and good side. That was where I always placed him, just mixed up in a badass crowd, because alone he was a big teddy bear to me. Long hidden in the back of my mind, because of our son, was the cold hard truth of what he had done. I thought he had heart or it's just what I wanted to believe.

I was living in an apartment now, to accommodate the boys and I. It was much larger and more affordable. Sable was five months old and Ashton was eight years old. I had become even closer to my stepfather and helped him hire a guy who used to work on the rigs in Alberta, who now lived in BC. He was a hard working man who had all the makings of a great, lovely soul. I was meeting more and more amazing people who weren't the bar-star, gangster type and felt it was where I belonged. I was changing into my womanhood and never needed any of the extra drama I once had, with always helping those lost mothers. They just seemed to be out to take, take and take some more. I still wanted to find a way to do what I loved most, seeing people smile, but raising my children was foremost in my mind. I had to worry about my own boys. I was happier on the whole as a person without all that. I welcomed the warmth of others, but hated the negative back talk all the time and found it drained me with the others that used to be in my life, because of my always out stretched hand of help.

My anxiety had subsided considerably during that transition of losing a few friends, almost as if the grey cloud had been lifted. They said I always acted as if I was too good for them. It wasn't that at all, I just wanted more out of life. I was twenty-six-years old. I was the only one with a car and always had to pay for everyone. I just had gotten sick of being used, and I wanted to finally be me. Whenever I had other friends or even Bible study with my older ladies they would mock me. I found it inconsiderate and rude. I was seeing how different perhaps I was. I loved people, would often envision what their lives were like. I enjoyed the casual conversations with older people, even the mothers and fathers at school. I was embarrassed by the way my old friends made me look. It was never that I didn't love them. I was just wise enough to notice I was never going to be like them, I just wanted to be me.

My stepdad really liked the person, Blake, he hired whom I had introduced to him. It was nice to be around people who were like me. I offered Blake a room to rent from me, so it would be easier for him to get to work. Strictly, on a friend basis. He wasn't a crutch like my other friends had been. He was a true friend who built me up, and did not bring me down. He also worked sixteen-hour days, so I barely saw him. My boys loved him. He was an exceptional example for my sons. He was my guy best friend, someone who had been where I was and done that and who had just grown up.

During my life-change, I had also met another girl, who could babysit for me, if I ever needed it. Her name was Desire, she was such an old soul that girl, with responsible, caring parents. They lived beside the golf course of Morgan Creek where I had kind of grown up, when my parents came into money with my father's new business.

She reminded me of me, would constantly have friend issues, as I had and would come to me for advice. She made me feel special. I consulted with her mother about many things. Desire was the prime example of a genuine soul, who gave a friendship all she could give. The dramas of teenage years: she had a huge crush on my Blake, which Blake and I would laugh about, as it was cute.

Damien was trying to become more active in his relationship with his new son, as well as Ashton, never separating the two boys at all. They would often lie upon the grass outside and visit. I started seeing a change in him, not so much the party, party, party guy. Perhaps it was that we were finally developing a parental relationship. He would often compliment me on my mothering skills as well as my cooking expertise (which was usual). He looked at me with respect for eliminating my friends and since the pregnancy not being seen out, for casual drinks, or even dating. I felt as though it was a sly remark, but a compliment no less. I often wondered if back then, he even knew me, or if I even allowed him to truly know me. I never had the urge to go out, hadn't for two years now. I was just not into that lifestyle and much had changed from my early twenties to now. I was surer of myself, slowly accepting that my family, no matter how well I did, I would always bare the butt end of jokes to them. I had my own little family to worry about. I was surrounded now by self-sufficient people, who took care of themselves as I did for my sons and me.

I was happy, but still I would keep mum with Damien, smile and nod, watch and learn. I was reluctant to be myself because he had done and said many harsh things to me that often played in my mind. I didn't have the courage to once again address the Damien and Kane issue, as I believe I had just tried to forget about it. It had affected me to the core. A year had gone by since then and I didn't want to even look at the fact that it was a sick joke on me and my precious son. Evil and corruption, could just stay away. I will never allow that around my children, so I just chose to ignore it, as I had learnt to do with many things when I was seeking to forgive the wrong doings of others.

Onwards

If you make a mistake, learn from it that way you can grow into the person your meant to become......

ONE DAY I received a phone call about a hockey game. Damien wanted me to attend as he had box seats at GM Place. He said it would be good for me to get out, as I hadn't since our son was born and he offered to take me. I called up my little friend, Desire, and asked if she could babysit. I felt very sure about going as it would be nice. I knew Blake would be home sometime shortly after I had left, so my boys would be okay. I was excited, it seemed like such a nice gesture, a simple evening at a hockey game and wasn't the wild life he used to try to bring me to before.

Damien lived the fast life, a go, go, go, sort of life, doors open, with the best of seats. People loved him/ them, people who were interested in that life anyhow, even the jewelry was fat and huge, the type you'd see on a rapper, or very rich folks: that you wouldn't know if it was costume jewelry or not, it was always about the bling. I was so over it. Limos were limos to me, rings were rings, and life was life.

The hockey game, (even though he had thrown in there about the box seats), seemed simple and laid back. Something a father would do. I was excited and would be home before 10:30 p.m. I dressed accordingly, no heels or dresses, just nice and classy, with jeans and boots and a nice sweater, so I would be warm. I felt great, when he pulled up I was ready. Desire gave me a quick hug and wished me a good evening, continuously setting my mind at ease that she would be fine. My Ashton was excited to just spend time with Desire as they had a bond that carries forward to this day. Sable is still the baby in all of our lives no matter how big he gets.

As I jumped into Damien's lifted ford F350, he seemed short with me, a look I had once known, and with a flittering of nervousness my stomach did a flip. He said I was late, we had to go, or we would be even later. I passed it off as my first-night out jitters. I was downstairs as soon as I had heard the honk, but when he acted that way, I knew he was blaming me. Instantly I regretted accepting his invitation. He gave me the once over and snorted, saying I should've dressed better, but we didn't have time, as he sped away.

To me he was back to being his old way with me and this was the first time I had been alone with him since that Mexico fiasco. I was nervous, no longer the girl who dreamed of a knight in shining amour, just a girl who was more aware and realistic. I continued to shrug it off as I tried to look forward to the game. We never talked much on the way down to the event. He was too busy, making a point of showing his disappointment in me, speeding trying to beat lights. As I held onto the side door when he turned a corner, he then tried to pull me close. I just smiled and stayed where I was. I was not getting wrapped up in him again, trying to keep boundaries.

He never once mentioned the boys or asked how they were. He was very much on his own kick, it set me on edge. I should've trusted my gut instinct, made an excuse and jumped out of the truck. He was sort of scaring me with his silence, driving and mocking glances.

Now I was in a huge city away from my suburban neighborhood where I lived. His mood spoke volumes, something had set him off or someone.

As we arrived at GM Place, he jumped the curb, parked without direction to a stall, handed the guy who was in charge of parking, some money and walked to the door directly across the street, as If he had done nothing wrong. I smiled at the parking guy, giving him a look of, I'm sorry.

When we got up to the box, it was packed with girls all dolled up in mini- skirts, bikers, and a few baller types. They all said hey, and hollered. Everyone was full of smiles and hugged me. The members knew who I was and treated me with utmost courtesy as I was the mother to one of their brother's children, it was nice. They never treated me as he did.

The girls had no idea who I was, and shunned me. You could honestly taste the icicles in their eyes as they completely blew me off, until one of them must have found out that I had one of the Angels sons, when all of a sudden, they were trying to get me to talk with them. It was awful watching the fakeness. I felt even more so out of place as Beast completely ignored me.

Half way through the game, I walked out of the box and went to sit in the lounge, ordering a coffee. That's when I heard Damien on the phone, fighting with his girlfriend I presume, as he was saying Baby, Baby. He must have noticed me as the lounge was directly across from the booth's glass door. He walked in and tried to put his arm around me. I smiled being nice, grabbed my coffee and walked with him back into the box. Just as I was going to sit down on the leather couch, in walked all these girls from the next box over, with huge silicone boobs and bleached blonde hair. One of them I knew, although it had been years since I had last seen her. She hugged me fiercely saying she has a picture from a few years ago of Damien and me, on and on she went. She asked if I had my boobs done. I said way before, but I'm nursing now. She was shocked to find out he and I had a new baby. Something set Damien off then, because he had the predator green-eyed glare as he watched her talk to me. He didn't like it, at all.

As the game was over, everyone started asking if Damien was going to Brandi's, a popular strip club in Vancouver. I didn't pay attention. I just wanted to go home, as I felt out of place, as though he had just officially announced I was his baby mama, unlike before when it was known we were dating. It was different, like I was in trouble for mixing with all the girls. I didn't know and could only speculate, but radars were going off inside me. I wanted to be home in the comfort of my children's arms and our cozy home. This was not what I envisioned for my first night out.

As we climbed in the truck, he was dead quiet. We started driving and he reached for me, to pull me close. I knew I didn't want that, we were approaching a corner so it was easy to slide out of his way and put my seatbelt on. I tried to laugh and say his driving was crazy, to make it not a direct, hurtful, shy away. He looked at me and saw right through it, as he often did. I was cornered as I had not leaned on him like I used to in front of people or casually snuggled into him when we were together that evening. I was making my boundaries known, in such a nice respectful way. I was being a mature adult, with a normal calmness. I could understand it, if he felt as if we should perhaps try to be together, but my heart wasn't into it, I wasn't into it. The feeling of security and trust was gone from me, the feeling of lust was over. I was finally happy just being me.

I now know what had set him off. I was okay with the girls he was hugging and saying hi to, I was not upset with his phone call, nor did I show any sign of interest in him. I never showed any sign of being jealous, nothing. I was happy with him and had inadvertently let everyone know tonight when he had brought me out that we weren't together, only had a son together, not a family.

I wasn't seen with him when I was pregnant. I had done it alone and never once did I stop to think of what he had said or if anyone knew. I guess the club knew because I had received a lot of hugs and congratulations, and they loved the name I had picked, "Sable." It was shouted about with promises of pictures soon for everyone. They were all so nice, no judging just perfectly amazing respectful comments and congrats.

I had inadvertently made it known we were not together, but I was okay with it, not upset in the least. I was happy with how things were. I had always shown respect for the club, always, even back in the days before Sable. I had even stuck up for them with crazy girls. I always felt as though I belonged, never that timid girl who would be reluctant around them. I was a solid girl who knew how to stand on my own two feet, as well it was in me to always keep every one's secrets, as they were not my secrets to share, and never would be.

I didn't treat Damien in any crass manner, especially in front of people on my first night out, at a Canucks game no less. It would have been rude. I was a silent person with him, always smiling, even though more often than not I felt like crying around him, at how uncomfortable he made me feel, or shouting at him for his lying, cheating ways. No not me, not Kerri, around him I smiled and allowed him to be the full-blooded male he was. I had fallen into a routine with him and he never really knew me. I believe I never allowed him to know me, my old friends were right. I was starting to see it, and that man I had once thought hung the moon and the stars was gone.

He asked then in a soft tone, "Hunny come, undo that seatbelt and sit beside me, in my arms as we drive home, how we used to do it." Now, I had to say how I felt, I didn't think he would do that, I gave no indication of perusal with him this evening, often staying at a distance. I looked at him as nice, soft and mature as I could be, "I just want to be friends, Damien."

In that exact moment, without an inkling of preparation, he back handed me, so hard and so fast, blood splattered on the passenger window. I was dizzy as I lost my sight for a few minutes as blood poured out of my nose, down my face. I was speechless. I had no warning at all. He just lashed out at me without a word and hit me so hard my head was still spinning.

I was shaking, as I tried to cover my face. My body numb, he grabbed my hair and leaning into me, still driving, said, "You're bleeding all over my f*&%%# truck! Clean it up! Don't make a mess, cover yourself!" he yelled.

I thought I was going to puke, I didn't know what to do. By now we were going 200 km down the highway, dark as night. The city lights had already passed as we were heading towards White Rock, maybe I did lose consciousness, I will never know.

It was a dark highway, at night, he reared off at an exit and screeched to a halt. "Get out. Get out of my F*#!ing truck. You're making a mess." I was so shocked, I jumped out of the truck, still in a daze, lucky to be alive and shut the door not knowing what to do as he sped off, I just listened, like a good girl. My face couldn't handle another blow like the one I received.

I collapsed right there and cried. It had happened so fast, I didn't know what I did, I had no idea where I was. I was scared and tried to wipe my face and clean as much blood off, it was smearing my sweater and clothes. Cars were speeding past. Panicky, lost and alone, I reached into my purse and tried to call Blake. I couldn't believe he answered. I tried to give him a brief description of where I was. He said he was about half an hour away. He was on his way and he would start driving towards me. I would have to call him again, until we found each other.

I cried so hard after that call, just a mess on the side of that highway exit. I didn't realize a police officer had pulled up, saying he had received calls about a girl along the highway in distress. I didn't know what to do, there was no way, after all I had been through that evening, I was having Hell's Angels after me or Damien.

Shocked into reality, I gave them a fake name," Kerri Maloney", and said my car broke down, the hood when I opened it, had whacked me in the face. I did my best to convince them and even phoned Blake again, in front of the one police car and gave him the exact location the policeman gave me. He then reluctantly drove away. I saw it in the police officer's face that he never believed me. It was enough to stop the tears, smarten up or I was going to be questioned further. I knew in that moment of clarity, I had now seen the true side of Damien. I couldn't allow him around my children.

I've been hurt before, abused, but never the silent kind, out of nowhere like that. The clarity in that moment was so precise, the evolving of all the doors opened, the realization he lived to hate me, and torment me. I could never see him, ever again. The gruesome moment of my precious sons and when they saw their mother with a broken nose or black eyes, after Dad had taken her out. I thought of Ashton asking if he could go to the game, it all flooded my painful vision of such ultimate humiliation. I could get over this, the pain of the blow he dealt me was nothing compared to the repulsive, dreadful way he treated me, the mental and emotional abuse I had already received from him were foremost in my mind. He was sick.

I couldn't believe the father of my son had just left me on the side of a highway in the dark hours just before midnight after hitting me in the face because of me wanting to be friends. I was crushed in such a mind-blowing and daunting way.

I couldn't see my mother until I healed. I had to find a way to hide this from everyone around me. I had to find a way to be strong, because I was. I knew the difference between right and wrong, and what he did was wrong.

When Blake arrived, he looked at me and helped me clean the blood off my face. He was shocked, he just let me lie down in his truck with my head on his lap as I silently whimpered. When he parked in front of the apartment, he and I sat outside looking up at our windows as we watched my babysitter cleaning up waiting for us. She knew what had happened as Blake had told her why he had to rush out. She was waiting to help me. I was mortified that my fifteen-year-old babysitter, no matter whether she was an old soul or not, had the knowledge that the father of my baby boy had hit me. It was embarrassing.

When we got to the front door, my thought of a way to explain to her wasn't needed. She opened the door and hugged me in an enveloping, embracing moment of her strength that I never knew existed. She snuck me into my room and cleaned me up, tucked me in and dimmed the lights as she brought me my baby. Our bond was formed that day, a bond of knowledge and an unforgettable experience. She had such a nurturing way about her, that she was no longer just my little babysitter, she was my friend, and Blake my hero.

I woke up the next day with two black eyes and a throbbing headache. My phone hadn't stopped going off and as before when I looked, there were numerous messages from Damien, saying, I will never forget,{ "You can't hurt me like that, Baby. You shouldn't act up like that. I'm coming over."}

I panicked and shut off my phone and locked the doors. A few days went by before I checked my phone again only to find songs playing on my answering machine.

When Ashton saw me, he knew. I could see it in his eyes, the disappointment and sadness that his mommy was hurt. I did what any parent would do; I lied to my son. I said mommy had an accident and fell down the stairs.

He tried to be my caregiver that day and played with Sable. My angel, my lifeline, my two gifts gave me the courage to move forward and healed me. It was the three of us, as it always had been. I had gone on one date with Beast, not as if I would ever do that again, or was in a relationship with him. We could move on, no big deal.

A few days went by and the messages were getting to be more music and songs of love, to worrying where I was and why no response. I didn't care. I had the people in my life I wanted. I did for a moment wish Stella was there, even just to make me laugh, make a joke about it all and dance around skit acting.

My sitter was constantly checking in on me after school every day and staying until Blake got home. If not for those two beautiful people, who knows if I would've become depressed. They gave me wisdom and courage. They never allowed my laugh and smile to fade away. They and my sons were pillars of strength for me that I owe so much.

I wore dark glasses to school, to drop my son off. I felt disgraced. It was during that week I met another dad from school who had tried to date my old roommate. He said hi, a very dominate sort of male, a police officer actually. He lifted up my glasses and saw my black eyes. He asked what had happened and I never said a word, I didn't have to. He shook his head, and then said" I was one of the best mothers at this school, as I had often volunteered, he had noticed." It was such a wonderful compliment from another parent. We formed a friendship that day, an unspoken friendship. Often every day after, that as I picked up or dropped off my son, I would get a huge hug, or a wave of hello. He never judged me, It was revitalizing to my soul, an acceptance of sorts.

I had gotten through the week, and my eyes were starting to go from purple and blue, to yellow and green. I will never forget the evening. There was a knock on the door and Ashton answered. It was Damien. He scooped up my son, swung him around and handed him a bag of presents (the best toys a child could ask for) and said, "Hey son, I'm home."

My innocent son was happy he was there. I was never a parent who belittled the father of my children to them. I knew the consequences of such actions, the havoc it can create in a mere child's mind and heart, so Ashton was loving the attention and relishing all his new toys. The joy of a father figure was what he needed as I also believed he secretly craved it, because of how his dad was.

I was shaking trying not to allow the tears to pool in my eyes and looked away from their moment. Then he came up to me and whispered in my ear, "I'm not leaving and you shouldn't ignore me! I was worried about you, Baby, you're mine and you know it."

It was sick and twisted how he did that. The look on Blake's face was horror seeing him there and he went to bed right away, avoiding the whole situation. Blake had no idea what he had said, only that he was there... I did notice the concern and compassion in my best friend's eyes and that was all I needed.

Damien wasn't too upset to see Blake, but definitely wondered why I had a guy roommate. It was awkward to say the least. I tried to ask him to leave. He took the hint, saw what he had to but stayed for a few hours not budging, then when he had marked his territory as a dominant animal would do, he left. From that moment on, he would just come over whenever he pleased, almost every day. It was a rough few months of not knowing when the Beast, as we all now called him, would just pop by as if he owned the place.

Blake and I would talk a lot about it. I always felt safer and better having Blake living there but not wanting to cause an uproar. Damien now knew Blake worked for my step dad, so he just gradually accepted his presence but you could see the mechanisms working in his mind, how it would bother him. I loved that Blake was there, we made perfect roommates as we had the same home values.

Never once did I let my mother or family know what had happened that night at the game. I was scared of what Damien was capable of and slowly felt trapped. I had seen firsthand how he can hurt someone and would not allow that to happen ever again to anyone else I cared about. I should never have covered up that incident, because it made me allow Damien to be around for the children looking so righteous and amazing.

He would often just fall asleep on the couch, and brought so many gifts to do with the house that he had never done before. He even gave me a year's worth of child support cheques: on the amount he felt was adequate ($150.00 a month). It was almost a direct pun the amount as it's only enough to buy diapers a month.

He was making his presence known by being a bully and telling us how it is, what he knows, opening up as if he was part of our elite circle. He would often grab me to kiss me in front of the kids, who would giggle and laugh. He knew I was repulsed and then he'd get up and walk out.

I would see so much of him in appearance similar to Sable, often with the one argument, of my son having my blue eyes, the windows to his soul. Damien would argue that no, they would turn green like his: all his kids did that. He was firm on it, but it would bug him. I would just turn around scoop up my baby boy and instill so many loving words into him that by wish and power, by sheer force I would never allow it. My son's eyes are still my blue, like Ashton's blue with our souls.

My voice was gone with him. I was scared to ask him to leave and often I would just fall into the routine of homemaker. Being ridiculed by him was second nature. He would say things like, "Wow, look at the look on your face, EWEE," or "Mommy needs a nap," and force me to lie down, when I was wide awake. He just started controlling all the things around me. It was sickening, he would grab his phone out of his pocket on a daily basis and follow me around, recording how I looked, how disgusting my face looked. It was such a degrading thing, I would often feel sick. I started going to my doctor's a lot, constantly asking if I had this or that. I made more appointments to see my family doctor, during that year than ever, thinking I was constantly continuously sick.

My sitter Desire, was onto it, as she would sit in the hallway at times and hear the derogatory remarks he made, then she would walk in to stop it. She stopped by bringing her friends over for confirmation of what she was hearing. She asked what they thought about it. When she walked in to stop whatever was happening, he would be all smiles, hug her and start building me up or her. She would tell me how atrocious it was to watch and would catch herself falling for it.

She said she had never seen anything remotely close to it before, neither had her friends. She was a mess, seeing and watching me accumulate bruises and the way I was being belittled, but she couldn't let a day go by without stopping by saying often she couldn't sleep at night because she was worried about us.

I never spoke out of turn again, it became part of life, and he was daddy to both the boys now. An unspoken truth of who he really was, was hidden.

I fell into that strangeness, almost an acceptance of who Hell's Angels are mentality, what I could and couldn't do with a man such as that. Because if any other guy were to do that, I'm sure Blake would've spoken up or someone else. It is an aura of authority really, you become entrapped or enslaved by a situation you can't get out of with a man like that, whose nature is already abusive. Sometimes you have no control or say over it.

Not all Hell's Angels are like that though, the air of authority is there but not the abuse. I'm sure with a Police Officer it would be the same. Abuse is in the eyes of the beholder or their nature. A Vicarious situation, a web of deceit and control. It happens in the beginning from remarks to actions, some worse than others. You are the only one with the strength to get away. I did not have that. I was in the midst of my own worst fears playing on me from childhood, from the degrading remarks, to now the use of them by the father of my child. I wasn't blind to it, just did not have the strength to fight it. When someone who is naturally abusive gets any sort of power, it will increase their dominance and add to the ignorance of who they are. Often individuals who have that tendency will become more and more abusive.

I didn't know how to get away, or how to leave because I was in my own home. I was lost, my only lifelines during this time were my sitter, nanny Desire, my Blake and my mother. My shield and the only strength and love I had went to my sons. I shielded them, built them up and all I had went into them. In turn they became my true heroes. I would spend hours and hours guiding them to the good and enlightening them about how wrong certain things are. I would instill so much love into them , that in turn the good prevailed in my sons.

My mother saw it and she would often become my strength during this time. She would allow me to vent to her, even helped me search my house for wires and recording devices to see if he listened in. We shut off all phones because somehow he knew when I was starting to get courage and say things, or stand up for myself. He even somehow knew when we talked. He knew things otherwise spoken discreetly between my mother and me that he never should have known. I felt as though he was always there, even when he wasn't. My mother felt the same.

My refuge was my son's school, as well as being a mother, all my love and I mean all my love went into my boys. I did everything from building blocks with them, sewing to events, to the every Friday night grease night, snuggle night. Ashton was growing into a fine young man with a best friend that he was inseparable from, two birds of the same flock. Sable was Sable, he was baby bam bam who loved girls, everyone loved him, and the sweetest caring strong boy you'd ever see.

It was around a year and a half after Sable was born and many doctor appointments later that my doctor who was becoming a friend noticed the change in me. He started asking if I was okay. I was sad, often thinking I was sick as that was what Damien would tell me, snapping pictures of the looks on my face, showing me what I looked like, saying I needed help but when I went into the doctor's, I wasn't sick.

I made a choice then and confided in my doctor about what was going on, as I had no one to talk to. I couldn't go to police or I would be a rat and beaten. My family didn't like Damien, or so I thought. My mother knew I was walking on eggshells constantly. My doctor became my friend and I would forever thank him for eventually saving my life. I knew or I thought, I was going to die and needed someone to trust. If I hadn't reached out to him one day to document the abuse, I don't believe I would've lived. I was scared, so scared for my boys and where they would end up if something happened. I knew I was slowly losing me and this time I was going to catch it, fix it and not fall. My doctor continuously reassured me that he wouldn't call the cops and gave me supportive counseling. He would allow me to sleep in his office a few times with the lights off, after the nights when Damien had kept me up all night, asking me over and over the same questions, to the point of exhaustion, until I answered in the right tone and with the right answer.

Ashton started noticing the remarks, innuendos and abuse. He would often shadow me around Damien. I was lost and grasping at straws to breathe and remain me. I was suffocating. My sons became like the air I breathed, and I was only living to keep them safe. If I had not had them, I do not know how I would have survived to be here now, writing my story to help others, writing my story to save our youth to not fall onto a path that is so hard to get off, and to girls who are influenced by the bling, one day you wake up and the bling is not so bright, the heart and the good are brighter than anything in that world..

I started noticing how he controlled other people, not just me, but everyone. A former partner he treated like garbage, even telling him how to act and how to speak. He was becoming a nightmare, at one point he told his partner to go to a doctor and say he was bipolar and needed medication, which the doctor gave to the guy. I was horrified; this man was a genuine soul. He didn't need any medication. It was sad to watch, but reassured me that I wasn't the only one.

I was now part of Damien's everyday life. It was sickening to watch the control and manipulation, how people bowed to him daily, which built the beast up even more, justifying all his actions. The partner then came to me and said it was the best thing in world, what Damien had him do. He had never felt better. I should go and convince my doctor I needed it. Stating that Damien had even sat with him in the doctor's office and helped me explain what I needed, anti-depressants. He told his own doctor, "Damien saved me." My mind shuddered at the thought of how much control Damien had over others, it was frightening. My heart wept in that moment once again, to see a grown man with so much light and goodness in him being monopolized by Damien.

I was watching all the goings on around me, how people were treating me, my life and my self-worth was slipping into a deep hole. My only refuge was my doctor, the school parents, teachers and certain friends.

Damien drove me to my doctor one day, coaxing me on how to talk and what to say was wrong with me, if I hadn't noticed how he had just done that to his partner I wouldn't have realized what was going on, so when I went into the clinic and by the time my doctor came in, my mind reeling and all I know knew. I burst into tears. I told my doctor everything.

He gave me what I needed, self-worth. He said to me, "Kerri, you are the happiest girl I know. When you come into this office, you make everyone smile. You have such a brightness about you, you don't need anything." In that sentence, he gave me a moment to hold onto, for the darker days to come. He gave me hope, he gave a piece of me back that had been stolen, a me that I always knew was there. He gave me a spark to a little glow that was in me, just to hold onto.

I shared with my doctor, my own personal hero, that Damien was outside and what he was making me do. From that moment on, he helped me acknowledge the truth I had always known, a truth of right and wrong.

When I walked out, I told Damien in the most powerful voice I had, "I do not need anything," and went on to explain that I took a test, all the testing I could get, and I wasn't a person who needed bipolar medication. "I won't be taking any or going back for more." He was livid. He snapped pulling my hair back, choking me as he went to rant in my face that I didn't see the right person! It was as if he was trying to make me look unstable. My eyes were slowly opening. I needed heart to survive; I needed my dreams back and I needed my beliefs, I needed to be able to *Kerri-On....*

He hit me with a blow that I had always known, a blow that rocked me to the core, then a verbal one. "Even your family thinks you need it!"

It hurt to know that he was getting validation from the family that had always put me down and ridiculed me. It hurt unlike any fist in the face I could ever get. I knew they said that about me, but to hear it from someone else, a person who abuses me as well was a moment of clarity, a moment of realization that I was now with a man who controlled everything, from how I spoke, to what I did and seeing the truth in his words (facing a truth that my family treated me like he did with their careless words), he couldn't control my heart, (my kind heart) he only broke it as did them.

A few more months went by and my roommate, Blake, moved out. I couldn't understand why, but yet I could. I knew he couldn't handle all the garbage of fake smiles, walking on eggshells or the abusive manner in which I was being treated, and knowing there wasn't much he could do about it, being who this man was. My security was gone, my lifeline, my best friend. I thought I was lost.

Overwhelming Loneliness

To share with others that they are not alone, to enlighten the world that we are human, with thoughts, dreams, and visions. We love, laugh and cry. We might mess up, but we are all only waiting for the right hand to pull us up, or the belief that we are something and someone. WE are waiting to be the name we were given.

A FEW MORE months went by with more slander and mimics from Damien, hair pulling and grabbing were just normal. Then all of a sudden, one day he came home to say were leaving for Mexico. It was a family wedding and I had to attend with him, as his own family would be there, even his brother and brother's girlfriend. I was petrified and reluctant to go, as I never wanted to see that place again.

The horror of my past experience was coming back to haunt me, but there was no way to get out of it. He had already booked the tickets. God forbid I would make him waste money. I panicked, was very scared and tried the card of no one to watch the boys, which didn't go far, as he had me call my sister Sabrina who lived in Alberta, right in front of him to ask her. Of course, she would say yes. That's who she was. I didn't want my boys to go there. I didn't want them to hear the slander that was often spoken about me by her. I loved her but I knew firsthand the implication of her words.

I had never left Sable with anyone before and leaving him for a week had never even crossed my mind. I was horrified. My sister was a good mother, but controlling with the yelling and screaming she does makes me feel sorry for my nieces and nephews. I wouldn't trust anyone else with my boys, other than my mother and there was no way she was able to do that. She was going through her own issues lately of anxiety and depression and divorce. It wasn't fair to her. She had often been put down by Damien, even to the point of him sending her to my room while he forced me, then ranted and raved for me to sign over my car to his brother, the one asset I owned. Since then, my mother was staying away now.

We were off to Alberta to drop the boys off to stay at my sister's. I was freaked. I hated being alone with him by this time, because no one knew the torment I would go through when he was in one of his moods. I would have to stay up all night, until school hours, or until I said what he wanted to hear, practice it, say it the right way tone with the right attitude, whatever thing irked him at the moment. My mental exhaustion was unbearable.

Hiding it all from my children was slowly killing me inside. You could now visibly see it in my face. I was ugly from the inside out, no matter what frills or gimmicks I put on. The eyelashes I was becoming addicted to could no longer cover the pain that was evident in my eyes and features. The life was being sucked out of me, even my losing weight showed it. I looked sick.

When we arrived at my sister's, I cried that first moment seeing her after all this time, almost two years since she had first seen my newest baby boy. She hugged me as my tears welled up. She could instantly see all I was going through, with her I knew I couldn't hide it. She hated Damien and wasn't afraid to say it to me. She asked me to be careful and told me my boys were safe with her. I didn't want to leave my sister's, I felt at home. Her concern was evident, but she was used to putting on a fake smile or façade living in a small town where everyone talks about you and knows your name. She grinned and bore it, laughing at his jokes, even the ones aimed at me, and listening intently to his conversations.

Sabrina wasn't fooled, but also she was so used to her own opinion which was already so strong about me, she would laugh or say things right along with him, even though it hurt me. Then when she would see it upset me, she would say, "Suck it up, Kerri, GOD!!!" In those statements, she had no idea it fed Beast, gave him more of a right to talk to me as he did, gave him the feeling that he's allowed to. I heard myself in private talks with my family, saying to them, "Please don't do those things in front of him. Please, it makes him worse." Somehow they would all forget, or not validate me and be out there slamming me, laughing at me, right along with him.

When I was alone with him, he would taunt me, "Wow, hey, I'm not the only one who sees it. Your family even sees it. Get help, Kerri, no one wants you." That would dig into my very heart and rip me apart. Was he right?

As we left for Mexico, my horrible intuition was setting off my own radar. I wanted to stay. I felt as though my chest were caving in, panic came at me like a ton of bricks, so much so that as we boarded the plane, I barely noticed these girls I guess Damien knew, who were strippers and were also on the same flight.

I didn't care, by this point the caring about that had stopped. He had made arrangements to go with them to Coco Bongo's sometime while we were there. I wanted to go there, probably the only place I wanted to go. It was a theater enactment place, in the fine arts. I loved theater, plays or books. I was excited to see the show they put on, as I had seen many pictures from it. I knew I did want to do that, perhaps the only thing I wanted do. The Moon Palace was absolutely breath takingly exquisite (resort we were staying).

The first few days of Mexico were relaxed with the wedding coming and going and I was often left alone. I made sure for any purpose whatsoever I had enough money on me that I could run, did everything he wanted as not to upset him. As we were getting close to going home, my homesick feeling increased and I was excited. I just wanted to go curl my arms around my babies and love them like crazy. I could feel them missing me as I was missing them.

Damien had gone golfing, so I went down to get something to eat at the buffet downstairs because it was such a gorgeous day. I grabbed my romance novel, put on my white sundress, (that was long and touched the ground, it was beautiful) that I had bought for myself the day before and went downstairs. I sat by the pool and read for an hour tops, then stopped and watched a horse carriage wedding take place complelty awe struck and started back up to the room. As I got there, the door flew open, an outstretched hand grabbed me and pulled me inside. I was freaked out.

Damien was livid. He was screaming at me that I was a whore, fucking whore, how could I go out in that dress. I didn't know what to do. I couldn't understand why he was saying that. I hadn't done anything, it was mid-day with the sun shining bright. He had gotten up to go golfing earlier. I became hungry, went down to get food, ate and then came back upstairs. I said, "I didn't do anything, please stop," and I tried to hug him to calm him down. He was shaking and red in the face.

I didn't even go swimming, nor did I wear a bikini as I had never felt beautiful enough to do that. I was always shy, as he would often tell me that I was fat. I wore a nice sundress and was only gone perhaps an hour. I went over everything in my head and couldn't understand why he was saying these things. I never talked to anyone, other than the driver of the resort who drove me back to the room.

He lost it, undeniably, horribly lost it. He hit me so hard in the face it left a mark on my cheek. I tasted blood again. I was scared and tried to curl into a ball, I knew the impact of his blows. I was still by the front door and wanted to run but didn't have the courage. I had seen him upset, mocking even, or that stunning blow out of nowhere in the beginning, but never like this. He was screaming profanities at me that were so mean and low. I had never felt so small in my life. He started ripping off my sundress, I had no idea what he was about to do but my mind screamed, with it getting stuck around my neck and arms. I screamed out in horror, as pain sliced through my neck and arms as he tore it off me, as much as it could be torn off. When he realized I was gushing blood and it wouldn't tear off anymore, he pulled even harder, tugging at it, then just like that, he left, just like that. Gone.

For hours, I huddled in a corner, crying my silent tears wishing him to stay away. I was scared to leave the room, as I had no idea where he had gone. I couldn't understand why his brother or his brother's girlfriend never came to help me in the middle of that. No one came, it was like no one cared. No one ever stopped him from hurting me. As I got up and looked down at my arms, I realized I was close to needing stitches. My lacerations were deep and pussing out, yellow fluid and blood, in criss cross lines, and welts had formed around them. I couldn't have a shower, as I thought their water would leave parasites on me or in me now and I could die.

I was not just horrified, but very frightened. I kept repeating to myself we leave in the early morning, make it until morning. I never wanted to go through my airport incident again. I knew I couldn't ask police or anyone for help. Once again, helpless and alone, I phoned my sister to ask about my sons, my only salvation, my only healing was with them. I cried to her and explained what had happened, not all of it, just what I needed to unleash my hurt.

She said, "We will be here, care bear." For once in all these years I heard the concern in her voice. I heard her take me seriously and the love in her voice, the voice was of a mother to me, not just my sister but my mom. When I had been all alone many years before, abandoned by my mother, it was my sister who took that role, my sister who saved me from my desolate state. I needed her like nothing else; my boys were safe.

I knew if I played my cards right, I would be home tomorrow. I was hanging up the phone, as Beast walked in. He never acknowledged me, not even a look. He jumped in the shower and started getting ready. He was going to Coco Bongo's, it was our last night and that was the plan. I didn't want to go anywhere, I knew I was safest in the resort, with every fiber of my being I knew I was safest there, and I knew it.

As he stepped out of the shower, he looked at me and snorted in disgust. He saw the marks and gave them a cool stare as he walked out, not a word to me, nothing, just gone. There he stayed out until nearly dawn. I heard him come in, crawl into the bed as I was sleeping fully dressed in case of emergency with a housecoat to cover my now infected arms. My neck was killing me, but I couldn't see it, which was probably better, as I had only a few bottled waters I was able to rinse my cuts with.

He tried to pull me into him, and I just lay there, non-responsive, trying not to vomit, shake or give any indication that I was awake…..

As we got to the airport, of course, I was pulling all the bags. We made it through the security and my overwhelming sense of safety came alive. I had not a problem dumping his bag beside him, and blatantly sitting away from him. He gave me a deadly stare as if looks could kill. I knew I was safe now. I knew I was boarding that plane. I was going to make it home and alive. I was not thinking of the consequences after, I didn't care anymore, I needed a doctor to look at me, at my arms and neck. I knew I needed stitches, there were lines upon lines of gushing yellowish dried blood within welts. It was gross and throbbing.

I never did anything but eat and relax. I was sick of hurting and with the company of other people, I knew I was safe enough to be me. He started making sickening jokes about me, to the girls, who had originally boarded the plane in Vancouver. It was sick watching him laughing, then he would walk up and whisper, "Whore," any other derogatory remark in my ear, blatantly defaming me like I was a joke, better yet a piece of nothing.

As we boarded the plane, I couldn't control my reaction, or myself any longer. I grabbed my pop and poured it on his head as he sat down. I didn't care anymore, it was the first time I had ever stuck up for myself, but I couldn't take it anymore. That look of mortification and horror on his face was worth it, very much worth it. People had to choke back laughs as they saw what I did. I smiled in that moment a genuine smile that had long been forgotten, and with a deep breath I sat down, stuck in the seat beside him for a six-hour plane ride ahead. I felt more alive than ever after I did that. I knew I hated him, which is such a strong word but in that moment I did. It was the first time I had ever stuck up for myself with him, the first time I ever talked back or out of line. I was beaming.

He would lean into my ear and say, "Wait, whore, until we get home. You're getting it, you will be sorry," over and over every few minutes, in between his loose gander, and smiles and chats with everyone, he would whisper his threats. What more could he do to me? He had victimized me from the very beginning. But in my mind, I still thought I had the best gift of all from him, the best part of him that ever was, his son, Sable, our son. I would take all the pain in the world for my baby boy.

I wasn't worried anymore, a person can only take so much. His brother and brother's girlfriend looked at me on that plane, as if I was crazy. I didn't care, no one knew the hell I had been through and no one acknowledged the continuous bruises or pain on my face and demeanor, the once proud, healthy mother was withering away, gloom settling within all my features.

No one would stand up to him, or for me, with a man who wielded so much power, a man who was everyone's dreamy friend, a man with the patch and personality of a monster. I was on my own and I knew it, like the air I breathed, being hit and screamed at a door away from his family, and no one had come to help. They all acted as though everything was normal, that it was okay for him to do that. I knew, if it was another man, who never had a Hell's Angels patch, someone would have stood up and helped me. But not with him, they had no idea how much they fed his ego. They fed his own reasoning that he was okay the way he was, no one told him the truth, and that it was wrong what he did, no one!

Home

Everyone, no matter what, has to work for what they want most in this life, or when they have it, often times it is taken for granted, to work for something makes the value worth so much more.

WE ARRIVED IN Vancouver and I was so excited. Now I wanted to get to my sister's. I wanted my boys! I wanted that true genuine feeling of love, my baby boys were what kept me going, implanting the love deep within my chest, no one or nothing could take that away, ever!

I left him as I hurried along the corridors to that checkout. He acted all nonchalant, when in fact he was watchful, he knew I was about to bolt. As I was waiting for my luggage, he came up and whispered in my ear, "If you go, Bitch! I will hunt you down. You will never see your children. I will make you look like a whore on Hastings Street and you WILL Die! "That stopped me dead.

The strength I had, anger, pain and the victimized state I was in when I finally I cracked and had poured that pop over his head was dissipating slowly. I knew, I would be alone with him again, never able to call cops, I'd be dead! I couldn't put my family through that. I could never allow what he did to me, to happen to them, to anyone. They wouldn't be able to handle it, the pain of abuse, it would hurt them. I had to be the one to take it, to take it all, no one would ever be hurt because of me. It felt like a cold rush of water icing my veins as I faced the truth.

Then with his flip side, he pulled me into him, and said, "That's a good girl. You know I love you. Feel better now, Baby, get it all out." It was as though it turned him on seeing my strength come out or was it that I was finally cracking in front of everyone and looking like a loony person. I was tired and alone. I was defeated anyway I looked at it.

As we got in his truck that was parked at the airport. We had to drop off his brother so he kept me close putting on a show of complete love and laughter, making fun of what happened on the plane. They were laughing.

I even had to have my laugh at myself, because I truly meant that, it did feel good. No one knew the arms and neck lacerations I was covering up, no one but him. They were my shame. The bruise on my cheek was nothing new. I always had bruises now, supposedly because, as Beast would say, I was anemic.

We dropped them off and I was alone, needing a doctor and my sons. He pulled into our place as by now he just sort of moved right in, and said "He was going to take a nap, then we would drive to get the boys".

I went into the bathroom and started cleaning my wounds with everything I had, Polysporin, peroxide and bandages. He came in then and tried to help, saying, "You should never have worn that sun dress," and that he was sorry he couldn't find me. I cried as he tried to help me. He said, "I'm sorry." He acknowledged a wrongdoing finally. It was a moment of truth that was acknowledged. I had found in those moments when those who had hurt me did that,

I wept. I allowed myself to openly show my hurt, it was a form of self-healing in me.

When the weeping stopped, I told him my family was going to see this. He never said a word, the moment lost. Then he laid me down and was as gentle as possible as he let me sleep in the comfort of my pure white dani down comforter. That was his feeling of love and guilt mixed in him, he was a picture perfect man whom cared to anyone on the outside. Me, I was torn into pieces, my strength came to me as I lay there a few hours later. I looked at him and said, "I'm scared. I am starting to hate you. I'm scared I'm going to lash out at you. I hate you for all this." I was not angry or mean but with the sincerity of a soul crying out. I told him I had visions, to stop all the pain. It scared me, I wasn't like that.

He looked at me and smiled. He kissed my tears and said he would never do that again. He loves me so much, he would kill for me. He never thought he would fall in love again, or with me, that he wouldn't let me go, and then true to his word he said, "Let's go get the kids, baby." I wanted to trust him, to believe in him. How can he have such an abrasive manner and a tongue so brutal with his words and control, so hard when he hits, but yet understand me.

Finally, when after all these years I had been silent, never being myself around him as my friends would say, finally I had opened up, because I had nothing to lose. I said what I had to say to him, in a kind gentle manner. I bared my heart wide open, for all the hurt and pain over the years, the victimizing and premeditated plans he had. I told him what I felt inside. He acknowledged me, he spoke to me and after all these years, said he was sorry. I wanted to believe him, but I knew it wouldn't change. I knew it because in the words I would kill for you, I knew within my very bones, it would take life or death to leave. I knew he would only kill me, no one else.

All I wanted were my little angels in my arms, their mommy's arms, to fill up with all the love I could instill in them, my angels, my lifelines, my own mini copies of me . The excitement I had wanting to get to them was extraordinary. I had to go to the doctor, but he never allowed me, purposely forgetting as he hit the highway at a fast pace, trying to do his own little thing to make things better.

As we pulled up to my sister's, I will never forget them in the front yard, playing outside. When Sable looked up at me he stared, stood still in his spot and let one tear slide down his cheek. He was upset I had left him. I felt his inner turmoil. Also in that moment, I saw his character, his strength, his wisdom and the pain because Mommy had left him. I ran to him and whispered over and over, "Mommy will never ever leave again, my baby. I'm sorry." He was upset, he clung to me and his tear was just that one tear. He was just like me, my baby was me, the child who, when you see someone or something, you show the love in happy tears, in character. I knew I had done something right with my baby boy, his true nature shone in that moment. I had long ago learnt to feel from others, see what they saw and could tap into their feelings. It was who I was, who I believe I always was, I loved the good and was drawn to it, like an angel.

As my Ashton came barreling up the driveway, he swung himself at me and held on for dear life. I was the one the boys wanted. My angel Ashton was my rock, my balance and my little man who helped me not to fall. It was a lot of pressure on him, but I never allowed him to see that's what he was. I just soothed him with words such as, "Ahh, mommy has the piece of her puzzle she was missing. I love you my son, just love you, finally I'm complete." As him, Sable and I clung to each other.

They never ran at Damien like that when he walked up, didn't look at him, the three of us were a team and I knew it that day more than ever. It was my reward I, thought, for my suffering, whatever had been going on I was putting all my love into these two little men. That was all I needed in life. My sister hugged me and I saw her face put on that fake smile I've seen so many times as she addressed Damien. He scooped Sable out of my arms and took off to be a father.

When all was settled, she and I went into the garage and had a cigarette together. She looked at me and shook her head as tears welled up in her eyes.

She wrapped her strong, dominant arms around me and said, "A blind person could notice your bruises, Kerri!"

I lifted up my sleeves to show her what he had done and she cried as she looked. She was aghast, in shock. I asked about my neck and if they are the same on my arms, just missing the tattoos of my children's names by a millimeter. She shook her head over and over in disgust. She vibrated then, she hated him, hated him, she couldn't look at him. She showed her love to me in a way of disgust and anger. She didn't understand why I was idly sitting by as he played his games.

We had a standstill then. She didn't understand why I couldn't leave, she couldn't understand. I tried to reassure her that I would be leaving but there had to be a way to do it, a way that I could leave safely. It was then that my seed of leaving and planning took fruition.

I didn't want to leave my sister's house, she was my safe zone. As we drove away, my silent tears cascaded down my cheeks as we waved good bye. He saw then where my strength lay within my family, children and others, or so he thought. He knew they knew the truth finally and if I had been more perceptive, I would have known not to share that with him, in my eyes or upon my face. He would use all their own ill-gotten thoughts against me. I was blind to the lengths he would go, but yet, when I looked at our son, I couldn't help but wonder if somewhere Damien was a lost man, who needed to be held accountable for the destruction he left in his wake. A man who never had proper guidance or the inklings of love and commitment, because I could see the difference as night and day between him and our son, Sable Baby.

I carried those scars on my arm for years and as I look closely right now, as I'm writing my life's events to help others, I can still see them winking at me in such strength and courage. They are a reminder of all I have been through to become the caring soul I am. I truly love each of you no matter your mistakes. I shall not judge anyone as I have been there! You are not alone.

Less than a month later, Mother's day came and went. I received a pair of extraordinary diamond earrings from my sons. I was shying away from him, collecting the presents were a burden, knowing my gain was someone else's pain. With my knowledge of the circumstances taking root in my mind, I was shutting him off, not caring too much other than for my sons. My life goal became making my children's lives perfect as well as my home. I had a safety plan in progress, by opening up slowly to people I could trust.

To Have & to Hold

LATE ONE NIGHT, I was checking my email. I had received the most beautiful email from the dad at school, wishing me a happy Mother's day, saying I was one of the best mothers he knew. I was replying saying thank you so much, with a radiating smile on my face, when Damien came around the corner. He noticed me smiling and then, look hesitant and leaned over to read it. He hit me so hard in the face that I hit the wall.

I fell to the ground in a daze. He had rocked my senses, as blood poured down my face. He was livid, but I had nothing to hide, all the parents had the other's emails. Ashton was his son's big buddy at school.

I couldn't think, my head was swimming, it felt as if he broke my nose. I was terrified; I had nothing to hide at all. I tried explaining that to him, begging on the ground, in front of him, but to him as he drilled me for answers, this guy was a "COP" dad at school. He was doing what he does for a living, already seeing the bruises, and knowing who I was with, he built me up by sending that, nothing more, a dad who didn't judge me, a human being and a parent at school. I tried to tell him he wasn't hitting on me, just being a parent. My son had a huge impact on his son and all he did was compliment me, Damien wouldn't listen.

People are people. I believed parents at school are parents at school, no matter what. I didn't care what he did for work, even though he was a CNN police officer, he was a human being to me, a person. I just happened to be checking my email when the boys were in bed, only he and I were up. If I had anything to hide, why would I have checked the email then, begging him to understand?

He knew I had nothing to hide. He had me under lock and key. He just couldn't control his aggression, or Damien just hated me. He dragged me across the room by my hair and backhanded me again and again as he had me by my neck and throat. I knew I was now going to die, I felt it in my bones. I tried running to the boy's room when he wasn't looking, as he stopped to go through the computer and then came back and slapped me some more. I was screaming for Ashton, "Get up, Get up," and pulling Sable out of bed in his diaper.

I was almost at the door with Sable in my arms and Ashton leaning on me, ready to head to the car and get them out to safety. He was going to do something so irrational, I saw it and felt it in every blow he gave me, from words of degradation to the force of his hands.

He came at me through the kitchen and this time he had a knife. As the boy's heads were within my arms, me protecting their eyes, he flashed it to me right then. He said, "Put the kids to bed, Hunny," in a sickening voice. "Let the kids sleep. Oh Hunny, look at your face. Did you hurt yourself?" That was when Ashton looked up and saw the blood. He started shaking, he knew what was happening, my son knew. I saw and felt his quivering body.

I put Sable down and went with them both to the bathroom as calm as I could be to get a cloth. I whispered to Ashton, "Don't worry, Mommy will get us out of here, Baby. Keep Sable all snuggled." He nodded to me, now on alert. Damien watched from a distance I couldn't see him as my room was connected to bathroom. I put them in their room, which was just across the hall from the front door. As I was trying to calm Sable, I grabbed my phone and gave it to Ashton, "Keep this close son. Call Nana. It was only a few more hours until sunrise.

I went back out their bedroom door as Damien grabbed me again with a hand over my mouth and dragged me into the front room, taunting me. He said he's going to have the computer checked by "specialists ", to see if I'd done anything wrong. He told me I was done, a rat goof, and the club was going to kill me. Continuously threatening me with his club.

He then, by knife point, put me on a chair in the middle of the room, and said he would be calling everyone in my family to explain my existence, my worthlessness and the truth that he wanted them to believe. It was time for everyone I loved and held dear to know the truth about me! I should now phone my sister and all my family telling them, "I'm a liar, that I needed help. I was wrong about him to all of them. I've been needing help for a long time." I had to say I was sorry for lying all these years about my mentality and that, I was sick in the head and needed medication. To cover my own behavior, I had lied about him, leaving bruises on myself to make him look bad, when he was really helping me.

I vomited on the floor. I couldn't help it, I was sick and terrified that I was going to die. He told me, as he wiped my body in my vomit and spit, that he was going to kill me in the bathtub so he wouldn't make a mess. The children wouldn't be so upset to see their mommy like that, dead. I vomited some more. I was shaking so much I thought I'd have a seizure. In my mind, I screamed to my sons, I love you, I love you and silently hoped Ashton would call for help.

After a while of obscene comments and hitting, he put me back on a chair, and forced me down as he grabbed a jacket and said there was a gun in it. He forced me at gunpoint to say what he wanted, to tell my family I was a screw- up. It was sickening. The pain of trying to write this is very hard to let out, as it's an indescribable feeling of such a humiliating, life-threatening situation. I was shaking in such fear, because he said, "If you don't do it right or your voice shakes, you're dead, you're going to die."

He then grabbed the knife and started explaining how I was going to say it, as I had to hold onto the phone. This torment went on for hours. I knew Ashton had my phone if he needed help. With everything inside of me, I knew I had to get away, I had to get away. It was late and everyone would be asleep. I don't know how long things went on in such horror, but I tried everything from begging, "Please stop. I never did anything. I have never emailed him. I don't know how he got it, probably from school. I'm begging for mercy. Please stop, please stop. You can check the computer. There is nothing in there, nothing," so he did check it for hours as I sat there, too scared to move.

He looked through every part of that computer, until he hit MSN Messenger where he found people that had been my friends for years on there. He snapped!! One of my friends had his shirt off in a picture. It was my fault. He swung at me relentlessly. Blood was dripping from my swollen face again, as he hit me so hard the chair fell to the floor with me falling over on it as he hurled things at me, choking me and telling me how worthless I really am.

It woke up my now sleeping son who came in and begged him to stop. Damien sent him to his room. The birds were chirping by now, daylight hours had come. There was no way school was happening. I had to get out of there, my son, by now finally realizing what mom had said as a cover up , that his mother needed help, he finally phoned Nana, who phoned family.

Damien once again forced me to phone my sisters at knifepoint or gunpoint where I still hadn't seen it, but he was acting it out to the fullest.

My senses were dulling after so many hours. I was shaking and sick, beaten and torn. I had to phone her and she answered. I tried to talk the way he told me to, telling her what he told me to say as I couldn't hold back the tears. "I lied about him, it's me Sabrina." I couldn't do it, I couldn't talk after all the hours of suffering I had gone through. She started asking me questions to assure herself that I was okay and that he was right in front of me. She said she wanted to speak to him. As she got on the phone, I watched completely shaken up. It went on and on, the conversation. As I watched I knew it was my chance to run.

I knew it was now or never and run I did. I swooped my two boys into my arms, one in a diaper and one in jamas. With the car keys in my hands, I ran through that door and I didn't stop running. I was scared he was going to track me. Did he hang up quick? Was he chasing me? My chance, my hope to survive came, when his defenses came down on trying to convince my family about me. I hoped he was still on that phone with her.

That run was fearful when I didn't know if my legs would make it. Ashton was shaking so hard I thought he might need a hospital. Sable was crying scared by my mad dash for safety. Mommy's panic of pure terror was crippling him. I looked up towards the balcony where we lived as I saw him watching me, still on the phone with my sister, yelling. I will never forget, "Oh, honey, don't scare the kids. You were only telling the truth. Come home, Honey." He was the most demented male I had ever met.(I made it outside)

I jumped into my car as he looked over the balcony. My children were horrified not knowing what was going on, but enough that no child should have had to witness or be part of it. I watched the rear-view mirror as I drove away in complete shock. In my mind I was sure he was having me followed. I had to ditch this car in order to be safe.

I was very scared as I drove, from his threats that he could track me anywhere, that members and prospects were watching the house already so I couldn't leave. I bolted, driving in circles, around and around. I finally arrived at the ferry terminal but it was an hour before it would get there, and we'd be able to get on. I was scared they would find me that he had me tracked. I drove to the line-up and waited. We went into the terminal store area because I had to get glasses to cover my face and buy clothes for the boys. I was in a state of numbness. I needed to be visible to people, so I felt safer, so my boys would be safe.

My mother was waiting on the other side, telling me she loved me on the phone. It was all going to be all right, she was strong for me, and when we boarded the ferry for the 2-hour ferry ride, I still didn't feel safe. I was horrified at the thought that they were on the boat waiting for me. We snuggled under a blanket as I told them stories of princes and princesses. *(I never told Ashton what it was about. I shielded him from it. I couldn't imagine taking away how proud he was finally being a big buddy, to the dads son at school).*

When we heard the signal for Duke Point terminal, I was starting to unwind. I just had to make it to Mom's house. When I saw my mother waiting outside for us, I collapsed in her arms. I was drained and suffering. She saw my bruises and told me to go have a shower and lie down, "Kerri, I will take care of the boys." She wiped away anything they might've heard or seen during that flight to safety with the nurturing of a grandmother's touch.

She held me that morning with the love I needed. She gave me hope, she allowed me to fall asleep as exhaustion overtook me. I was a mess and had nowhere to go. I knew I couldn't stay there as that could only last so long, and I wasn't putting anyone I knew in danger. His rage or demeanor could change in an instant. I couldn't go home. I was lost in the turmoil of survival. My children had just witnessed something no child should ever see, even if they were protected and only noticed the panic. They could now see the bruises dad had left and they felt the terror of flight. My son had phoned for help, my poor sons. I was a horrible parent. To me I was everything he had said I was.

Even though I had received that compliment earlier that evening and it was now one of the few compliments, I received from people on being such an amazing mother, to myself I wasn't, I thought I had failed. I thought I had tainted my children with the horrors of violence. I felt as though my once-safe haven was now my nightmare, from being his girl to the mother of his children as he now stated.

I was a mess. I was nothing, barely hanging on. If it had not been for my sons, I would've succumbed to the torment he had given me. I had felt as though that's what life had thrown at me. I was meant to be that emotional, degrading, punching bag for people. I was nothing inside, my light had faded and barely glowed by this time.

My salvation was the love I had for my sons, my only refuge was my romance novels, I had no friends and not a place to belong. My mind was reeling, how could I receive such a compliment and then be so utterly trapped. I had let my children down; I knew it. I couldn't allow this to continue, but I had nowhere to go, nowhere to run. I wasn't going to put my family through anything that might get them hurt, and I couldn't allow my children to be around people who thought slamming me at every turn was a joke. A joke too much and a laugh too hard, on an already ridiculed degraded person isn't normal. I would not handle that well, as a person can only take so much. I was clinging onto the only thing I knew, love, hopes and dreams.

I shut my phone off for a few days, just to get a grip on reality. His messages were daunting to read. I hated my phone, hated the connection to my seclusion. It was from hate to love in the flash of an eye, with him. When I finally had the courage to turn on my phone, messages flooded in. He supposedly had the computer looked at and everything was fine. He was sick in his mind, never understanding that what he had done was not normal. Then he sent a picture of a wedding dress. I will never forget the feeling of defeat as I looked at that message. I was appalled, so was my mother. That was the first time I heard her say, "He makes me sick, Kerri Lynn, sick." It was only confirmation in my eyes that he felt I deserved all he gave to me.

I also couldn't understand what my sister had said to him, something was said to make him feel justified in his behavior. I was now opening my eyes to the inevitable, the thought perhaps flickered in my mind but I was barely able to grasp it. Maybe somehow he felt it was okay to put me down, because others did. Maybe it was allowed because I allowed it. Perhaps I was allowing people throughout my life to take advantage of me, without even knowing it. Maybe I was the one who had to look at myself, at who I allowed around, who I tried to please, and what I was doing wrong. Perhaps I was the one who really did have the problem. Maybe I did need help, or even deserved it.

I knew then he had seen the love in my eyes for my sister that day a while ago, he was using his deadliest weapon yet. My love for my family..

Opening my Eyes

People often wonder why others get angry, sad or upset. It's an Emotion, a lonely emotion, sad emotion when no one understands your truth...Only you do....

I HAD TO do this the right way, leave the right way, in my mind, because otherwise people would get hurt. I could never live with myself if anyone I loved, or who maybe didn't love me, ever was hurt. I hated hurt, pain and suffering. I would openly weep with anyone who was sad, lonely or afraid. I could tune into their sorrow and feel it, as I have been there.

I couldn't allow my children to fall into the wrong hands. I swore when I was a little girl that I would have a family one day of my own. I would love them no matter what with no separation just a normal family. Now my children were my world. I was stuck with a sociopath, a man who under all the horrible abusive behavior had goodness in him just not for me. If he could just get help, anything. I wasn't strong enough to think that perhaps this was just who he was. I was in denial about him because I had such a special treasure from him, a boy who if he ever hurt anyone would cry, a boy who had so much love in him, our son.

I knew after the many incidents thus far, that Damien could very well end up killing me. I knew I had to be strong for our children, never for me but for my sons. I had to survive, as I was their only hope.

While I was staying at my mother's, I received a message from Stella, after such a long period, it was a hello and she missed me. I don't know if it was all the negative experiences that allowed that door to open, but open it did. It was a relief at that moment to hear from her, not that I let on all that was going on. It would have been an embarrassment, to the children and me. I hated allowing people to see my weakness, somehow it always was used against me. Perhaps it was only the people in my life during these times, but at that moment, I realized I needed her.

I told her I was staying with Mom never hinting at anything bad. She had met someone, they had started a family and had a little girl. I was proud of her. We knew we were each hiding something or we wouldn't have reached out to each other, but what a wondrous feeling I had just knowing my best friend was now around. That message lead to a dozen more that day. Even my mother was smiling every time I ran down the stairs to tell her something new Stella had said.

I believe my mother found relief in my re-acquaintance with her during my dark days with Damien. My mother said, "Well, at least now I know you will have someone closer, because I live farther away. I could see the strain in my mother's eyes, knowing she couldn't do anything to protect me from a man like that. What I didn't understand was, how come my real father had never once tried to protect me, ever. My eyes were slowly opening to a new thought process, re-evaluating my life. Finding where this cycle began and how to end it.

I had to get home, while I knew Damien was out of town, at least to get some things, so I was leaving my mother's after staying there for a few weeks. My bruises were still there but barely visible. I made plans to meet with Stella in the next few days as well. It made the homecoming that much less daunting and safer.

I knew Damien was over his rage but I never knew for how long. I had a refuge with my mother, but after the last incident, I couldn't put her or the children through that again. I had to be smarter and find a way to make everything better, for everyone. I had drilled my sister on what she and he talked about as I made my dash for safety. I was always worried about anything anyone said to him, because he'd make it somehow justifiable or use it to hurt me down the road. The more prepared I was, the better.

It was a sick way to live, but my only way, as I had no options, none that I knew of. She said something that triggered me, my sister, "I agreed with him, Kerri, I couldn't handle being with you either," it hurt to know that. In my heart I knew that one day he would throw that at me, in some form or another. I knew then, that no matter how much pain or suffering I was in, even happy or sad, scared or alone, my sister didn't really respect me. She may say she loved me, but in her way she would always have a harsh opinion or a small heart when it comes to me. I saw that my family wasn't all like me, whereas if someone had hit my sister, I would be the first to scoop her up and take care of her, nurse her back to health and happiness. All I received was a careless comment, a tell-you-what attitude and whispers behind my broken back. I was feeling more alone than ever from my siblings and family. Everyone heard the incidents but they didn't understand the living with it, as I had too. They didn't understand I was trapped inside, or that I needed to be given a different type of strength, Love/Belief in myself.

When I arrived home, I saw my doctor and explained what had happened without going into big detail, but enough that should anything happen, my boys would be protected. I was nervous going into my apartment. It had memories of something so horrific that I wasn't yet ready to face it. I would put that on a back burner until I was strong enough to deal with it. I walked in to make sure everything was fine and was surprised to see the house so clean, shining, with even the beds made. He was good to his words over the last few messages; home was ready for us whenever we wanted to be there. I just wanted to pack and leave, to start over.

I told the boys they could come up, and my nanny brought them up, as she had met me, as soon as I had arrived back. She knew about everything I was going through. She had heard the remarks, as well as seen the bruises. She saw the control from the man who could hold a smile anywhere and any place. She was part of my strength, a huge part of my strength. She wasn't really a nanny, it just became what we all called her. My boys loved her, not only as the only person I would allow to watch my children, but as my friend.

She knew about Stella and was reluctant for me to meet up with her, but she was young, so I thought she had no idea about all Stella and I had gone through. From the outside looking in, I guess she knew trouble when she saw it, as opposed to me always accepting people's faults and weaknesses and falling into the hopelessness of being taken-advantage-of once again, she was taught better. She couldn't understand how I could give people so many chances, she hadn't yet fully understood me, for that was who I was, I cared about humanity.

I was home a few days and the nanny stayed with us. It felt safer and better for the boys to be back on their routine again, and me as well. The only thing I had was my children and our home. I would converse a lot about what to do, where to go, forming a plan and escape route all the while just wishing things would be normal and we wouldn't have to run. The limelight of the whole-family dream had long since faded. My dreams were robbed by the nightmare of living with Damien who just moved in slowly but surely, staking his claim.

He came home. My stomach did flip-flops as he walked in. He said he wished I was in Calgary, he had planned a surprise for me. I was strong, not into hearing the pettiness anymore, false promises and beautiful kisses, with such a gentleness you would never guess he could become that way. No one, but a select few believed me or understood his capabilities. He was the ideal best friend and guy outside of the home. He was a poster child and a dominant loving friend.

I told him if he didn't leave, the boys and I would and that all this isn't healthy. My bruises may have almost healed, but my mind never would. What he did was sick; it was too much. My voice was a voice and finally after all this time it spoke. With as much determination and forcefulness as I could muster, I told him it was over and one of us had to go.

He called my bluff and said he's not leaving, not in a scary way, but in a way that said he was testing the waters. I started packing up a few items, in a way not to raise alarms. I would stay in a hotel before I would subject these precious boys to any more garbage. My stepfather was on alert ready to pay for it or anything else I needed to help.

He tried to pull me onto his lap, kiss and love me. The way he always did, but the time away had healed me, more than he could have. He had done and said too many hurtful things. It meant nothing. He had taken such a huge part of my life already, I had wasted so much time on a never-ending story, it was time to say goodbye while I had the chance.

I was ready, and told the boys we were going on a journey, a trip, making it sound fascinating and exciting. We walked out that door and down the hallway. I had heard his pleas, his sorry s. Then I heard, "Please just turn around, you have to turn around, Baby." I knew not to, I knew to keep going, but his voice was the one I did love, the one that had originally melted me. I heard his pain.

I turned, slowly stopping and turning, halfway already down the hallway, almost at the exit. I saw him, right there on his knees on that dirty apartment floor begging me, to give it one more chance. He was on bended knee, a man pleading for something he knew was lost, a man who was hurting. Arms spread out. In his hand was a ring that glittered all the way down the hall. In the moment I turned around, he asked me, "Would you marry me, Kerri Lynn Krysko? I love you like the air I breathe."

Ashton my son, just smiled, so happy to hear me being proposed to. He was all excited waiting for me to say ," **Yes**", his heart as big as mine, his soul that of a child who dreamed of happily ever after. Sable was giggling not knowing what was going on, but his daddy crawling on the floor made him giggle even more so loudly. I had to shush him to stop, now both my boys were smiling, they both had such a light in them.

Me, being firm, made me look despicable and rotten, or perhaps that was how I felt.. To see this big tough guy asking, no begging, me to marry him, was a delusion I swear. It was too much. I asked him to get up, just get up, as I walked part way towards him to show compassion, but also to say NO!

He pleaded with his heart on his sleeve, a look in his eyes. I was becoming embarrassed, as I shooed him back into the apartment.

He went down on bended knee again, with a huge speech on all the reasons we should get married. When I was reluctant to answer, he kissed me so gently, the kind that takes my breath away. He always did that, he always made me see what I longed for. It is the using my weaknesses against me, so to speak. My mind did a 360 as I relived the horrors in my mind of the last beating.

He knew, he always knew when he had done something wrong, but somehow he justified it. It was only a matter of time before he forgot about it, and then the taunts would continue, "I will break you Kerri, tame you and build you into what I want, Whore, Whore, Pig, Pig" Squealing in my head. Then slowly he would follow me around with a camera phone to take images of the look on my face. If I wasn't happy or gleeful, he would start trying to control my mind, not just my body. It became a sickness, a humiliating existence for me. I was slowly suffocating, looking for any means to escape, but each time I knew, I would have to take it to the end for us to survive. There would always be that controlling man, or maybe the overwhelming need to die was inside me. The only one who knew the true nature of his abuse was my mother, and a few others knew just pieces of it. The mother who, when I was a child, had thrown me away, the one who had hit me herself, was the one to embrace me, and help me try to heal my wounds. I tried to hide this sick abuse from my children but the lack of weight and personality I had was showing. The bruises from the constant grabbing and choking were all too visible to see. My mind was reeling as all the events went through my mind as I looked at him, pleading on the floor before me. I knew, if I walked away right now he would follow. I knew if I said NO, he might just punch me in the face in front of the two boys watching, who were relishing in such a nice moment from dad. Now he was waiting for me to say YES. I was scared, reluctant to say anything as these events took hold of my mind. This was a man who got everything he wanted, a man who people bowed down to, and a man who had forced himself on me many nights, in my terror and horror, a man who was the father of my child, a man who hurt people to get ahead, a man who truly and utterly never really thought he did anything wrong. This man was now asking me to marry him. I watched him spew his speech. I was caught now, in a battle for my life, my visions of married life coming true, as he slipped the ring on my hand, his plan had come to fruition. I knew within my very heart that he only did that because of the terror he had put us through. I knew in my heart that another nightmare was just about to begin if I said "Yes". Now I really had to find the courage to live, and in that moment I knew, as I looked at my two sons, that I couldn't let them down, couldn't let them witness beauty and pain together. I would find a way, even if he had to hate me first. I knew I had to give it one more try, before I ran away becoming a fake identity, in a foreign land far away.

The life of his girl was long gone, the life of fast cars, catering employees, prospects and supposed friends, were now only a comical thought. It was over for me. The presents were nothing more than material to be had, that I would throw away. My life and only existence was for my children. A girl's dream of marriage was for me a joke, no longer the visions I once had or dreamed about as a girl.

Kerri-ed Away

Book 2

The Road to Truth & Freedom

A chapter preview

IF I WAS happy, he would be upset and grill me for the reason. I now gained my only courage with others around me, finding a way to speak out about the crimes he had committed, begging to be heard, any way to be heard, to be saved, but no one would listen, no one would hear me, no one who surrounded the boys and me. The people who were around, family and friends would all listen to him. We would go unheard, only to listen to the skepticism in their words behind our backs, their doubts and how I was looking more and more unstable. How it was my fault, how I needed help, somehow the people that meant the world to me, turned their backs. They couldn't understand what I was seeking, how I really needed help. I needed help with love and understanding. I needed his taunts to be lies about my family. I needed to see their support, compassion and I needed their love. Lack of it was holding me back from our freedom, our life and our happiness. It was holding me back, from being who I always longed to be, from my true strength, my true character and the truth. I was only as alone as the people who surrounded me.

In my darkest most daunting hours trying my best to break free of these chains, I had no one but me to rely on, no one but the boys and me. We knew the truth, we knew his words, and we knew his threats. Only we knew the walls of control that were surrounding us, only we behind closed doors knew the power in his lies and twisted games.

In that truth we found the freedom we sought by me taking the most riveting, harshest looks around me, and finding the answers I had long sought and I previously couldn't face. It was okay to be alone, it was okay to start over and it was okay to let go of the people who brought us down.

I would talk back, or even toss something on the floor. I was a lunatic to other people. No one could understand that I wasn't allowed to have a voice or comment, or any emotion but one, the fake smile or nod of a broken woman. He would whisper in my ear, "Whore, c'mon act up some more, you're only proving me right!" Then, I would run to hotels or transition houses for a night, many nights, just to get away. I knew when he'd torment me or was going to blow, whenever someone wouldn't pay him on time or something went wrong, anything, and everything was my fault.

Sex became a chore, a time I loathed. His touch repulsed me, his demands were disgusting, I couldn't feel anymore, nothing. I knew he was unfaithful, I didn't care, I just wanted his lies to stop, everything was, his, his, and his! It was always about him.

His control escalated to such bizarre behavior it was uncontrollable. He needed to prove me even more unstable. Following me some nights to hotels, he almost kicked the door down, freaking outside, for me to beg him to calm down. He would throw me on the bed, my children screaming in horror as he shoved pills in my mouth, whatever tranquilizer he had at the time, to calm me down, to make me weak, do his bidding and then would dumped water all over my face, until I swallowed. He said, "Don't worry, they will find you on Hastings Street. They will find you one day dead." He attempted to control me by getting everyone around us to think I was causing the problem. My son, Ashton, was the only one who knew the truth. I had nowhere to go. When I went somewhere, because of who he was, I would be asked to leave. Transition houses turned me away.

I started paying a psychiatrist to see me, every week because he thought I was getting help, when in fact I was unleashing all he was doing to me and formulating a safety plan to leave, so we would be okay. My life wasn't my own.

I was driven by a force deep within me to save my children. It kept me alive. I Documented the abuse while at my doctors, often times skittish. When my doctor came in, he would just tell me over and over he believed in me. I wasn't myself. I can't stress this enough.

It was a whirlwind of demonic behavior, a manipulation that ran so deep it was difficult to follow. It was hard to explain to an average person or you'd look utterly loco, the whole story completely unleashed.

I did not do these preparations for leaving, to sink him or hurt him. I did them to live safely and healthily for my children, and to keep them and me, safe. No one believed me. They all thought I had lost it, while I was trying to tell the truth, screaming the truth as they looked at me with skepticism. I changed yelling and screaming, to begging them to please, believe me. I was crying out to my family, my sisters and they didn't bat an eye. They only said, "I see where he's coming from. I'd be on crack if I was with you." They would tear my heart out with their words, and crass behavior. My pain continued with no one to run to, everyone was somehow influenced by him.

My children had no one to run to, if something happened to me, they wouldn't have anywhere to go, to be safe. My family had all turned their backs on me and in turn on them my sons. I had to live. I knew staying with him would mean death.

My last attempt was to finally see if maybe I was causing this, if I was going crazy like he said. I took a friend with me and tried to check myself into a hospital. A psychiatric nurse and doctor sat down with me. I told them everything from tossing things off the table, to him drowning my face in medicine, trying to force it down my throat, from the anxiety to the horror. I didn't hold anything back. If I was going to lose my children because I was sick, I needed to know that. I begged them to check me into the hospital and examine me. I held nothing back. At the end of a four-hour interview, they looked at me as my tears were pouring down my face in sadness and defeat. They said words that partially instilled a belief in me, a voice of truth and compassion that saved me. I will not forget them.

"You are one of the most abused women we have ever seen. You are slowly killing yourself inside by staying. You need to pack a bag and leave, a safety bag. You need to live for your children as you have been doing. Knowing who he is, you need to do it carefully. We are not checking you into this hospital. You do not need a mental institution. You need to live. Find the courage and here are take these resources to help you (pamphlets). Save yourself and your children." No one understood, transition houses wouldn't house me, no one would.

"Why not," I asked, "even for one night check me in. See, I need to sleep. I am exhausted." They wouldn't, they just wouldn't do it as my friend held my hand beside me (not Stella), begging these nurses to help. They gave me strength, these two Women, at the hospital. They gave me something I had been hearing whispered in my mind. They gave me hope to believe in myself once again. They gave me the will to do the battle, to survive and live, no matter what my family or anyone said about me. I needed to live and to believe in myself, for the sake and safety of my children. I believed.

Everyone, including my friends, the ones I had left that is, had to go. I had to find myself again, the girl that was lost long ago. I needed to start from the beginning, when I started dating the guys I did and learning why. The one I needed to start with was ………

My purpose had lead me back to the beginning. I was accountable for all the choices I had made as an adult and was ready to deal with the "WHY", I dated the people I did. I was now ready to deal with the childhood that had long been forgotten. I only needed to start setting things right from where I had allowed myself to be swept into the life of bad asses and gangsters. These people who replaced my family, who gave me a sense of belonging, who looked past the realities of real life, normal laws and infractions, everyday hustle and bustle.

I needed to find myself there. Then and only then, could I truly live the way I was meant to without the shackles of ridicule, pain and loneliness. Digging into my past I found them. I needed to go back, to relive all the paths that shaped me, and choices I made. The moments which I believed had inadvertently lead me on a road to hell.

I searched for months trying to find him, until one day I received the call, in one of my only times alone. I know where the person you're looking for is, he is at Surrey Pre-Trial, up on charges.

He was shocked to see me, floored really, and he just stared at me through the glass. He didn't say a word just looked at me. It was weird being confined within Cells, knowing you can't get out. I had a different kind of claustrophobic feeling, a safe one. The buzzer rang and the doors were sealed as I sat in front of the glass, waiting. In he walked. ......*ACTION*...........

My closure was coming, and my self-healing was beginning. It no longer scared me. It was a driven force of recognizing a corrupt situation or soul.

With Love N Dignity,

Kerri Krysko

Gratitude

YOU PEOPLE SAVED me, saved my children, none of you even truly knows the love within me as I express this. As I speak, I have tears rolling down my face in the sheer joy, of now being able to say thank you. Without any of you, I would not have found myself. From my heart I embrace all of you to say thank you, thank you, thank you, you truly saved a lost girl, a lonely woman and a loving mother.

It was hard to get my children on a schedule, as their dad would often want them up and keep them going until all hours. There was no set bed time, so it was there that I started. Every night at 8:00 p.m., I would drive all over town, talking to my children until they became tired, showing them all the beautiful homes, the people in them, whether they were just eating around a table or clicking their lights off for bed. I showed my children the normality of life. I showed them that these homes didn't have fighting. They were happy and peaceful with normal lives and schedules. I showed my children life as I drove down the quiet city blocks. I showed them LIFE.

We would tell stories of each of you, as we drove, about how you'd just gotten home from a hard day and were reading stories before bed, just beautiful, lovely stories, until my littlest boy would fall asleep. In the beginning, it would take two hours, but eventually only fifteen minutes, six months later. I gained a normal routine by allowing the goodness of your lives to filter through and trickle into ours, and anonymously truly loving all of you and inwardly thanking you, for just being you.

As I had settled into bedtimes, I had also enrolled my children in every activity I could find with the help of government funding. As I never had money, it wasn't worth the price I'd paid to get it, so to me it meant the world being able to do that. I kept us so busy there wasn't time to wallow in sadness. But it gave us a chance to associate with people and in that I gained trust and my children gained courage. I would often visit with the parents of the school children, and in my own mind be admiring their structure, valuing them each differently and looking at all their strengths. I started believing again, and dreaming. For that I thank you, for giving me the time, accepting me and just even liking me. It gave me confidence.

Sable started preschool again, and his teacher took me aside one day and said words that built my inner soul up even more. *"The difference in Sable is amazing, we're proud of you, Kerri."* It was hidden from everyone before, and I beamed, truly beamed inwardly. Thank You, to all the teachers, I knew I was doing all the right things, was doing them with just the three of us, no family or friends (as he had me blacklisted). I did it with just my sons and me. I cried that day my first tears of happiness that had been long forgotten. It touched my heart and soul that kept me pushing and fighting, touched me to the point of now knowing acceptance and the value of myself. Thank You.

My children were healing and I was healing just from the gentle words of praise and kindness. Ashton was able to gain his friendships back because the abuse had been so bad, that certain ones weren't able to visit any longer. With his best friends back, it was a beautiful feeling of acceptance and triumph, and the human nature of understanding. I thank you my Tristan and Jacob, the little men who knew the difference between right and wrong, the men who dragged a bigger man than them off me, time and time again. With my son, you boys have proven to be bigger men, in character and substance, than you will ever know. *Carry that with you throughout your lives and you all will move mountains in your own righteous ways.* For that you gave my son the courage he needed to be himself again, the courage to trust again and not be frightened, the courage and love he needed. I will forever love and thank you boys.

Every step I took brought me closer to finding myself that lost girl of long ago. We had no one save ourselves, that first year, no hangers on like before, random friends. I had only the society of store clerks from Walmart, who would talk to me whenever they let me in late at night to shop. I was afraid to be out, I didn't know how far the malicious rumors had gone. They told me to write a book and share my story. You ladies gave me hope to help a world, the hope to be someone. You ladies were my only friends and I really love each of you. Also thanks to Starbucks workers, teachers and parents. You all showed me the world that I had envisioned was there, with your simple acts of kindness, understanding and love.

My doctor allowed me to come in just to talk, to get off whatever was on my mind, off. I still had many insecurities within myself, so whenever I saw him it was revitalizing knowing that I had this person I could trust, a person who had stopped being just a doctor to me and was our own personal hero . I knew no matter what happened, Ashton could go there, get my records and they would be safe. *My doctor would keep them safe, because of anyone else within this small world he knew the truth, he knew the difference between right and wrong and he believed in me, cared about me and was our true hero. (that little belief turned into a soft glow that I am now able to radiate outwards) I know in my heart that he saved my life with kindness, caring, a non-judgmental attitude, he gave me my dreams and beliefs back. Thank you, I have a special place in my heart for you, as do my children.* You were what I needed in my dark hours of torture and self-inflicted sadness. You sir, indeed saved all of our lives. You have done what no one I knew had the courage to do. You found me inside a haze of turmoil; you saved my very soul, thank you so much. I can't explain how high I hold you in my mind. You are the stars where wishes are made and answered, you saved my children and my very life. Thank you for allowing me to tell the secrets I kept hidden until I was ready to share them. Thank you for allowing me to trust again.

Without his gentle persuasion or pushes, I don't believe I would have survived many more years. He brought out the truth in me; brought the girl I always was out, the hidden person inside, that others mocked. He gave that girl validation, gave me hope and gave me my dreams back. His nurses gave me love, understanding and genuine warmth. For their hugs and kind eyes I thank them, they are beautiful women, who truly are in that field of work because they are exceptional people. I thank them and truly love them.

We all have a purpose in life and some people stay for a short while and others stay forever. I know that my angels, God, and energy or a better/higher power saved me. My angels came in human form, with feelings that go back to the basics of seeing, hearing and believing, the power of a gentle smile, validation even a hug , a warm kind hand, or gesture, conquers the most fragile person's demeanors, they give anyone hope, and even a will to survive.

A place where I belong, where my children belong, I found in all of you and for that I truly thank you. I took little pieces of everyone and all the good I found in just watching and learning, I learnt to slowly walk again. You all saved me, every last one of you, who took the time to notice a sad, lost lonely soul, who only needed love, kindness and a word of encouragement. In all of you I found myself, truly found myself, the self I was missing and not allowing out. The self that hid behind a cricketed smile, mocking laugh, tear-filled face, and bruised, broken body, that self and the voice was and is one that I shall forever allow to shine. That self is me.

My step-father a man who like me has been through so much, with his long talks and devotion, I was able to have *not just a father a friend*, my only friend for so long, *I love you dad.*

I realized we are what we make ourselves to be, we are only human with feelings, with love, with aspirations. We all have our own stories and most of all we all have each other if we allow it.

If this could help others understand the diversities of life and truly embrace the knowledge I shall give you to help others, that is what I hope. I know by writing this I am hurting a great many people in my life, but who aren't really in my life, for that I am sorry. Truths hurt and I will have to live with that, *but I love you so much. You all have no idea that at certain moments in my day, I just stop and wonder, and ponder, always with you and never far, thank you for allowing me to live.*

I hope people can take my knowledge, what I have been through and practice it within their own lives, learn from the mistakes of others, own their truths and grow from it. We are all human, we all make mistakes, we are only what we allow to shape us, and most of all we are not alone, only as alone as the people who surround us.

I want parents, siblings, teenagers and anyone else to know <u>you are not alone</u>. If you need help, look around you, enjoy the view, the kind praise of a person, you will see a individual, a stranger even, that you can trust, in that you will find hope, and also find yourselves. Be careful who you label or you judge, you never know if that person is truly what you are saying, or just a simple person, a sad person looking for love to fill an otherwise empty void.

I say what I say because even though I was with a Hell's Angel, it doesn't mean they are all like that, or even every police officer is righteous and perfect. Evil and meanness comes in all forms from a parent to a preacher, only we as people can and will change this world, with acts of kindness and goodness. We are all humans, we all bleed, we all hurt and we all suffer our own personal demons, we all have a heart so we need to use that heart to spread the love and save a soul one day at a time.

Thank you everyone for all you've done and for just being you. Allowing me to find me with a dignity of self-worth, because now I know my name is Kerri and I am proud to be me.

With Love,

Kerri Krysko

Book 2

Coming Next Year

About Kerri Krysko

KERRI KRYSKO IS a nurturer of many people, no matter what background, age or status, she will not hesitate to give a hand to those in need, even at the sacrifice of herself. She has a passion for decorating and bringing out the beauty in any broken item, as that is what she sees. She enjoys nature, and watching the world flourish around her. Kerri has 2 wonderful children whom own each half of her heart, she bases her life around them, and couldn't have accomplished all she has without them.

CPSIA information can be obtained at www.ICGtesting.com
Printed in the USA
LVOW08s1530111113

360873LV00003B/606/P

9 781460 217641